ARCANE

GRAVE CARGO

JAMI GRAY

Copyright © August 2020 by Jami Gray
All rights reserved.
Grave Cargo - Arcane Transporter
Celtic Moon Press
ISBN: 978-1-948884-38-9 (ebook)
ISBN: 978-4-948884-41-9 (print)

Cover Art: Deranged Doctor Design
www.derangeddoctordesign.com

WHAT READERS SAY...

About Arcane Transporter:
"Taking a refreshing approach to fantasy magic, this fast-paced, economical thriller is told from a highly likable perspective." —Red Adept Editing

About PSY-IV Teams:
"This story is an emotional roller coaster, from betrayal, anger, fear, love..." —InD'tale Magazine

About the Kyn Kronicles:
"...a fantastic paranormal action novel is quite possibly the best book I've read this year. I could not put it down, and had to exercise serious self-control to keep from staying up all night to finish it." —The Romance Reviews

About Fate's Vultures:
"...if you like your characters with a bit more bite, with secrets, with hidden agendas, and all those sorts of things, and your worlds are a far more deadlier place, then this is for you." —Archaeolibrarian

ALSO BY JAMI GRAY

ARCANE TRANSPORTER

Ignition Point - novella

Grave Cargo

Risky Goods

Lethal Contents

THE KYN KRONICLES

Shadow's Edge

Shadow's Soul

Shadow's Moon

Shadow's Curse

Shadow's Dream

PSY-IV TEAMS

Hunted by the Past

Touched by Fate

Marked by Obsession

Fractured by Deceit

Linked by Deception

FATE'S VULTURES

Lying in Ruins

Beg for Mercy

Caught in the Aftermath

Fear the Reaper

ACKNOWLEDGMENTS

This writing business is not as easy you may think, so there are quite a few people I need to offer my humble thanks.

To my supporting cast - DeAnna, Camille, Dave, Monica, Nana, and Joanna - because you all never say no when I need your eyes and input.

To Red Adept Editing - without who these jewels would not shine so brightly. Big thank you to Stefanie for the notes!

To the beautiful artistic minds of Deranged Doctors who can take my scattershot approach to cover art and create stunning covers.

And as always, to Ben, Ian and Bren - no words will ever cover how grateful I am to be yours. You guys are the only reason I'm still having fun with this whole roller coaster ride.

To my readers - you are the reason I keep putting my fingers to the keyboard. It never fails, when I start to wonder if I'm writing into the void, you'll give me a nudge to let me know you're there. Thank you, thank you!

This is for those who crave fast, wild roads and unpredictable curves. Don't ever slow down!

CHAPTER ONE

THE SHRILL WHINE of approaching sirens tore away the last bit of sleep-deprivation haze that the comforting scent of roasted beans failed to clear. I winced at the ear-grating sound, and my hand, the one holding my nirvana in a cup, jerked. Scalding caffeine erupted from the lid and splattered across my skin. Muttering a word best not used in public, I quickly shook it off and then blew across the cup's tiny opening in the lid. Taking a cautious sip, I watched the blue-and-white police car rush by as the rumble of conversation inside the corner coffee shop died away. We all stared in that uniquely urban, yet morbidly fascinated way as another unit, complete with flashing lights, chased the first up the street. Out on the sidewalk, morning commuters slowed and craned their necks to follow the action. A deeper, harsher blast followed, and like extras in some bad TV sitcom, everyone turned to watch an ambulance bring up the rear of the emergency-response caravan.

Not an unusual activity for the narrow maze of downtown Phoenix. Between impatient drivers and equally impatient pedestrians, both of whom were firm believers that traffic signals were mere suggestions, navigating these streets was not for the faint of heart. Chances were good someone had dared a yellow light with disastrous results.

Crappy way to start your day, I thought with a tug of empathy. Typically, I would be happily ensconced on my eighth-floor balcony, blearily eyeing the morning comings and goings, safe from the havoc below. But this morning, the combination of a late-night delivery job and the fact that my roommate, Lena, had failed to replace our caffeine stash left me with no other option if I wanted to function. Somehow, I'd managed to throw on clean—I did a quick check—yep, clean clothes and navigate the handful of blocks necessary to get my fix. Luckily for Lena, I was in a forgiving mood and had ordered her favorite drink. No one liked dealing with the caffeine deprived.

"Rory, your Italian espresso is up."

Thinking of which. I hopped off the stool and nabbed Lena's coffee. "Thanks, Van."

Busy recharging a simple warming sigil etched into the counter for an unclaimed order, he gave me a quick smile and called out the next name. The irritating itch of active magic ran over my arms, but with my hands full, I tugged my personal shields closed, shutting it out. Shouldering my way through a trio of twentysomethings in the midst of debating the finer points of casting a hex, I headed out into the morning rush of pedestrians destined for class or work. My walk home was accompanied by the chaotic choir of buzzing traffic, the echoing discordant clangs of the nearby light rail, and the continuous crash-bangs of ongoing construction. Despite that, it was a beautiful Tuesday morning. A slight breeze chased away the edge of heat that would win later in the day. Give it another month or so, when summer really hit, and I would think twice about making the trip on foot.

A block from home, my phone vibrated against my hip with an incoming text. Since my hands were full and my front door was nearly in sight, I figured it could wait. Sticking to the sidewalk, I rounded my condo's manicured landscape, which was a strangely attractive combination of rock and tropical garden. The pretty picture was marred by the ambulance and two squad cars from earlier, now parked at an angle in front of the high-rise. A hulking mass of a fire engine had joined the party.

Various uniforms dotted the scene, one of which was stringing up fluorescent-green crime-scene tape and closing off the lobby entrance. The use of green instead of yellow tape spiked my curiosity. It indicated magic was somehow involved. I was too far away to tell if they had warded the area for containment, but considering the bystanders stood in scattered clumps a safe distance back in the parking lot, it was a reasonable assumption. A collection of familiar faces huddled under a nearby awning, their attention focused on the unfolding drama. Deciding to join them, I made my way over as I took in the passing pedestrians doing the looky-loo thing. A tall, dark-haired figure caught my attention, and before I could react, his long-legged stride took him around the corner, where he disappeared. That could not be who I thought it was, because there was no reason for him to be anywhere near here. I started to pivot, intent on proving my point, but the sound of my name had me turning back.

"Rory!"

"Hey, Ang." I shifted direction and went to the bench where my neighbor with rainbow-hued hair held court in the midst of a writhing mix of canine bodies. "What's going on?"

Angie wrestled with the leashes of the overexcited dogs she walked every morning before her university classes. Today's motley trio included a laid-back chocolate lab, a bouncy Yorkie, and a black-and-white fluff ball of unidentifiable origins. With her hands full, she used her chin to indicate the hive of police activity. "Someone dumped a dead body in the lobby."

Her voice carried, and from behind me, the frighteningly efficient sixtysomething Martha, who lived a couple floors below me, corrected, "They weren't dumped, Angela." She left the nearby group in the shade to join us. "I think whoever it was collapsed."

"Collapsed or dumped, they are definitely dead," Angie shot back.

Martha's eyes narrowed. "And exactly how do you know that? Pets aren't allowed in the lobby."

Neither were dead bodies last time I looked at my lease. I set Lena's cup on the bench, freeing up a hand so I could give ear scratches to the lab that plopped down at my side.

Angie rolled her eyes. "Don't worry, I didn't take them inside. I just finished their walk and was out front, answering a text, when Colton ran out yelling at me to call 911."

Not recognizing the name, I looked up and asked, "Colton?"

"Over there." Angie pointed to where an officer was talking to a young man who kept shifting his backpack and his skateboard as he talked. "He lives on the third floor. He's a kinesiology major."

Her pointing finger turned into a little finger wave as Colton looked over and caught us watching. Even from where we stood, there was no way to miss his pale face or freaked-out expression. Someone was definitely rattled.

"I hope it's not someone we know," Martha murmured.

I sipped my coffee, thinking the odds were not in our favor. Despite the high number of college students drifting in and out of the area, our condo was fairly new. It was built in the last couple of years and boasted a hefty security warding, one they advertised as "top-notch magical security for privacy." The price tag for that particular extra was one in a list of many, and it made the place irresistible to young professionals, retirees, and seasonal students from well-to-do families. It was also one of the reasons why I had a roommate.

I eyed the green crime-scene tape. "Whoever it is, they had to be a mage."

Martha turned to me with a puzzled frown. "What do you mean?"

I lifted my coffee in the direction of the taped-off lobby. "Green crime tape. It means whatever went down was magical in nature, and if magic is involved—"

"So is a mage," Angie finished with barely concealed excitement. "What if they were working for one of the Arcane families and got caught in the crossfire?" Her enthusiasm increased as she forged deeper into her drama-filled story. "Or maybe the mage was being hunted by a Cabal assassin. You know, like a real-life thriller?"

"You need to cut back on your entertainment viewing, Angela," Martha chastised in her best teacher voice as she sat on the bench. She repositioned Lena's cup, moving it out of the way. "Not to mention that Cabals are pure fiction."

Undaunted, the younger woman dug her heels in, committed to her romanticized version of events. "You never know. It's not like that type of information is shared with the public." She caught my gaze. "What do you think, Rory? You've got an inside track to that world, what with your job at the Guild and all."

Inside track? I nearly laughed but choked it back. I had to agree with Martha—Angie spent way too much time with a TV. "I think your version is better suited to one of your writing classes." That earned me a pout, but undaunted, I kept going. "This is a bit too..." I searched for something more tactful than *sloppy* and *embarrassing*, only to come up with, "Public for anyone at the Family level to be involved."

A series of sharp yips erupted from the bouncy Yorkie and was answered by the black-and-white fluff ball, both interrupting Angie's speculation. I followed the dogs' focus and watched as our impeccably dressed building manager walked over with a uniformed officer at her side.

As they approached, Angie scolded softly, "Sit, Petunia. Sit, Tully." Both dogs ignored her, pulling at their leashes. Meanwhile, the lab at my side leaned deeper into my legs, content to brush the ground with its tail.

"I get the feeling I'm going to be really late for work." I chased my muttered comment with another sip of coffee.

Martha gave me a tiny smile of commiseration.

"Ladies and gentlemen." Natalie, the building manager, stopped near Angie and her canine charges, close enough the black-and-white fluff ball decided to plop its butt on her shoe. Natalie gently shifted her foot aside and gave us what she probably hoped was a reassuring smile but didn't ease the lines of worry fanning around her eyes. "Thank you for your patience. Sergeant Abrams would like a moment of your time."

The nearby group shuffled closer, and all eyes turned to the steel-haired male standing stoically at her side. He moved in front of Natalie and said, "I know you all have places to be, but we'll need to collect your contact information and statements." He waved over a couple of younger uniforms and turned back to us. "We'll do our best to get you out of here as soon as we can."

"Can we get inside?"

I couldn't see who asked the question, but I was glad someone did.

The sergeant was shaking his head. "No one enters or leaves, not until we clear the scene."

A rush of complaints and questions erupted, only to be cut short as he barked, "People, I understand, but this is an active crime scene. I'd suggest you make other arrangements, because you probably won't be able to access the building for at least a few more hours."

Natalie and the sergeant moved away a little. The younger officers split up and began pulling people aside. One officer started with Angie, which wasn't a surprise. He probably preferred not to have the dogs underfoot. Angie and her entourage followed the officer to a spot out of earshot. Someone called Martha's name, and she gave me a subdued goodbye and headed over.

With everyone occupied, I pulled out my phone and sank onto the bench, next to Lena's coffee. Swiping the cracked screen, I thought yet again how I really needed to get it fixed. Of course, after living with it for six months, I might be able to hold out until it was time to upgrade the phone.

I checked my texts and found a message from the Arcane Guild's contract coordinator with a request for an update on last night's job. *To call or to text?* If I called, I would be pulled into a conversation filled with "I don't know" and "I'm not sure," so I sent a text indicating I was running late. If I was still a full-time employee, my dodge might cause me trouble, with a warning about managing my time. Thanks to my recent transition to paid contractor, it might be grumbled about, but not where I could hear it.

Text answered, I called my roommate. Lena's phone rang twice then went to voicemail. *Hmm, she must still be sleeping.* "Hey, wake up, lazy ass. You're missing all the excitement." I looked to her cup sitting next to me. "I got you an espresso, but chances are it'll be cold before I can get it to you. By the way, you better call the Guild and tell them you'll be late. Call me when you get up."

I had conquered two levels of the game on my phone and

finished my coffee when a polite "Ma'am" gained my attention.

I looked up to find the officer who'd been talking to Angie was now closing in. I got to my feet, pocketed my phone, and waited for him to stop in front of me. "Morning."

"Morning." He waved me back to the bench. "We can sit if you prefer."

"Sure." I retook my seat and put Lena's cup on the ground, by my feet.

"Thank you for waiting." He sat down, keeping a polite distance between us. "I'm Officer Marco Alvarez."

"Rory Costas."

"Rory, do you happen to have your ID on you?"

I pulled out my phone wallet and handed over my driver's license.

He took it and studied it. "Do you live here?"

"Yep, on the eighth floor."

He lifted my license. "This has a different address listed."

I winced. *Dammit.* "Right, sorry." Much like fixing my cracked screen, updating my license was on my list of to-do items that I kept putting off. "I moved in a few months back and haven't had a chance to get in and get it updated."

He studied me for what felt like forever, and I tried not to squirm. The truth was, I'd moved in more like six months ago. He made another note and handed my license back. "You'll want to get that taken care of soon."

"Of course."

"If you wouldn't mind, can you take me through your morning?"

I did just that while he listened. He asked a few questions when I mentioned Lena, but otherwise kept making notes. A familiar voice interrupted us as we were finishing up.

"Rory, what are you doing here?"

Recognizing the rumble of bass, I twisted around and shaded my eyes against the sun. "Hey, Detective Brenner."

Sun-touched skin crinkled around sharp brown eyes. "Hey, yourself." He turned to the officer, who was now standing, and nodded. "Alvarez."

"Detective." The young man looked back to me. "Thank you for your time, Ms. Costas. If we have any more questions, we'll give you a call."

"Okay, so am I good to go?"

He nodded.

I tried a smile. "Any chance I can get up to my condo?"

"Not until the scene is cleared, sorry."

I knew it was a long shot, but... "I had to ask."

That got me a small smile in return. "Understood." The officer turned to Brenner and jerked his chin up, and Brenner returned the gesture.

I watched the young man walk away. Brenner sat down on the bench, taking Alvarez's place and bringing a whiff of cologne with him. It was the same scent he'd worn when we met six years ago. "So." He stretched out his legs and leaned back, laying his arms along the back of the bench. "I didn't know you lived here."

My grin wasn't big, but it was genuine. "Um, yeah, moved in a bit ago."

I sat back, some of my tension fading. Brenner and I had met when he was a patrol officer. Actually, he'd ended up investigating a dispute that involved a Guild client and a package with questionable ownership. Since the Guild was a mercenary storehouse that employed the magically adept, they didn't take sides on anything. That made my job as a Transporter pretty straightforward—ensure packages got from point A to point B. Asking questions, such as who was the legal owner of said package, wasn't in my job description, but it was in Brenner's.

He propped his ankle on his knee, his gaze drifting over the ongoing interviews. "Did the Guild give you a raise?"

Not quite sure why we were indulging in chitchat, I played along. "Kind of. I finally paid my training loans off, and my friend needed a roommate, so it was a win-win for both of us." I looked toward the front doors. Lights still flashed, but other than the uniform holding the line, no one else was visible. Deciding to indulge my curiosity, I asked, "What happened?"

Brenner followed my gaze. "A call came in, and the first responders hit the scene." He turned back to me, all signs of lightness gone, replaced by a stoic grimness. "The code came as a 451-M."

It took a moment for my brain to translate the radio code. "Magical homicide?"

He gave me a nod. "ACRT is on its way."

When magic was used to commit a crime, the Arcane Criminal Response Team, or ACRT, was called in to contain any magical fallout. Maybe Angela's theory of Family involvement wasn't so far-fetched after all. "Any idea of who your victim is?"

"We're in the process of ID'ing him now." Something worked behind his eyes, leaving me unsettled, and I wasn't sure why. "How long did you say you've lived here?"

For the first time, my anxiety churned. "Almost seven months." When he didn't say anything more, I pressed, "Why?"

Instead of answering, he asked, "Are you still working for the Guild?"

"Yes, on a contract basis."

His gaze sharpened. "Any recent jobs involving known Family associates?"

It was my turn to go cryptic, as I didn't like where this was headed. "You know how it works, Detective. All Guild contracts carry a confidentiality clause." In fact, those nondisclosure agreements were ironclad. To break one would require a hell of a warrant. Not to mention the Guild paid a pretty penny to a team of lawyers well-known for their ability to block said requests.

Brenner's smile was more of a grim twist of lips. "You do realize your non-answer is an answer?"

Giving myself a stern reminder on professionalism, I held his gaze without flinching and fought back my urge to snarl some pithy comeback.

He sighed, dropped his foot and sat forward, bracing his hands on his knees. "Just do me a favor and don't take any out-of-town jobs, okay?" He waited for my nod before he stood.

Studying him, I took my time doing the same. When we stood side by side, I asked softly, "That bad?"

He ran a hand over his close-cropped brown hair. Worry deepened the harsh lines in his face, cracking the official hard-ass mask. "Worse." He patted my shoulder. "You be careful."

"Will do." Apprehension tightened my shoulders as I watched him walk away. I turned, dumped Lena's now-cold coffee and my empty cup in the trash, and pulled out my phone.

Still nothing from Lena.

That apprehension sank a little deeper even as logic tried to hold it back with the reminder Brenner had called the dead body a "him." I typed out a quick text, hit send, then waited for a response. My screen stared blankly back.

Don't panic. Maybe she's in the shower. Maybe her phone is dead. Maybe—I cut off my line of spiraling thoughts. It did me no good to stand around and drive myself insane. Since getting back inside my condo was out, it was time to go to work. I followed the walkway around the condo to the residents' attached parking garage.

My faded jeans and T-shirt were a far cry from my typical business casual look but wouldn't cause more than a few raised eyebrows at the Guild offices. Besides, I didn't have any runs scheduled for today, hence my lazy morning. My initial plan had been to go in late and catch up on my reports. The late part still held true, so up next was filing my reports. If I was lucky, Lena would be at the office.

I crossed in front of the entry gate. Recognizing the familiar teal mohawk visible inside the parking booth, I raised a hand in greeting. "Hey, Shane."

"Hey, Rory." Shane stepped out and met me. "Did you hear what happened?"

Since I wouldn't be able to get by without answering, I stopped. "Yeah."

Excitement and interest animated his face. "Did you see anything?"

From anyone else, that question would have been considered tacky, but Shane was a year away from completing his degree in criminal justice, so it was to be expected. "No, I came in after the first responders got there."

Disappointment dimmed his excitement. He looked behind me as if he could see what was happening from our tucked-away location. "Sucks to be stuck down here sometimes. Nothing exciting ever happens."

"You're young still." I patted his arm in mock sympathy and moved around him. "I'm sure you'll get more than your fair share of excitement."

"Maybe." He didn't sound convinced.

I headed toward my parking spot in the back. Despite the dim lighting, my baby was a sight to behold. She was a rebuilt 1968 Mustang Fastback, sporting a beautiful coat of midnight-blue paint complete with white racing stripes, dark-tinted windows, and five hundred fifty-one horses under the hood. A year after winning it in a street race from an overconfident college student with more money than sense, I still got a charge at seeing it parked in my spot. I beeped the aftermarket alarm and slid behind the wheel. The previous owner had sunk a lot of money into blending modern convenience into the classic interior of this racing-edition beauty, and now I reaped the benefits. The engine growled to life, the sound echoing off the cement walls.

Pulling out of the garage, I headed to work. As I navigated traffic, I tried to remember if Lena had been home when I stumbled in just after midnight. It was dark when I came in, and I had tossed my keys in the bowl on the island then headed straight for my room. I couldn't recall if her door had been fully closed or partially open. Our condo boasted an open floor plan with our bedrooms and their attached baths split on either side of the living space. Everything was quiet, and I'd made an effort to not disturb her because she could be vengefully cranky when her beauty sleep was interrupted.

Thinking about it now, had it been too quiet? As if maybe Lena hadn't been home? Unlike me, she had a thriving social life. In fact, recently, there had been a handful of nights where she hadn't come home—a sure sign she'd met someone. Although we did our best to let each other know where we were, there were times when she'd come in doing her walk of fame—she refused to call it shame, and I couldn't blame her —and only then would I realize she hadn't been around.

Doesn't explain the radio silence.

I soothed the worrying voice with the reminder that Lena was not only an adult, but a Guild-certified Key who could handle herself. She knew how to spot trouble, especially since it took a special kind of vindictiveness to create some of the curses she'd dealt with throughout her career. Because her client list was much more volatile than mine, the Guild ensured all Keys, or curse breakers, were trained in self-defense, both mundane and magical. So yeah, Lena could take care of herself.

But if she didn't text me back or wasn't at the office by the time I got there, I would be putting my skills to use and tracking her ass down.

CHAPTER TWO

LOCATED in the upscale part of town, the Guild offices were housed in one of the many multi-storied glass-fronted corporate buildings lining the Camelback corridor. I could never quite figure out how a magical mercenary storehouse managed to share building space with lawyers, financial institutions, and corporate giants. It wasn't so much the high-end rent demanded by the building's location, which was easily paid by the commission the Guild made off their employees; it was the unsettling dichotomy of the building's occupants.

At any given time, a combat mage reeking of magic and covered in undeterminable things could run into a briefcase-carrying lawyer or a buttoned-up number cruncher. And it wasn't just the varied employees; even the clientele was jarringly different. There was no telling who would turn up looking for help from the Guild or what trouble they would drag in behind them. During my ten years of punching the Guild's clock, none of the building's other residents ever made a peep of dissent about our business or clientele. Of course, that could be attributed to being afraid of pissing off the motley crew the Guild claimed. We did have a well-earned reputation of payback. Whatever the reason, the strange arrangement worked.

Like most Guild employees, I skipped the elevator and used the stairs to access the second floor, where our offices were located. I walked down the hall, passing thick doors locked tight in wards, and pushed through a door bearing "Arcane Guild—Western Division—Arizona Office" etched into the glass. An instrumental rendition of a song that normally carried a hefty bass line played through the lobby speakers. I bypassed the cluster of chairs with the accompanying end tables sitting on either side of the door.

To my left, a harried-looking man with a pet carrier at his feet perched uncomfortably on the edge of a corner chair. He was so wound up that I almost expected him to pop up at any second, as if launched from a cannon. Thankfully, it didn't happen. Instead, his attention shot to me as he rocked forward. When it was obvious I wasn't the person he was expecting, he settled back down and returned to staring at the pet carrier. Whatever was in it was vocally unhappy, hissing and rattling the cage.

"Morning, Rory." The man sitting behind the front desk didn't take his eyes off the screen in front of him as his fingers danced over the keyboard.

"Hey, Evan." I waited until I hit the desk before saying more. "What're you doing here?" Normally, the front lobby was manned by one of the trainees, not one of the Guild's best electro mages.

"Daria called in. Seems she zigged when she was supposed to zag and ended up in urgent care with a dislocated shoulder last night."

"Urgent care? Wouldn't it be faster and easier to call in a healer?"

Without looking from his screen, he said, "Probably, but would she remember to zag next time?"

Recalling some of my more memorable training experiences, I conceded his point.

Under the short silver-touched brown hair, a forbidding frown darkened his face, turning him from friendly corporate greeter to ruthless raider. "Suck it, jag off."

My lips twitched at his snarl. I leaned over and saw his screen was filled with a war-torn battlefield. "Who's winning?"

A spectacular explosion lit up the screen, obliterating the action. Evan's frown turned into a feral smile, and he finally looked up, light dancing off the clear lenses of his glasses. "Me." Something in my expression must have given me away, because his brown eyes narrowed with speculation. "What's wrong?"

For a brief moment, I considered sharing my worry about Lena but thought better of airing my paranoia. At least not yet. Unwilling to go into detail about my morning, I stuck with "Long morning." Thankfully, he didn't push, and I decided to shift his focus. "You do realize you've got a customer waiting?" Since my goal wasn't to embarrass, I kept my voice low so it wouldn't carry.

He leaned to the side, looked behind me, then turned back to me. "Yeah?"

"Might want to tone down the trash talk."

He waved my point away. "Trust me, he's more worried about other things. He's waiting for Adrian, who's currently finishing up a phone call with another client."

The yowls behind us grew in strength. This time, we both looked back at the waiting client. A sweep of color flooded the man's face, and he muttered, "Sorry."

"No worries." I gave him a commiserating smile before turning back to Evan. I widened my eyes in silent query.

Evan leaned in and lowered his voice. "Someone cursed his dog, who likes to dig in flower beds—" Another distinctly feline, not canine, yowl cut him off. "Into thinking it was a cat." Humor lurked in his eyes as he added, "In heat."

I winced. "Vindictive neighbor?"

He nodded.

"Why Adrian?" Like Lena, Adrian was a Key adept at reversing curses, but where Lena preferred the variety of private assignments, Adrian leaned toward the corporate jobs.

"The guy's homeowner's insurance is covering the bill." A thin layer of exasperation colored Evan's response.

Ah, that explained why the poor guy and his feline-identifying canine were stuck in the lobby. Adrian liked to milk his corporate accounts because they paid by the hour. Behind us, the hexed pup started caterwauling, then a nose-curling stench blossomed through the lobby, followed by an embarrassed exclamation from the cat-slash-dog's owner.

Evan sighed, bent down, and dug through a desk drawer. He came back up with a roll of paper towels and rounded the desk. "Any chance Lena's coming in soon?"

My faint hope of Lena beating me to the office sputtered out. "I was hoping she was in already."

Evan shook his head as he headed over to the disaster area. "Nope, haven't seen her this morning."

My anxiety spiked, and I decided after I filed my report with the director's office, I would be digging through Lena's locker for clues. *Unless...* "Is Sylvia in?"

"Yeah." He tore off a handful of paper towels and handed the roll to the embarrassed client. "But I think she's in a conference call."

Scratch that idea. With the director unavailable, I could squeeze in a quick search of Lena's locker and maybe ease my mind. "Got it. I'm heading to the back."

Evan lifted a hand in acknowledgement then turned to help with the cleanup.

Behind the desk was a deceptive-looking door that separated the calm public facade from the inner sanctum of chaotic mayhem. Thanks to the myriad of magical situations handled by Guild personnel, accessing the operations area meant bypassing multiple security wards. Dealing with the redundancy of the wards on a daily basis was an irritating but necessary precaution. The initial ward was built into the door, specifically the doorknob. I grasped the handle, endured the itchy buzz of a magical scan, and when cleared as an authorized employee, felt the lock release. I pushed through the door, crossing the threshold, and triggered the uncomfortable sensation of the secondary ward. Much like walking through a clinging curtain filled with fire ants, it left behind a stinging impression, which was still highly prefer-able to the lethal response incurred by an unauthorized entry. I'd once witnessed that. The memory still made me shudder.

As magical mayhem tended to sleep in, mornings were typically calm. Today proved no exception. The low hum of conversations spilled out of half-opened doorways that led to the more private offices and conference rooms. Somewhere, a phone was ringing. Workstations—some with computers, some without so employees could utilize personal tech—dotted the main space. The odor of burnt popcorn hung on the air, and I wrinkled my nose to hold off a sneeze. I threaded through the workstations toward the employee lockers, intent on snooping through Lena's stuff.

Next to the double doors leading to the locker room was a large whiteboard. I stopped and scanned the names. Finding Lena's, I noted three green checkmarks and one black *X*. Three open cases, one closed. I was listed toward the bottom, with one black *X*, a green checkmark that I took a moment to switch to black, and a blue circle indicating a potential contract that hadn't been there yesterday.

Nice. I made a mental note to check in with Adele, Sylvia's right hand, for the contract details. *But first, Lena's locker.*

Pushing through the doors, I hit the cooler temps of the
office gym. The relative quiet disappeared under a wash of
bass-heavy music and the distinct sound of a body hitting the
ground—hard.

I edged around the mats where a red-faced bruiser was
sprawled on his back, relearning how to breathe. His oppo-
nent, a seasoned combat mage, stood above him, hand down
to help him up. "Like I said, easily distracted."

Bruiser took the offered hand and let the other man haul
him up. Once on his feet, Bruiser rubbed his jaw. "That was a
hell of a punch, Gabe."

"It's called a bolo for a reason," Gabe said.

Oh, ouch. I winced in sympathy. I'd been on the receiving
end of Gabe's sneaky hook during my hand-to-hand training,
and more than once, I'd left with the bruises to prove it. I
kept moving through the narrow path between the mat's edge
and the nearby weight machines.

My passage caught Gabe's attention. "Hey, Rory. You're
here early."

I half-turned and kept walking, now backward, toward the
lockers. "Had a report to file."

Gabe cocked his head, and a grin eased the strong lines of
his face. "In the gym?"

"Ha, ha." My heel snagged on a weight machine. I caught
my balance and gave Gabe my back, calling over my shoulder,
"In the office, but I needed to check on something first."

I pushed the door to the women's locker room open and
slipped inside. As the door swung shut behind me, the gym's
music faded, replaced by the drone of a hair dryer. Turning
away from the mirrored sinks, I went to the empty area
where the lockers and benches sat. Snooping in Lena's locker
wouldn't get me in trouble, but I didn't want to waste time
fending off the curious while I indulged my growing paranoia.
It helped that our lockers were side by side. Even better, we

had exchanged combinations for our locks since there were times we needed to nab something and bring it home.

I had her locker open in moments, but my search didn't take long. Not that I was sure what I was even looking for, but besides the workout clothes, makeup, hair ties, an extra set of office wear, a yoga mat, and a towel, there was nothing to calm my worry. No note with my name on it, no random address, *nada*. I muttered an oath and closed the locker a little harder than necessary.

"You okay, Rory?"

I spun around, my pulse spiking before leveling off. "Dammit, Nat, don't sneak up on me like that."

The curvy sun-touched brunette armed with a hair dryer grinned, but her eyes remained watchful. "You do realize that's part of my job description, right?"

"Okay, ninja chick, but unless you're spying on me, give me a warning." I sat on the cement ledge that served as a bench and fiddled with the lock. "I'm too young to keel over from a heart attack."

Natalie laughed, opened her locker, then tossed in her hairdryer. "Let me guess. Lena borrowed something and forgot to return it?"

"I wish," I muttered as I replaced the lock. I waited until she closed her locker before saying, "I've got a question for you."

"That sounds ominous." When I didn't return her grin, Nat's humor was replaced with a predatory sharpness. "What's wrong?"

See? That was one of the drawbacks of being with the Guild. It didn't take long to go from laid-back to lethal. "I don't know that anything *is* wrong."

Her jaw firmed, and she folded her arms over her chest. "Something's bothering you, so spill."

"Okay." After sucking in a deep breath, I did just that,

recounting the events of the morning—the dead body, Detective Brenner's strange behavior, and Lena's continued radio silence. "I was kind of hoping she'd be here, but she hasn't been in yet." I was a bit relieved to see my worry reflected in Nat's unsmiling face. *At least it wasn't just me.* "Tracking people's your thing, so tell me, am I overreacting here?"

"I don't know." Nat sank onto the bench, arms braced on her knees. "We both know the value of listening to our instincts. If yours are telling you something's wrong, they're probably right."

That was exactly what I was afraid of.

"Have you tried tracking her phone?" Nat asked. "That would be the first and easiest step."

"I was going to ask Evan, but I'm not keen on pissing off the director and using Guild resources for a personal matter." I used air quotes on the last two words.

She shook her head, her tone wry. "Still getting used to the contractor gig, huh?"

I nodded.

"Right, then." She sat up, slapped her palms against her thighs, then stood. "Go get Sylvia's permission to have Evan track Lena's phone."

I tapped my foot against the floor. When I caught my nervous tell, I stopped the motion and curled my fingers into fists. "I'm not sure it'll be that easy."

She cocked her head, puzzled. "Why not?"

I grimaced. "I think Sylvia's still upset about me going from employee to contractor."

Nat waved my worry off and rolled her eyes. "I doubt that. If anything, she's probably secretly doing a victory dance. She makes more money off of her contractors than her employees."

Nat would know. Unlike me, who was barely starting my contractor road, Nat had long since left me in the dust. She was one of a handful of contracted Hunters and reputed to have astronomically high retrieval rates. On top of that, it was rumored she was on private retainer for one of the moneyed elite Arcane Families.

But the Hunter wasn't done. "You're the best Transporter in the state, which means Sylvia can hand-pick your Guild assignments. The more elite the job—"

"The higher the pay, and the bigger her commission," I finished.

"Right." Nat smirked, but it faded as she studied me. "Look, Sylvia may be a hard-ass, but there's a reason she's held the director position as long as she has. She actually gives a damn about her employees. You and I both know she considers her contractors the same as employees." She leaned in. "If you think something's up with Lena, go talk to Sylvia."

Firmly chastised, I stood up. "She's my next stop."

"Good." Nat pulled a backpack out of her locker and looped it over a shoulder. "If it were me, I'd go through Lena's desk, find out what she was working on." She shut the locker door and then turned back with a small frown. "Have you thought that maybe she's with her mystery man?"

I blinked. "Mystery man?"

"Yeah." Now it was Nat's turn to look uncomfortable. "Rumors are she's been seeing someone recently."

Reminding myself this wasn't gossiping about my best friend but cultivating leads, I asked, "You have any idea who?"

Nat shook her head as she shifted the backpack higher on her shoulder. "No, you know how it is, office gossip. Probably just jealous nellies."

I wasn't so sure, especially considering Lena's recent behavior—huddled over her phone like it contained the answers to life, late-night conversations behind closed doors, and even later nights coming in. "Maybe." But even I didn't sound convinced.

CHAPTER THREE

I WALKED with Nat through the now-empty gym. We parted ways as she headed out, and I turned toward the director's office, which dominated the far corner of the floor. Reaching the inner sanctum of the director's office meant first getting past Adele, the scarily efficient and fairly intimidating executive assistant. On top of zealously guarding Sylvia's tight schedule, Adele also managed the Guild duty assignments. A fortysomething woman with grown children and a corporate "O" something of a husband, she was intimidating as hell, more so than Sylvia herself, and everyone treated Adele appropriately.

"Morning, Adele." I stopped in front of the desk and waited for acknowledgement.

It didn't take long before Adele looked up from her screen, her cool professionalism shifting to warm acknowledgment behind the purple tortoiseshell frames. "Good morning, Rory. How are you?"

"Good, and you?"

"As well as can be expected." Her bright gaze dropped to my empty hands, and an amused eyebrow rose. "No report?"

It was a well-known fact that anyone who turned in assignment reports late did so at their own risk. Adele's patience did not extend to those who—and I quote—"waste my time by not managing theirs." Guild agents who wanted to continue being assigned solid assignments did their best to be prompt with paperwork. Otherwise, they might find themselves dealing with a dog who thought it was a cat in heat.

"I'm actually going to file it now, promise." I made a crossing motion over my heart and returned Adele's grin. "You know I wouldn't dare disappoint you. It's not good for my health."

Adele laughed. "I knew there was a reason I liked you. You understand the importance of respecting the system."

"I don't know if it's so much respect as fear. I've seen what happens when someone fails to meet your expectations."

That earned me a sly look. "Better to be feared than loved."

"If you say so." Since I was already standing there, I asked, "The assignment board indicated you had a job for me?"

She turned to her computer, fingers moving with scary speed. "Not me. That one came straight from the director."

And just that fast the stars aligned. "Any chance I'll be able to steal a few minutes to get the details?"

Proving her legendary status, Adele didn't even consult her calendar before answering, "She'll be on the phone at least another twenty minutes, but she has fifteen before she needs to leave for a lunch appointment."

"I'll take it."

"Can do." Her humor drifted into her normal professional demeanor, and she set the appointment on her computer. "Will you be nearby in case she finishes early?"

"Yep, I'll just..." I waved a hand back toward the front, where the computer stations gathered.

"Sounds good."

I didn't go far, just to the nearest unassigned workstation with a sight line to Sylvia's office. If there was one drawback to being a contractor versus an employee, it was the paperwork. As a contractor, covering not only your ass, but also the Guild's, required copies of copies versus the single report I'd filed for years. I pulled the completed forms off the printer and was adding my signature on the last copy when Adele called my name. I looked up to find her motioning to Sylvia's door.

"Better catch her now."

"Thanks." I tucked my forms into a folder, handed the whole deal over to Adele, and headed into Sylvia's office.

The stylishly dressed, statuesque woman stood near one of the long windows stretching along one side of the office. She carried an air of classic elegance that disguised the ruthless mind within. With one hand braced on the window's ledge and the other propped on her hip, she turned as I entered, speaking into the headset half-hidden in the chestnut strands pulled back in a sleek chignon. She sent a perfunctory smile that eased the normally austere lines of her face and waved me to one of the two chairs in front of her desk.

I took a seat, doing my best not to listen in as she went back to staring out the window. She made a couple of noncommittal noises between longer pauses, obviously letting whoever was on the other end do all the talking. Based on her frown, whatever they shared did not make her happy.

To give her the illusion of privacy, I studied the office. The clean, minimal lines felt like stepping inside a high-end IKEA display. The only jarring note was the cluttered desktop. A couple of coffee mugs were hidden between piles of paper and folders. Colorful sticky notes peeked out here and there. A half-melted candle sat in the middle of a copper plate, probably used for a scrying spell. All in all, her office was the antithesis of my borderline-compulsive need for organization. Every time I had to sit on the other side of Sylvia's desk, I got antsy.

Today, though, I was pretty sure those ants had more to do with my worry about Lena than Sylvia's personalized chaos. It didn't stop me from nudging the pen holder until it lined up with the desk's edge.

Sylvia tossed a pair of wireless headphones onto a pile of folders, dropped into her chair, angled it to the side, and crossed her legs. "Sorry, it was the directors' quarterly meeting." Her head dropped back as she pinched the bridge of her nose. "They should consider calling them what they actually are—quarterly bitch sessions."

My lips twitched. "Ahh, but isn't that why you make the big bucks, Madam Director?"

She lifted her hand and pointed a maroon-tipped finger my way, shaking it in mock threat. "If you aren't careful, I'll assign you as my proxy."

That did make me laugh. "I'd never make it out alive. Maybe you should sic Adele on them."

She gave a delicate snort. "That would be something. Not only would she keep them on point, they'd be too scared to argue with her." She sat up, a crafty yet pleased smile chasing away the remnants of her earlier frustration. "You know, that's not a bad idea." Wicked humor lit the coffee-colored gaze. "And I'll be sure to share it was your idea."

A small squeak of panic rose as she lobbed my teasing back at me. "Whatever I did to piss you off, I'm sorry."

Her laugh was short but genuine as she settled back in her chair. "I'm guessing you're here about the pending job?"

I shifted my shoulders. "Mostly."

She watched me with avid interest. "Mostly?"

Despite the friendly banter, I couldn't squish the niggle of apprehension about my impending request. "I'd like to ask Evan to do a trace on Lena's phone."

"Why?" The one word carried a cool sharpness indicating I was now addressing the director.

It also served as a reminder that I should have led with an explanation. A fumble I was quick to correct. "This morning, I came back from a coffee run to discover my condo was shut down for a magical homicide investigation. Authorities were still processing the scene when I left, so they aren't letting anyone in or out. I tried to reach Le—"

Sylvia held up a hand, palm out, cutting me off. "Back up, Costas. Magical Homicide?"

"Yes, ma'am."

"Anyone we know?"

Considering the Guild tended to touch on all things Arcane, the question was valid. "No idea. Like I said, I arrived just after the first responders arrived." Since it looked as if details were going be required, I filled in the blanks. "I didn't see the body, and no one I spoke to seemed to know who it was, either, but I caught that the victim was male. You may want to reach out to Detective Brenner for more information. He was waiting for ACRT to arrive when I left."

Sylvia snagged a pen and jotted something on a nearby sticky note. "How does Lena connect to this?"

"Since it was an active scene, they weren't letting people in or out, which meant I couldn't get back into my condo. So I tried calling Lena to let her know what was going on." Realizing I was sitting on the edge of my seat and leaning forward, I forced myself to ease back. "She never answered."

Sylvia tapped the pen absently against the sticky note. "And you automatically jump to the worst possible conclusion that Lena is in trouble?"

As hard as it was, I stifled my wince. Hearing that assumption aloud cut uncomfortably close to the truth. "Not initially." As a defense, it sounded weak, but determined to get my point across, I kept going. "I got home after midnight, and the last time I talked to her was before I headed out for my job. I've been trying to reach her for the last couple of hours with no luck. It's not like her."

Sylvia studied me for what felt like an eternity, then she asked, "Could she have turned her phone off? Perhaps overslept?"

I shrugged. "Maybe, but I'd feel better if I knew for sure."

She frowned. "Was she planning on coming in to the office?"

I shook my head. "The board indicates she just closed a case and is working another. I'm assuming if she had been home, she would've called in to check for messages and then headed out to do the fieldwork on the next job." That normally consisted of knocking on doors and in-person interviews, not hanging in the office. "But I can't shake the feeling that something's off."

Her lips thinned, and whatever her thoughts, they were hidden behind an inscrutable mask. Finally, she gave a small nod. "Have Evan trace her phone and make sure she's out there. Let me know what you find."

Relief coursed through me. "Will do."

She set aside her pen. "Good. Moving on. Are you free tonight?"

The way she asked left me with one answer. "Yes."

Her tight smile didn't reach her eyes. "I need you to do a run."

I took out my phone and pulled up the customized app where I kept my assignment details. "Rating?"

"Basic transport."

Sounded easy enough. When she didn't elaborate, I looked up.

Sylvia's dark gaze pinned me in place. "Client is requesting a level-four NDA."

My relief went up in a puff of smoke. A high-level nondisclosure agreement meant the straightforward transport was more a combination of armed escort and driver.

Sylvia confirmed my suspicion when she continued, "You'll meet at the given location then drive the client to the destination. Once there, you'll accompany them inside, wait until they're done, then return them safely home."

"Threat level?"

"Moderate, but nothing active."

If the client wasn't under an active threat but expected trouble, it meant they were moneyed, so appearances would be crucial for this assignment. "Is the client providing the vehicle?"

"No. You've been authorized to use a class-three vehicle."

I blinked and continued noting the details on my phone. A class three meant the car would be protected by non-military-grade armored doors, bullet-resistant glass, and a low-level aegis ward set to minimize magical threats. All standard for personal security. "Do you have the client's contact information?" When she didn't answer immediately, I looked up to find her watching me, her thoughts clearly on something else. "Sylvia?"

She gave a small head shake, throwing off whatever thought she had. "Before I share that, if you agree to the job, your pay will be the standard rate plus twenty percent."

My checking account would love me, even after the Guild took their cut. Before I got too excited, hard-earned cynicism shoved to the fore. "What's the catch?"

"At this time? Nothing."

"But?"

"But..." She drew out the word. "If the client is satisfied

with your performance, the offer for a retainer position may follow."

"A retainer position?" That meant the client had to be tied to one of the Arcane Families. They were the only ones with the money and need for privacy that would drive a request like this.

Her reluctant nod had me reconsidering my options. I made a point of steering clear of the powerful magical Families for my own peace of mind. A decision that worked well for me up until six months ago, when I took an under-the-table delivery job, only to learn I'd been unwittingly drawn into a kidnapping-blackmail scheme involving the local Cordova Family. On the plus side, that fiasco had allowed me to graduate from employee to contractor and move out of my barely livable apartment and into the condo I now shared with Lena. The downside? It put me in the crosshairs of the Family's Arbiter, Zev Aslanov. No one wanted to mess with an Arbiter, no matter which Family they served. Arbiters existed to resolve messy situations broiling behind the public curtain. Although six months had passed in blessed silence since that night, momentary twinges of worry that Zev would show up at my door haunted me. Some of those twinges had nothing to do with worry.

"Rory?"

My name jerked me out of my spinning thoughts, and I managed to say, "A retainer position is quite the offer."

Sylvia eyed me shrewdly. "Is it something you would consider?"

Personal biases aside, it was a rare career opportunity, one I'd be a fool to reject, and I was no one's fool. "Yes."

She continued to study me for a long moment with an uncomfortable intensity that left me in no doubt that the wheels were spinning in her ruthless mind. As the moments ticked by, apprehension and nerves dug deep claws into my chest, making it hard to breathe. Finally, she looked away and riffled though a haphazard pile of papers. I managed to suck in air without being obvious about it. She pulled out an over-sized sticky note and held it out. I pinched the paper and went to pull it away.

Sylvia held tight, her gaze searching mine. "Be certain about this."

Her question revealed she had noted my desire to stay under the radar with the Families. I appreciated the chance to reconsider, but the reality remained that to succeed profes-sionally, earning a retainer position would be key, and that meant working with the Families. "I am."

It came out stronger than I felt, but believable enough, because she let go of the note. I drew it back, sucked in a big breath, and read the note. It took a moment for the letters to make sense, and once they did, I couldn't figure out why Sylvia was concerned. Yet something about the name nibbled on the edges of my memory. I frowned. "Sabella Rossi?"

Sylvia's gaze sharpened. "Do you know her?"

I shook my head. "It sounds familiar, but no, I don't think so."

"I'd be surprised if you did. She's keen on maintaining anonymity whenever possible."

That not only sounded ominous but also made me ques-tion accepting the job. "Why?"

Clearly hearing the suspicion in my voice, Sylvia gave me a grim smile and sat back. "Because Sabella Rossi is the matri-arch of the Giordano Family."

CHAPTER FOUR

"*THE* GIORDANO FAMILY? As in one of the originating Arcane Families in Europe?" The thought of dealing with one of the biggest and oldest names in magical society had me alternating between clapping in nervous giddiness and fighting the urge to throw up. *Talk about stepping out of the shadows and into the spotlight. Hell, I might as well just roll out the red carpet.*

"Yes, that Family," Sylvia confirmed. "And if you want to be specific, they're from Italy."

Italy or England—wherever didn't really matter—but it did explain Sabella's NDA request. Before I could censor, an inane question escaped. "What is she doing in Phoenix?" Color rose under my cheeks, but at least I didn't compound my gaffe with a face-palm.

Still, it earned me a raised eyebrow and Sylvia's dry response. "She prefers our winter to hers."

Since I was already stumbling down my unintended road, I kept trotting along. "With summer around the corner, is she planning on heading back soon?" That made me realize another possible challenge to this job. "If she's looking for a retainer, she may want to ask someone else. I'm not looking to move overseas." It would suck to lose this chance, but Lena would never forgive me if I bailed on her and our lease.

This time, Sylvia's humor escaped in a small smile. "I'm glad to hear that, but a move is not required."

It was my turn for skepticism. "Italy." I held out my left hand. "Phoenix." My right rose on the other side. I eyed the space between. "That's a hell of a commute."

Sylvia laughed. "Sabella resides here half of the year."

My interest stopped pouting and perked up. "So, if this escalates to a retainer—"

"*If* she makes the offer," Sylvia stressed, "you'd be on call when she is in residence."

Excitement bubbled, edging out my personal concerns. Being on call for half the year could work. "Makes sense." I added Sabella's name and information into my phone and handed back the sticky note. Then, despite my best intentions, my paranoid concerns got the better of me. "Why me?" It was a legit question that didn't reveal my real worry, as there were a couple of established Transporter names whose shingles had been hanging up long enough to lose the shine mine still held.

Sylvia took the small piece of paper, spun her chair so her back was to me, and dropped it in the paper shredder. When it fell silent, she turned back to me, her face unreadable. "Sabella and I have been friends for years. Recently, her driver retired. Now that she's ready to deal with finding a replacement, she asked me for a recommendation. I gave her your name."

Humbled and shocked, I stuttered out, "Th-Thank you." When Sylvia's expression turned puzzled, I added, "For the opportunity, I mean." Because that's what this was, a unique chance to get a very solid, very big boost on my career plans.

"Understand, nothing is guaranteed." There was a wealth of warning in her voice. "That position is yours to earn or lose."

"I understand." Boy howdy, did I get it, but damned if I wasn't going to make the most of it.

Sylvia's austere mask fell away and was replaced by her customary professionalism. "Sabella is expecting you this evening at six thirty." Her *"Don't be late"* came through loud and clear.

"I'll be back here at a quarter after five to pick up the car."

"Good." She got to her feet and came around her desk.

I stood up and followed her to the door. With her hand on the knob and in profile, she stopped. "Let me know as soon as you get ahold of Lena. I want to know where she's been."

Her request caused a twinge of guilt. Bringing my concerns to the director shifted Lena's situation from worried friend to professional concern. "Will do."

I left Sylvia chatting with Adele about her lunch appointment and beelined to Evan. Back in the lobby, the lingering stench of ammonia made my nose wrinkle, but the identity-challenged dog and his owner were nowhere to be found. Behind the dual computer screens, Evan was on the phone. I went over and leaned against the desk's edge, waiting for him to finish.

It wasn't long before he hung up. He used his foot to shove his chair back far enough to study me. "You want something."

"I do."

He folded his arms over his chest. "Bring forth your query."

Normally, I would have indulged in our typical back-and-forth, but my anxiety made that impossible. "I need you to track Lena's phone."

He dropped his arms, and behind his lenses, his eyes narrowed, hiding the flash of something I couldn't identify. "You know how the director feels about the frivolous use of company resources."

"It's not a frivolous request," I muttered then added, "I already cleared it with her."

His gaze hardened. "Is Lena in trouble?"

The sharpness to his question made me pause before I answered, "I hope not."

He turned to the computer, his fingers flying over the keyboard. The bloody battlefield disappeared from the primary screen to be replaced by strings of indecipherable code. "Number?" He shot the question out without looking away from his screen.

I gave it to him and scooted around the desk to stand just behind his shoulder. "Maybe I'm being paranoid."

"How do you figure?" he asked absently. A map popped up on the secondary screen, and with every keystroke, the map adjusted.

Fascinated, I watched the map shift, zoom in, then shift again in a dizzying spin. "Nat mentioned Lena had a mystery man."

His fingers slipped on the keyboard, and the map on screen zoomed out and stilled. Evan cursed. A couple of clicks later, the rapid adjustments continued. "She have a habit of blowing off work for a man?"

"Nope," I answered, noting his reaction. "Which is why I'm having you track her phone." As the minutes ticked by, anticipatory tension had me wrapping my arms around my stomach, hiding my fisted hands. There were no beeps or lights or anything to tell me what was happening. After what felt like forever, I finally broke. "Evan?"

His broad shoulders hunched as he all but hissed, "Shush."

The tension continued to ratchet up until I wanted to scream.

Evan's muttered "Dammit" was followed by his fist slamming against the desk next to the keyboard. He shoved back hard, which forced me back a step in tandem. He dragged a hand through his hair, leaving it mussed. "There's no signal, so I'm assuming it's not active."

I shifted to the side, so I could still see his screen. "If it's not active, it means it's turned off, right?"

"Or something." His tone was dire, his attention once more on the screens.

Frustrated, I snapped, "So what's next?"

"I'm going to see if I can track her activity before the signal dropped."

That sounded simple enough, but as the minutes stretched and it appeared Evan wasn't in a rush to share, I demanded, "Tell me what's going on."

He shot me a disgruntled look. "The program only goes so fast, Rory. It has to piece together the information from the towers her phone pinged off of, and with no idea how long her phone's been offline, it has to dig back hour by hour."

Gritting my teeth, I waited.

Eventually, the sprawling code slowed, and so did the dizzying map changes. When things appeared to finally settle, he hit a button on the phone and growled, "Kel, need you to cover the desk." He tore the earpiece from his ear, tossed it on the desk, then pushed back his chair and stood. "Come on."

I trotted along in his long-legged wake as we headed to the back office. "Tell me what you found."

He held open the door and waved me through the ward as he answered. "Her phone went dark around two yesterday.

Last known location had her over on the west side of the valley."

I barely clocked the sting of the ward as I stepped through. "Where in the west valley?"

He didn't answer. Within two long steps, he'd bypassed me and taken the lead. Moving determinedly through the workspace, he didn't slow as a young man all but ran out of one of the offices. Spotting us, the kid pulled up short. Evan pointed back to the lobby. "Handle things. I'll be back shortly."

Not waiting for a response, Evan kept moving, his voice harder than I had ever heard it. "Any chance she forgot to charge her phone?"

Even though he couldn't see me, I shook my head. "She's anal about keeping it charged. I'm not sure she could function without it." I didn't like his tone. "What about after two? Does she show up anywhere?"

"No." He stopped, pulled me out of the way of anyone walking by, and braced his shoulder against a wall bearing a nameplate that read "GIS-5." The door sported an electronic lock. "When did you see her last?"

"Yesterday morning." I kept my voice equally low. "We headed out at the same time. She mentioned tracking down a couple of promising leads for an assignment. If they panned out, she was hoping to close the job and call it a day. She mentioned dinner, but I was booked and warned her I would be home late."

He frowned. "She say anything about going out? About meeting up with anyone?"

There was an impatient edge to his questions that made me wonder if Evan was jealous. *Something to ponder later.* "No, but we tend to go our own way. Grown women, personal lives, you know how it goes." Yep, that was a definite hint of red rising under his skin as he looked away. I reached out and caught his arm. "Evan, tell me you can find her."

The half-formed blush disappeared, and his frown deepened. "Got one more option we can try." He straightened and motioned to the door. "The map room." He typed a code into the keypad then held his palm flat over it. A shiver of magic ruffled over my skin. The light went from red to green. He grabbed the handle and looked at me. "Did you know the Guild insists on tagging every employee's phone with an emergency loci spell?"

I shrugged. "I'm not surprised. It makes for a great emergency leash. Will it pinpoint her location?"

"Maybe." He twisted the handle and pushed open the door.

"Maybe?" I stuck to his heels as he strode into the windowless room. "What do you mean 'maybe'?"

Despite its outwardly bland appearance, the interior was an impressive sight. The three main walls were covered with interactive screens that mapped out the valley in crystal-clear satellite images. Various colored, blinking points dotted the maps. I knew enough to understand each flashing light represented a Guild employee. Compared to the others on the massive grid of the city, those pinpoints were few and far between. A double row of computer stations on narrow tables ran down the room's center. Half the stations were occupied, their operators barely acknowledging our entrance beyond their initial glance up to blink owlishly before turning back to their oversized screens. Empty junk-food wrappers littered the cord-strewn space between, and the scent of stale pizza hung on the air. It was the epitome of nerd nirvana.

Ignoring them, Evan headed toward the screen on the far wall without answering my question.

I followed with a hissed "Evan."

He waited until I stopped at his side and kept his voice

low. "What I mean is, the loci spell, it's magic based." He laid his fingers above the map's key in the bottom right corner. I recognized the layout of the west valley. He pinned me with a grim gaze. "You know as well as I do, if Lena's in trouble and that trouble is attached to a mage, we may be SOL."

I did not want to hear that we were shit out of luck. I wanted him to tell me where Lena was, but throwing a hissy fit wasn't just unprofessional. It would also get me nowhere. So I bit my tongue and kept my mouth shut.

Evan's fingers moved, activating the map's key. Arcane symbols in prescribed patterns flared to life, hovering over the map's surface, like a holographic overlay. Magic sparked, brushing over my skin as an unearthly glow simmered in Evan's eyes. In response to his magic, the satellite image on the screen changed with dizzying speed. He moved his hand, touching three distinct points on the map, then under his breath, he muttered an incantation that I didn't catch. The three points ignited in a blue-green blaze that raced along lines to connect them into a triangle. He lifted his hand, and for a moment, his magic hung there, connecting the three illuminated pins by the thinnest thread. They shimmered, as if plucked by an invisible finger, then stilled.

I held my breath, my heart pounding, hope rising.

He stared at the map.

The itchy feeling of his magic increased until I was rubbing my palms against my hips to erase the sensation.

The glowing lines flickered again, only to blink out, leaving the map unchanged. "Fuck."

Evan's barely there curse turned my blood to ice. My restless movement froze. "What? Where is she?"

He didn't answer. Instead, he touched the screen again. This time, the rush of magic was stronger, deeper, and left me gritting my teeth. Once again, the three points flared into brilliant life. The interconnecting lines ignited, only to flicker out.

"Evan?" His name came out sharp, because I knew what he was going to say.

His face was grim as he dropped his hand. "The loci spell is being blocked."

Yep, exactly what I didn't want to hear. Fuckin' great. Whatever Lena was tangled up in probably involved a high-powered mage, which meant tracking her by magic wasn't an option. We couldn't track what we couldn't sense. Fine, great, we just needed to go back to good old-fashion tracking. I studied the area lying within Evan's triangular parameter.

"That's what?" I traced where the lines flared. "Nine, maybe ten blocks?"

His hands went to his hips. "At least that."

So maybe two miles. Doable. "What's there?"

His magic sparked, and labels popped up as the screen zoomed in. "A couple of shopping centers, apartments, neighborhood—"

"Office park." I pointed to the cluster of buildings tucked between an apartment complex and a storage unit facility.

"Yeah, another one over here." Evan circled another collection of offices.

There were too many options.

Evan was obviously thinking the same thing. "We need to narrow it down."

"And we do that how?"

"Got an idea." Evan grabbed my arm and steered me toward the door. "Come on."

Evan let me go as the door to the map room closed behind us. Keeping pace, I asked, "Where are we going?"

He didn't slow. "My office."

Works for me. We crossed the floor and made a couple of turns before entering a quiet hall interspersed with unmarked doors. It was an area most forgot existed. Evan opened the last door on the end and disappeared inside. I followed. His office resembled a rehabbed supply closet. The lack of windows left the space feeling slightly claustrophobic and would've driven me nuts in no time. To help combat the smothering feeling, I left the door open.

Evan rounded the desk that dominated the space and hunched over, half-hidden by the multiple screens. The lone visitor's chair was piled high with unidentifiable electronics, so I leaned a hip against the small overstuffed bookcase and picked up the worn Rubik's Cube to work off my anxiety while Evan did whatever it was he'd planned on doing.

His fingers flew over the keyboard, creating rapid-fire clicks. "All right, Lena-bee, let's see what you were up to."

My fingers stilled on the fidget toy, and I glanced up. *Lena-bee?* Since I was fairly sure I wasn't meant to hear that, I refrained from taking Evan's focus away from whatever was on his screens. It would do me no good to pester. He would start talking when he was ready.

I managed to turn one side of the cube a solid green before Evan finally spoke. "Okay, I'm in."

I set the toy down and walked over to join him. "In what?"

"Lena's files."

Since only a couple of minutes had passed, I couldn't help but ask, "Aren't our files pass-coded?" Considering the clients we served, I would have thought the Guild's electronic security would be tougher than that.

He turned just enough that the screen's illumination reflected off his lenses, veiling his eyes. "Hello, electro mage here."

I shook my head. *Right, guess nothing is off limits to him then.* "That does not make me feel any better."

He turned back to the screen, his lips twitching. "Who do you think designed our security?"

"Point," I muttered then leaned in to see what he pulled up. "The whiteboard indicated she just closed a case."

"Uh."

"Uh?"

Evan looked at me over the edge of his glasses. "System says she has four open cases."

I frowned. "Four?"

Evan's fingers didn't pause, and his screens filled with files. "Yep, looks like she accessed this one"—he tapped a finger on his first screen—"yesterday morning, so we'll start here. The access dates on the other three go back a couple of days."

"Probably because those cases are in the initial stages of investigation." Bracing my hands on his desk, I read the information on the screen, feeling Evan do the same next to me.

I zeroed in on the noted contact name. "Who is Dr. Oliver Martin?"

Evan turned to his keyboard, the middle screen shifting as he typed. "Dr. Oliver Martin is a urologist with the Reid Clinic." An image of an older man with glasses and receding hair line, wearing the standard white lab coat, appeared on the screen.

Puzzled, I asked, "Why is he hiring a Guild Key?"

"He's not." Evan's attention stayed on his screens as he talked and typed. "At the insistence of his patient, the good doctor requested the Guild's assistance."

That still didn't make sense. "Why?"

"Because..." Evan's answer was distracted. "It appears his patient is trying to hide his identity behind a doctor-patient confidentiality screen."

"Can you do that?"

"If you have enough money, you can do anything."

"Can you—"

"Already did." Grim satisfaction broke through the harsh lines of Evan's face. "Keith Thatcher." On the far screen, a face popped up. Based upon the well-tailored suit and the glittery background, the photo was obviously taken at some upscale event.

I studied the image of a man in his early sixties. He sported a short conservative cut that blended grays and browns into an attractive mix above arrogant brown eyes. His face bore the lines of maturity expected of someone his age, and he had an arm around an equally mature woman. They were the epitome of a well-to-do couple, but there was something about him that I couldn't place. "Why does he look familiar?"

"Do you pay any attention to the gossip rags?"

"Do you knit?" I gave Evan an arch look, already knowing his answer.

A brief flash of humor lightened Evan's eyes. "At one time, Keith Thatcher was a financial manager for LanTech Industries."

The connection clicked, but not for the reason Evan assumed. LanTech's spectacular implosion months earlier was proof of what happened when someone crossed a major Arcane Family. "LanTech closed their doors—what? Four months ago?"

Evan nodded. "Yep, they lost the majority of their military contracts, which financially crippled them. Or that was the story."

There was much more to it than that, but since keeping my mouth shut had worked for the last six months, I wasn't inclined to share the details, especially since one of those details was my unintentional part in a failed kidnapping attempt.

Unaware of my thoughts, Evan kept sharing. "Just before Keith lost his job, he also lost his wife of thirty-plus years. The divorce was well underway before the LanTech mess, but it came to a head about the same time." An image of a couple came onscreen. "Meet Madeline Thatcher and Keith's replacement, Theo Mahon."

Madeline's name struck a chord. One of the bigger mover and shakers in the valley, she'd held that position uncontested for decades. She was striking. Her hair was a stunning shade of silver no dye could ever match, and it added depth to her timeless beauty. But it was the lean, fit man standing next to her that had me asking, "There's what? Twenty years between them?"

"Try twenty-eight." Evan's voice was dry.

That put Theo in his early thirties. I grimaced. "I'm guessing the tabloids had a field day with their relationship?"

"Considering Madeline's one and only son is three years older than her boy toy, you'd be guessing right." Evan leaned back and folded his arms over his chest as he stared at the screen. "But that wasn't the only reason they were all over the news."

I studied Theo's image. It was hard to miss the salon masterpiece of casual sun-streaked brown hair complemented by a close-cropped beard covering an angled chin and a grin filled with startlingly white teeth. It didn't take much to guess what other rumors were floating around about the May-December couple. "Let me guess—someone cheated, hence the nasty divorce?"

"Both someones," Evan confirmed. "But infidelity wasn't their only vice. Allegations of embezzlement were thrown around, but nothing ever came of it. The divorce was messy, but by the time the final papers were signed, Theo was a standard fixture at Madeline's side, and the ex had a hell of an alimony bill and no job. The son does his best to ignore them all."

Things like that made me grateful to be an orphan. "Can't say I blame him."

"It gets better." Evan hit a key and brought up a news article. "Last week, Madeline and Theo announced their engagement."

"Sounds more like a story line in a soap opera."

"Which is exactly what the paparazzi bank on when they print shit like this." Evan went back to playing with the keyboard, shutting down windows and opening others. "Who knows what the real story is there? What is important is why Keith doesn't want his name attached to a Guild job."

Oh, I can think of a few reasons. "Maybe he's tired of making headlines."

"Maybe." Evan kept shifting through various windows and files.

Instead of pursuing that rabbit hole, I focused on the more important one. "Dr. Martin submitted the case to the Guild, and he's a what? A urologist? They deal with kidneys and bladders and such, right?" I tried to make the pieces fit. The screen filled with what read suspiciously like a patient's medical file—Keith's, to be exact. "Is that what I think it is?"

"I have no idea what you think it is," Evan countered with studied nonchalance. "But this"—he pointed at a section—"is probably why the Guild—and by extension, Lena—was called in."

I read the mix of jargon and numbers, trying to make sense of it. "Looks like the doctor ran a bunch of tests on Keith. Most of which came back negative. Except this one. What does 'MC-GK required' mean?"

"If this MC is the same as the one used in police lab reports, I'd say magical contagion," Evan confirmed.

Which means... "GK? Guild Key required?" *If one plus one equaled two, then...* "Keith was cursed."

"Sure looks like it." Evan grimaced. "If I was to guess, I'd bet his most important anatomy part was targeted."

I winced. *Okay, that was... gross.* I turned back to the first screen with Lena's case file. "Where's her after-action report?" If Lena marked the case closed on the board, her final report should be on file.

"There isn't one." Evan started closing down windows, leaving Lena's case files up. "I'm guessing she was planning on filing it before she went MIA. Her last login to the case file was yesterday at 9:23 a.m. She's got a note here."

I leaned in, my hand tightening on the back of Evan's chair. "She's got a wrap-up appointment with Keith today at two." I checked the clock in the corner of his screen and noted the time: 12:18 p.m. My mind churned through options. "Any chance she's got a draft of the report saved somewhere?"

"Hang on. Let me see if I can check a few things." His fingers flew over the keyboard. "What are you thinking?"

"Lena changed the case's status on the board to closed, which tells me the case was all but finished. Yet there's no final report, and she has a meeting with the client. Maybe she hadn't filed the final report because she had a couple of loose ends to tie up first. If I can—"

"Yes!" Evan's exclamation cut me off. "Got something." A half-finished after-action report filled the screen.

I stifled my urge to echo his excitement. "Can you print that out for me?"

In answer, a printer in the corner powered up and began spitting out pages. "What's your plan, Rory?"

I collected the pages from the printer. "I'm going to keep Lena's appointment with Mr. Thatcher." I turned, papers in hand, and met Evan's gaze. "Do we have an address for him?"

He turned to his computer. "It's on his medical records."

I set the papers down and pulled out my phone, waiting for the address.

A few keystrokes later, he said, "It's 3598 East De La Vista West in Scottsdale." He pushed his chair back and stood.

I typed Keith's address into my phone. "Looks like I'm going to Scottsdale." I picked up Lena's report and turned to the door, only to pull up short when Evan blocked my way. "What?"

Arms braced against the doorjamb, he stared down at me, his expression steely. "I'm coming with you."

"No, you're not." It came out sharp.

He aimed a hard-eyed glare at me. "Excuse me?"

Instead of quailing under that dark look, I lifted my chin. "I need you here."

"Why? You and I both know the chance of Lena waltzing in is less than zero."

"I know." And that worried the hell out of me. Every instinct I had screamed my best friend was in serious trouble. "Which is why I need you to stay here. Look through her other cases. Find out if there are any other leads. If this doesn't pan out, I'm going to need a next step."

His gaze reflected the same mix of worry and frustration roiling in me, but his carried something more, something he was trying hard to downplay. He didn't back down. "You don't even know if she'll show up at his place."

Chances were damn high she wouldn't, but I was still going. "And?"

"Dammit." He dropped his arms and looked away, a muscle in his jaw flexing as he glared at something only he could see. "How are you going to play this?"

"I'll tell him Lena was unavoidably detained. After that, I'll play it by ear." It was the best I could do, considering I was flying blind. "In the meantime, you can update Sylvia."

He blew out a harsh breath and stepped aside. "Poking around on your own isn't smart. Especially considering the names involved."

I gave him an arch look. "Neither is hacking into confidential records, but that didn't stop you, did it?" When all he did was glare, I added, "I'm not exactly going solo here, since you'll be tracking my ass, right?"

He didn't deny it, but exasperation swept over his face as he shook his head. "Just be careful of whose toes you're stepping on, Rory, and keep your damn phone on you."

"Will do."

I hustled out of his office, determined to keep stomping on said toes until someone tripped and I found out where the hell Lena was.

CHAPTER FIVE

I LEFT Evan's office and headed straight to my locker, where I kept a spare set of clothes and a backup weapon. There was no way someone like Keith Thatcher would take me seriously if I showed up in jeans and a faded concert T-shirt. As for the weapon, well, it was better to be safe than sorry. In the empty locker room, I changed into dress pants and a blouse before tucking the 9mm Glock G43X in the concealed waist holster. Hopefully Keith wouldn't notice the not-so-professional black slip-ons that didn't quite match the rest of my attire. After a quick touch-up on my hair and a few swipes of makeup, I was as good as I was going to get.

I took a few precious minutes to read through Lena's after-action report. Curse breaking wasn't my forte, but I knew the basics. The convoluted magic could range from pesky to deadly, one-time usage to unending, and simple to complex. Reversing that kind of spell required untangling a complex web of power and intentions. That was why Keys, or curse breakers, were highly specialized. For Lena to be assigned meant the curse was target specific, and considering the players, that was not a surprise. The Thatchers definitely qualified as soap opera material.

Lena's notes were professional and impartial, but we'd been friends long enough for me to read between the lines, and the story was a doozy. Keith Thatcher had gone to Dr. Martin when he began having issues in the bedroom—performance issues, to be exact. After exhausting all available medical tests, Dr. Martin had advised opening an investigation with the Guild for possible magical causes. Once Lena was assigned, it didn't take her long to confirm that Keith had, indeed, been cursed. Determining who had set the curse and why had turned out to be the bigger challenge, especially as Keith was apparently keen on keeping the embarrassing details quiet. Her investigation began with the typical culprits: the victim, his ex-wife, and her brand-new fiancé.

First up was the man himself, Keith. He claimed the curse had to be Madeline's doing. He painted a picture of his ex as being vindictive and jealous, despite her apparent happiness with her new boyfriend and the fact that their divorce had been final for months. A divorce Madeline instigated. In fact, he was certain Madeline was punishing him for sleeping with her best friend, Vivian Ellis.

When Lena interviewed Madeline, she, of course, denied any involvement with the curse. When Lena mentioned Keith's affair with Vivian, Madeline all but waved it off as unimportant. Not only had it occurred well after the divorce, but Vivian had mentioned it as a joke to Madeline, who'd advised her bestie to go for it, but be sure to use protection as Keith was a man-whore. Madeline had warned Lena that if she thought the curse was set by someone Keith had slept with then dumped, Lena might be in for a challenge. Her ex was an ex because he couldn't keep it in his pants. Lena actually quoted Madeline saying, "If I wanted to make him pay for fucking around, I'd just cut it off. I wouldn't bother with a curse."

I thought I might like Madeline.

Lena interviewed Vivian, who not only corroborated Madeline's story, but shared that the singular experience was "far from memorable and not worth repeating." I skimmed the other interviews, including Keith's bed-hopping partners, his business acquaintances, and a handful of people who were considered friends. There were plenty of females and a few males who would justifiably want to ensure Keith's penis was out of action, but Lena had heard a rumor from a couple of different people that Madeline and Keith had ended up back in bed at some point in the last few months. Vivian had mentioned that Madeline had considered it an "oops" moment, and one of Keith's male friends commented that Keith hoped it meant Madeline would take him back.

Lena had even uncovered a recent police report of a domestic disturbance between the divorced couple at the son's home. Bolstered by alcohol, Keith had confronted Madeline about their one-night stand at a family dinner in front of the son, his wife and teenage children, and Theo. Things blew up, someone got slapped, words were exchanged, and the police were called. When the dust settled, Keith was taken away in cuffs, the son swore he was done with both parents, and Theo spent the night at a motel. However, the younger man's anger didn't last long, because days later, he and Madeline announced their engagement.

It had taken Lena a bit to work through the tangled maze of relationships and affairs, especially since she seemed to be having trouble pinning Theo down for an interview. It looked like she'd finally managed to meet him yesterday morning, but her notes were missing. Prior to that meeting, she had narrowed her suspects to Madeline or Theo. Lena still had a couple of questions for Keith noted, but knowing how Lena's mind worked, it wasn't hard to tell she was leaning toward Theo as the guilty party.

With the file in hand, I headed out. During the twenty-plus-minute drive to Keith's address, I went over my approach. I wasn't holding out hope that Lena would show for the scheduled appointment, but maybe I could get something from Keith that would help narrow down where she might be or what she might be doing. It was a hell of a long shot, but it was better than sitting around waiting.

Out of habit, I checked my mirrors as I drove, but nothing struck me as out of the ordinary. Maybe it was paranoid to think I would be followed, but the longer I went without hearing anything from Lena, the more I worried. Using my phone's GPS, I followed the directions to an upscale neighborhood. I wound my way through the neighborhood streets lined with large houses, shiny sedans and SUVs, and ruthlessly manicured yards. It was one of the newer planned communities that obviously catered to those who would call themselves "comfortable." It wasn't just the higher-priced rides or McMansions that gave it away, but the fact that the lots weren't sitting on top of each other, unlike many bedroom communities, where every inch counted. Here, people didn't have to worry that their neighbor could watch them and their neighbor's TV at the same time.

My GPS took me to a wide driveway that led to an over-sized architectural beauty that was a cross between an Italian villa and a Spanish ranch. The mix of whitewashed adobe and burnished red tiles sat pretty and polished under the afternoon sun. It wasn't the only bright, shiny thing in attendance. A real estate agent's sign was propped up in the meticulously kept front yard. *Hmm, looks like Keith is moving.*

I parked my Mustang next to a sexy black Audi RS that sat in the drive instead of in the triple garage then grabbed Lena's file. I got out, eyeing the gorgeous sedan, somewhat surprised by Keith's automotive taste. From what little information I had on him, I would have pegged him as a Benz type. I beeped my locks then scanned for any nosy neighbors. Luckily, it was early afternoon, and the street was quiet. A classic Corvette crouched in the drive next door. The gleaming cherry-red paint was dust free, with no car cover in sight. *What? Do they have someone come out and dust it every day?*

Living in the desert meant everything carried a layer of dust. Between that and the unrelenting Phoenix sun, keeping a car showroom pretty was damn near impossible. That was why I paid extra for covered parking for my Mustang.

Movement on the street was followed by the soft sound of wheels over asphalt as one of the latest electric sedans rolled by, its heavily tinted windows hiding the occupants. I turned, watching it head out of the neighborhood, and got my mind back on point. I followed the flagstone path to a front courtyard guarded by an oversized door laced in wrought iron to go with the Spanish-ranch vibe. I moved up the three steps, and as I went to ring the bell, I noticed the thick door was open a couple of inches.

A sense of foreboding crawled down my spine, but I tried to shake it off, knowing my morning had left me markedly off balance. I checked my watch, noting I'd made the appointment time with five minutes to spare. I stood there for a moment, logic urging me to turn around and call Evan. Instead, I tucked the file under my arm. Being careful not to touch the door, I leaned in and braced a hand on the doorjamb. I didn't need Keith calling the police on me. "Hello? Mr. Thatcher?"

Silence answered.

Okay, where was the client? I tried again. "Mr. Thatcher? My name is Rory Costas. I'm with the Guild."

Still nothing. I studied the partially opened door as tension coiled. In response, my magic stretched awake, covering my skin in a thin layer of invisible armor. My ability wasn't showy or intimidating, but it was a hell of a defense. Right now, not knowing what lay inside, I needed that kind of reassurance. The formal designation for what I wielded was Prism, but that knowledge was something I kept quiet, mainly because it was a rare ability often coveted and ruthlessly exploited.

A Prism's power acted like a magic-repellant armor, for lack of a better term. It wasn't impenetrable—a purely physical attack could breach it, or a relentlessly strong magical attack could eventually overpower it—but when facing most magical assaults, it would buffer the impact. On rare occasions, I had been able to turn the strike back on the originator, but it only happened when death and I were getting up close and personal. Right now, I had no intention of stepping inside without its protection.

Moving forward was a given, because I didn't need the skin-crawling apprehension to tell me something was very wrong inside Mr. Thatcher's house. My desire for answers about Lena's whereabouts smothered logic and had me giving the door a little push with my fingertips. The surprisingly thick door swung open silently, and the rush of cool air carried nothing more threatening than a pleasant floral scent. *"Come in," said the spider to the fly.* Standing in the open doorway, I clutched the file in one hand, the other fisted at my side, knowing this was a very bad idea. Despite my waning hope, I tried one last time. "Hello? Mr. Thatcher? Are you home?"

Nothing.

I looked over my shoulder, but the street and sidewalks remained empty. My gaze skated over the For Sale sign. Maybe I was overreacting. This place looked huge enough that if they were in the midst of a showing, they would have no idea anyone was here. *Yeah, even I don't believe that one.*

Taking a deep breath, I drew my magic close and stepped over the threshold, braced for anything. I stood in the tiled foyer under an unlit chandelier and waited.

Nothing.

Across from me, floor-to-ceiling windows that looked as if they could be pushed aside led into a stunning backyard. *Talk about bringing the outside in.*

Two arched entries branched off from the foyer. The one on the left led into what appeared to be a hall, and the one to the right opened into a great room. My magic vibrated against my skin, just as on edge as I felt. I strained my ears, trying to catch any indication of life, but all that came back was the soft hum of air conditioning.

With no other choice, I left the door open behind me and went to the left. I stepped through the archway and came to a halt as a wave of pins and needles washed over my skin. I knew that feeling. It was the same one I'd encountered when walking into a scene saturated by magic. For the longest time, I'd thought everyone got the same visceral warning, but careful questioning of friends revealed that wasn't always the case. It might be a side effect of being a Prism. Not that I would know, since information on Prisms, unlike other magical abilities, was nearly impossible to find. Trust me, I looked.

Gritting my teeth, I waited for the lingering traces of magic to abate. It was akin to standing at a beach's waterline, the echoes of power curling around my ankles like a politely persistent, thorny wave. Even the buffer of my protective magic couldn't keep it from tugging me forward. I stood fast, ignoring it, because whatever had happened here hadn't been caused by a run-of-the-mill spell. For a magical echo to be this strong equaled a highly complex casting, the kind that required years of training. Training a top-level Guild operative or a ranking member of an Arcane Family would have, and neither of those boded well. My pulse kicked up, and I swallowed against a dry throat. *What the hell has Lena been dragged into?*

Since the lingering power refused to relent, I forced my legs to work and moved deeper into the open space. I didn't have to go far to confirm that Keith would not be making this appointment. In fact, it would be safe to assume wherever Keith Thatcher was, he was in serious trouble. The living room was a disaster. What once must have been a glass-and-wood coffee table was now nothing but shards and kindling. Couch cushions looked like they had gone a few rounds with a shredder, one of the two chairs was overturned, and the area rug bore obvious scorch marks. Even more ominous, the tempered glass of the folding patio doors separating the living area from the back yard was all but opaque. Whatever slammed into them was obviously big and heavy enough to have shattered it. Something, say, like a body?

What happened here? And where was Keith Thatcher?

After skirting the mess of broken glass, shattered pottery, and splintered wood, I stopped in a relatively clear spot. Strangely, the violence seemed contained to the front half of the great room. Whatever had happened had occurred in front of the unlit fireplace dominating the wall to the left of the entryway. The mantelpiece hung at a diagonal, one end resting on the floor, surrounded by the shattered remains of whatever it'd once held. A low set of shelves that had once sat behind the couch had been smashed into pieces, the wood mixing with broken electronic equipment, torn books, and decimated knickknacks. At the room's far end, the kitchen appeared untouched. In fact, place settings were neatly arranged on the breakfast bar, and the barstools were tucked in place. The destruction stopped at the untouched seating arrangements that sat between the two areas. The entire scene was not only weird, but also disturbing on an instinctual level.

I studied the room carefully then picked my way through the debris, wading through the magical remnants hovering unseen around the chaos. The skin-ruffling sensation of expended magic got stronger as I moved closer to the center of the destruction, the echo of it rubbing like a painful scrape. So far, my power had kept it to nothing more than a nuisance. Not keen on triggering it to a more credible threat, I stopped moving and tried to piece together what had happened. It wasn't hard to picture what the room had looked like before. The couch facing the fireplace. The chairs positioned on either side, with the coffee table taking up the center space. All of the pieces carefully placed to create a casual but elegant area for conversation.

I toed aside a couch cushion to reveal a thick cut glass lying on its side. The glass's previous contents were now nothing more than a stain on the rug. Using my foot, I nudged some of the larger pieces of torn upholstery away. It didn't take long to uncover a second glass. Keith hadn't been alone, but had, in fact, been with someone he was comfortable enough to share drinks with. Someone he'd consider safe. I dropped into a crouch. The change in perspective helped. I reached for the first discolored spot on the thick rug, doing my best to ignore the unsettling sensation of lingering magic nibbling at my hand. My fingers brushed the stiff carpet fibers. Dry. The spill was hours old.

Without moving, I eyed the remains of the coffee table and the discolored marks snaking under the wreckage. I carefully crab-walked closer. I dropped a knee in a relatively clear spot and braced a hand on what was left of a chair. With my other hand, I used the folder to brush aside the clutter without disturbing the markings so I could study them. They appeared to be burnt into the rug. But when my careful movements actually marred the lines, I changed my assumption. The marks were more like ashes than actual burn scars. Yet there was something familiar about the lines, something I couldn't quite place. Tucking the folder under my arm, I reached out to move a piece of cushion foam away so I could see more of the strange markings.

"Do you always poke at dangerous things, Rory?"

I froze in mid-motion. Instead of going for my gun, I jerked my head up and met the dark gaze of the one man guaranteed to take any situation from bad to worse. "What the hell are you doing here, Zev?"

The six-foot-two slice of darkness stood in the entryway in jeans and a T-shirt that did nothing to disguise the threat he carried with him. As the Arbiter of the Cordova Family, that threat was undeniable. One of his dark brows rose in sardonic amusement. "I think that should be *my* question."

I straightened slowly, doing my best to ignore my racing pulse and not fidget under his stare. Heat rushed under my skin, and I prayed it stayed off my cheeks. "I'm here on Guild business."

He pushed off the wall and prowled closer, skirting the destruction. "Is that so?"

"Yes, it is so." *Wow, way to sound mature, Rory.* My rapidly pounding heart had nothing to do with seeing him again. *Nope, not at all.* I turned with him, uncomfortable with having him at my back.

He continued toward the patio doors and stopped, keeping his back to me. "So you've already called the police?"

There was something in his voice I couldn't pin down. "Since I just got here, no."

He shook his head then turned to face me. He folded his arms over his chest, the move tightening the material over his broad shoulders. "Guess that will make it awkward when they show up."

I jerked my wandering gaze from his physique and automatically glanced back toward the front door. "What?" The
question came out sharper than I intended, mainly because
his presence threw me off center. I turned back and caught
his arrogant amusement. Narrowing my eyes, I felt my
temper rise. "Did you call them?"

He shook his head. "Didn't have to. They were already on
their way."

Hearing that made my muscles lock in shock. "What?"

He nodded, his close-cropped beard doing little to hide
his smirk. "Yep, they should be here in the next five minutes."

I dragged a hand through my hair as I looked around,
trying belatedly to spot Keith's security but not really seeing
anything. *Shit, I must have tripped an alarm somewhere. Time for a
quick exit.* "Damn security. I need to go."

Zev muttered something I didn't catch because I was
already working my way out of the wrecked living room.
Unsurprisingly, he was on my heels as I headed out of Keith's
house. I could all but feel his breath on my neck as I stepped
over the threshold and back into the afternoon heat. My foot
hit the second step when a hard hand on my arm put a stop
to my retreat. "Not so fast, Rory. We're not done."

Of course we weren't, because that would be too easy.
Sighing, I waited impatiently while he pulled the door almost
closed. "Hurry up," I muttered.

"Chill. I took care of the cameras."

I pulled against his hold. Not that it did any good.

He kept a firm grip on my arm and hauled me along as we
rushed down the steps. "Let's go."

"What do you think I was trying to do?" It was snarky, but
that seemed to be the dominant tone of my interactions
with Zev.

He didn't answer as he all but dragged me to my car.
"Get in."

His grip disappeared, and I beeped the locks. I went to open the door but stopped because Zev had his hand flat against the door. I glared. "What?"

"We need to talk."

Talk? We need to do a lot more than talk. I released the handle and turned so we were facing each other, frustration and impatience making me reckless. "Here? Now? I thought we were trying to avoid the cops."

He closed in, reducing the space between us to miniscule. My breathing shallowed, mainly because taking a deep breath would breach the scant space between us. I wasn't ready to handle that on top of everything else. He leaned his head down, his voice a low rumble. "We're doing that, but you're going to follow me out of here so we can have this discussion uninterrupted."

Mmm, uninterrupted? Sounds good to me. I spoke over my purely idiotic, hormone-induced madness. "I am?"

His dark eyes held mine, his ruthless streak shining through with unmistakable clarity. "You are, because if I have to hunt your ass down, you won't like it."

All sorts of emotions churned through me. The hardest one to ignore was the immature desire to sink a knee into his balls in response to his patronizing tone. Adult that I was, I managed not to give in to the dangerously stupid urge. Zev's retributions were not to be taken lightly. Besides, I had a few questions of my own to ask. "Fine."

"Fine," he repeated before dropping his hand and stepping back so I could open my door.

I got in, refusing to look at him. I continued to do my best to ignore him as I started the Mustang. When my car quietly rumbled to life, he finally turned and jogged over two houses to a big, beautiful beast of a motorcycle. I reversed out of the drive and onto the street, scouring the area for signs of the impending police response, my fingers dancing nervously on the steering wheel. A million thoughts swirled, none of them landing for long, but under it all, a ribbon of dread and excitement unfurled. Because Zev was the Cordova Family's arm of justice and vengeance, his interest in Keith did not bode well. It meant the murky waters swirling around Keith were a hell of a lot deeper than I'd expected. And somehow, some way, Lena was involved. No way in hell would I be leaving her to the sharks. Zev's bike roared past, and I followed, determined to find out just what in the hell was going on.

CHAPTER SIX

I FOLLOWED Zev's bike out of the neighborhood and onto the main road. He didn't go far, just a couple of miles, before turning into one of the sprawling shopping centers that seem to populate every other block in this part of town. It was actually one of the nicer centers, complete with pretty little areas between shops to sit and rest before reentering shopping hell. He aimed his bike at one of the spots closer to the shops, while I pulled past and took the first available space farther down.

I put Lena's file in my glove compartment and locked it. For insurance, I touched the security sigil subtly etched next to the handle and activated the ward. Overkill, maybe, but better safe than sorry. I got out and walked through the bright afternoon sun to where Zev waited for me by his bike. He made quite the picture, all tall, dark, and handsome mixed with trouble. The last bit wasn't from his looks, so much as the air of lethal mystery hovering around him. Luckily, I had no desire to play Sherlock Holmes.

Liar!

Ignoring the irrational denial in my head, I stopped in

front of him and looked around, avoiding eye contact. "Interesting place to talk."

"Better than Keith's driveway." Without waiting for my response, he put his hand at the base of my spine and gave me a nudge forward. "Come on."

As we walked side by side, I did my best to ignore the completely inappropriate reactions his impersonal touch evoked. Not that my hormones were all that smart to begin with. Nope, they were brainless little bastards.

We wound through the eclectic mix of independent and corporate shops until we reached one at the end of the inside corridor. Rather than trying to blend with the rest of the storefronts, this shop sat proudly unapologetic, flouting its unusual glory for all to see. A garden fence decorated with live greenery and sun-faded ribbons ran along the path from the sidewalk to the door. A multitude of wind chimes muttered softly as we approached the door painted to look like wood. A reflective film designed to reduce the sun's glare covered the large windows, while fairy lights outlined the edges. A sign hanging from an ornate metal holder standing next to the door proclaimed it Haven's Corner.

The door swung open, disgorging a couple armed with yoga mats, coffee, and pastry-filled bags. I stepped aside for them to pass as Zev caught the door's edge, holding it open. Once the couple cleared the small porch area, he waved me through. Stomach-rumbling smells lured me into the AC-cooled depths. It was busy but not packed. Scattered through the shop were chairs, some with tables, some without. On either side of the counter, cozy nooks were tucked toward the back. Customers wandered away from the register to wait for their orders. We walked up to the high counter, where an older woman sat on a stool, armed with a pair of long knitting needles that moved with mesmerizing grace as they escorted an electric-blue thread in a lively dance.

With a welcoming smile that took years off her face, she watched us approach. "Zev, how are you?"

"Good, Maeve, good." He moved around me and leaned against the counter. "What's the pastry special today?"

Maeve set her knitting project aside. "Apple crumble."

My stomach chose to offer its opinion, loudly enough that Zev shot me an amused look before turning back to Maeve. "We'll take two, please."

Maeve got off her stool and headed toward the pastry case. "Drinks?"

"My usual." He turned to me in silent question.

I did a quick scan of the handwritten list of drinks and spotted a caramel-vanilla-chocolate mix that sounded good. "I'll take a Gypsy Queen, please."

"Of course." Maeve continued to bustle around behind the counter, prepping the apple crumble. "Here or to go?"

"Here," Zev answered, already pulling out his wallet.

Maeve bobbed her head then called out to the young man working with the plethora of coffee machines at the other end. "Max, a Gypsy Queen and a Marauder, please."

"Got it, Maeve," the kid shot back without looking up. Behind him, a couple of empty cups floated from the back counter and settled behind the one already sitting on the counter next to him.

Maeve handed over two small plates, two forks, and napkins. Since Zev was busy paying, I took them with a polite "Thank you."

We waited for our drinks and collected them, then Zev led me toward the empty nook area on the left. The high-back pub-style bench seats curled around a cozy table, leaving the area semi-private. Zev took one side, and I set the plates on the table before I took the other. Zev pushed my cup toward me as I busied myself with unfolding a napkin and laying it on my lap. My nervous movements stilled as a brush of magic swept over me. Zev's hand hovered over a carved symbol on the table. He pulled his hand back as the illuminated lines faded back to inert.

Recognizing the markings, I asked, "Soundproofing?"

Zev curled his fingers around his cup. "It's best this conversation stays between us."

I stabbed my fork into the apple crumble. "And which conversation would that be?" I held his gaze as I took a bite. Buttery cinnamon and tangy apple filled my mouth. *Damn, this was good.* I'd have to make a return trip, minus Zev's broody presence.

"The one about how Keith Thatcher ended up dead on your doorstep."

I choked on my bite, inhaling crumbs, which just made my coughing worse. I grabbed my drink and did my best to relearn to breathe. Finally, I found my voice and managed a squeaky "Excuse me?"

"You heard me." Zev watched me with a disconcerting calm, his dark gaze intent as he took a sip of his drink before setting it down.

I stared, a hundred and one questions running through my head while worry for Lena crested. A flash of memory—the disconcerting glimpse of someone on the edge of the crowd from the morning's scene at my condo—had me accusing, "You were there this morning. Outside my condo. Weren't you?"

"I was." There was nothing apologetic about his confirmation.

Not that I expected him to, but the lack of it still pissed me off. "Why?"

"Same reason you were poking around in a private residence," he continued with that irritating calm. "I was investigating Keith Thatcher."

Uh-huh, sure he was.

Before my disbelief gained traction, pitiless logic pointed out that Keith held connections to both Lena and LanTech, which meant there was a solid chance Zev wasn't lying. Well, not outright anyway, because his presence gave me a good idea who was driving Zev's investigations. I cut another bite, lifted the pastry-laden fork, and asked, "Why is the Cordova Family interested in Keith Thatcher?"

"Who said we were?" Zev sat back in the booth, one arm draped over the seat back's edge, the other on the table, his hand curling around his cup. He was the picture of casualness, his expression conveying aloof amusement. "Maybe my business with Keith is personal."

I shook my head, my brows rising in patent disbelief. "Nope, sorry, not buying it."

"And why's that?" Curiosity flashed in the depths of his eyes, there and gone. If I hadn't been watching, I would've missed it.

"If it was personal, you wouldn't let anyone, including me, know you were interested. The fact you're sitting here, making time with me, indicates that Keith was interfering with the Cordovas in some way." I brought my fork up and took a deliberate bite, never breaking our stare.

"You sure it's not you we're interested in?"

As a subtle threat, it was a doozy. My brain short-circuited for a second as those full lips surrounded by a sexy, way-past-five-o'clock shadow twitched and curved upward, but there was an underlying seriousness to his response that made my heart skip a beat. I lowered my lashes, hoping to hide my reaction. I tried to swallow my food but found it difficult as a slithering sense of foreboding left my mouth dry. Maybe it was best to stick to my drink while being dragged through this verbal minefield. With a faint sense of regret, I set my fork down, pushed the small plate away, sat back, and braved meeting his gaze. "Are you?"

He held my gaze for an endless moment before answering, "Maybe."

"Why?"

"Why not?"

Unsure if it was a warning or his twisted version of flirting, his answer left me even more off-kilter than ever. If an Arcane Family was interested in me, I was in a shitload more trouble than I realized. For now, I decided to feign ignorance. "I don't know what kind of game you're playing, Zev, but I need to get back to work."

"Is that what you're calling it?" he asked drily. "It looked more like breaking and entering to me."

Okay, he was damn good with sarcasm, but I held tight to my fraying temper and said calmly, "I was at Keith's on Guild business."

It was his turn to raise his brows. "Guild business? I thought you were working for yourself now. Wasn't that why you kidnapped my nephew?"

At the sting of rebuke, my hand fisted on the table next to my cup as a blush worked its way under my cheeks. The job that had involved Zev's ten-year-old nephew and brought the two of us together had been both a blessing and a near-disastrous mistake. The combination of mortification and defensiveness added a sharp edge to my voice as the hold on my temper slipped. "I didn't kidnap Jeremy, dammit." I took a breath, uncurled my hand, and wrapped it around my cup. "I'm not rehashing this with you. It has nothing to do with Keith."

Zev straightened in his seat and leaned in, his voice a low whip of sound. "You sure about that?"

His intensity sent an unsettling shiver down my spine, but I met his accusing glare head on. "Yes, I am." Even as I said it, my mind futzed with the puzzle pieces, bumping up against the one commonality between the situation with

Jeremy and the current one with Keith—LanTech, a company that specialized in magic-infused technology. "Unless there's something you want to share."

Oblivious to my mental gymnastics, Zev asked, "Like?"

"Like why Keith ended up at my condo this morning. Or why you're here now. Either one is a good starting point."

"I'm here because I followed you." His admission carried not one ounce of visible shame.

The fact that he'd completely ignored the first half of my question didn't escape me, but his answer to the second part was just as concerning. "Why are you following me?"

"I wasn't initially. I was following Keith." He lifted his cup, tipping it toward me. "Saw you this morning with the other looky-loos and figured since Keith was a dead end, I'd follow you."

I wanted to snarl in frustration, not just at his bad pun, but because he was deliberately talking in circles.

Before I could rip into him, he continued. "It was my understanding Keith recently signed a contract with the Guild. I had no idea you were involved. Though, considering your predilection for taking questionable cases, I shouldn't be surprised."

In light of how things played out the last time we met, I couldn't take umbrage at his assumption. However, I could level with him, at least on this particular point. I wasn't sure why I wanted to, though. "It's not my case."

His face blanked so fast, it was unsettling, and a predatory stillness invaded our small space, ready to pounce. "Excuse me?"

Unable to hold his gaze, I looked down at my cup as I fiddled with it. "The case belongs to my roommate."

The unseen danger level dropped a notch, or three. "Roommate?"

I tilted my head in acknowledgment, keeping a wary eye on him from under my lashes.

He continued to study me, his thoughts tucked well away. "So, she's a Hunter?"

"No, she's a Key." The Guild's mercenary banner stretched over multiple specialized crews. Six were publicly acknowledged: investigators known as Hunters; Hounds for tracking and retrieval; Sentinels for security; Keys for decryption and spell breaking; Spiritualists, which were mainly necromancers and mediums; and Transporters, who specialized in secured deliveries. Two other crews did their best work in the shadows, away from the harsh light of publicity: assassins known as Blades and the spy corp known as Scouts.

"Interesting." His gaze went behind me. I managed a not-too-subtle check, but no one was approaching. When I turned back, he asked, "And she's where?"

"Your guess is as good as mine," I muttered and went back to poking at the apple crumble.

"Want to explain that?"

"Not particularly, no." I couldn't forget Evan's warning that Lena's location was being blocked by a powerful mage, and not only was Zev pretty damn powerful, but so was the Family that held his loyalty. Until I knew exactly how the Cordovas were tied to the Thatchers, I wasn't keen on sharing much more with Zev.

He sighed. "Are you always this stubborn?"

Since the answer was yes, I declined to answer on the grounds that it would incriminate me.

He drummed his fingers on the table. "Fine, keep your secrets."

Considering his stubbornness could rival mine, I hadn't expected such quick capitulation. My gaze flew to his as I tried to find the inevitable trap.

As soon as our gazes collided, his smile was all teeth. "For now."

Yep, there it is. Unwilling to dig my proverbial hole any deeper, I went back and tugged on a possible link. "Did Keith have something to do with Jeremy's kidnapping?"

Zev sat back and studied me. "That's a hell of a topic shift, Rory."

"Is it really?" It was time to use Zev's annoying tactics on him. "Keith worked for LanTech. Jeremy's mom not only worked for LanTech, but was selling her research to their competitor, Origin, hence LanTech's and Origin's decisions to send two different professional retrieval teams after her kid. A kid who incidentally is the Cordova heir. Keith's dead. You're here. I'm just trying to connect the dots." I slipped my fork under a bit of crumble, brought it up, and stuffed it in my mouth. A safer move than adding "jackass."

"LanTech closed its doors months ago." His answer was really more like a half-assed dodge than an answer.

I lobbed it back with a noise of agreement as I swallowed. "True, but you're not answering my question. Did Keith have anything to do with the kidnapping attempt?"

"If he did"—Zev picked up his cup—"you would be chasing a ghost." He took a sip, his gaze locked with mine.

Yes, you're a badass. I get it. "I had to ask," I murmured.

The thing was, there were multiple ways for an Arcane Family to deal with a perceived threat. And six months ago, both LanTech and Origin, a biotech research company, put themselves on the Cordova radar. Lara, Jeremy's mom, had decided to sell her research for LanTech to Origin, despite the fact that selling said research violated numerous NDAs and ethical clauses. Both companies were keen on claiming her research, so much so that two weeks after her death, they'd kidnapped her only child in an effort to force the Cordovas' hand in obtaining that research. Not the smartest move on their part. When it came to things like justice and vengeance, the Arcane Families struck not only with lethal speed, but also ruthless accuracy. I held no delusions that LanTech's doors were shut tight because of anything other than the merciless retribution dished out by the Cordova Family.

As for Origin, I was fairly sure that their burgeoning financial woes touted in the news outlets could also be traced back to the Cordovas' displeasure. When the last grain of dust settled, both LanTech's demise and Origin's imminent one would be the direct result of their failed attempt to kidnap the heir to the Cordova Family.

"A word of advice, babe."

The endearment caught me unawares and left me grappling for balance even as I paid attention.

"If you plan on working with the Families, might I suggest you learn the value of discretion?"

Oh, I knew all about how to keep secrets, but sometimes a direct approach worked. Maybe not this time, but for Lena's sake, it was worth the attempt. Since Zev was blocking that investigative side street, it was time to backtrack. "Since you're so interested in Keith, does that mean you're going to be my shadow?"

Amusement and something I couldn't decipher sparked in his dark eyes. "I have a better question for you. How far do you think you'll get on your own?"

Unsure if he was truly curious or implying something ominous, I frowned. "What do you mean?"

He leaned in, his elbows situated on either side of his cup as he laced his fingers together. "You said this wasn't your case, which makes me wonder why a Transporter is investigating a Guild case better suited to a Hunter."

If he expected a response, he was shit out of luck. Unfortunately, he wasn't one to back down. He pointed a finger at me. "That right there tells me this is personal."

I stiffened in my seat. "What right where?"

"That stubborn chin lift and mutinous pout." I went to fold my arms, but he caught my wrist, stilling my movement. "Answer me honestly—are you really working for the Guild?"

With our past track record, his question shouldn't have caused a flare of hurt, but it did. I stamped it down, trying to ignore how his touch sank through flesh and bone, threatening to leave an indelible mark. With nowhere left to go, I met his gaze with a shaky defiance. "The Director is aware I'm looking into it."

"Is she now?" he murmured, his thumb brushing the inside of my wrist. "Tell me, Rory, how many investigations have you done?"

The answer to that was none, but I would be damned if I gave him that. "Why the interrogation, Zev? Are you worried I'm going to mess things up for you?"

His absent-minded caressing stopped, and there was something in his expression that worried me. "Actually, yes." Although his blunt honesty took me by surprise, a part of me was thankful he wasn't jerking me around. Well, not jerking me around *much*. Before I could formulate a response, he kept going. "If you follow standard investigative procedure, your next stop is going to be who? Madeline Thatcher?"

I gave a half-hearted shrug and tried to tug my hand free. When his grip tightened in warning, I heaved a heavy sigh and gave up. "Yes."

His gaze sharpened, reminding me of a hawk spotting his next meal. "Did you already call and make an appointment to see her?"

Feeling like I was missing something and not liking it one bit, I snapped, "It's on my to-do list as soon as you and I part ways."

"Yeah, good luck with that."

This time when I tugged, he let me go. I dropped my hands to my lap, absently rubbing at the lingering sensation of his touch. "What's that supposed to mean?"

"Exactly what you think it does," he shot back. "If you think she'll meet with you to discuss her ex-husband, you're in for a world of disappointment."

"If she refuses to meet with me, then I'll drop by her office or home. It's not like she can ignore me forever." So long as Lena was missing, there was no way I'd back off Madeline. I knew how to make a nuisance of myself until I got the answers I wanted.

"Actually, she can."

The certainty in Zev's statement pulled me up short. "What do you mean?"

"If Madeline Thatcher doesn't want to talk to you, she won't."

"She may run in elite circles, but she's not Family. Eventually, she'll have to talk to me."

"No, she doesn't." He sat back and flattened his palm against the table. "She may not belong to one of the Arcane Families, but she has allies—powerful allies—and that can be just as important as claiming a Family blood tie."

Pushing past my personal fascination with Zev and the confusing emotions that entailed, I studied him with a critical eye as my thoughts spun. I wasn't stupid. I knew how things worked in our world. The majority of the population could call on some trace levels of magic, but the strongest power users belonged to the bloodlines of the twenty-seven original Families. Generations of careful cultivation and genetic manipulation had ensured their progeny remained at the top of the magical food chain. It had helped even more when those Families took an active part in shifting the tide during the World Wars almost a century past. Now descendants of those Families enjoyed a glittery spot under the public limelight, even as whispers said they moved in shadows, shaping politics, dominating corporations, and pretty much ruling the Arcane society. It also meant anyone who wanted to thrive within the shark-infested waters, like Madeline had managed to do for years, needed strong ties of their own. Staring at Zev, I began to get an awful, terrifying idea. "So in order to talk to Madeline, I need allies of my own."

"Yes."

"Allies like you?"

He smiled, but there was nothing comforting or humorous about it.

My thoughts stilled and perched precariously on a dangerous edge. The trap was right there, but I couldn't see another path around it. Thinking of Lena, I asked, "What's it going to cost me?"

"You'll owe me a favor."

A thousand and one reasons why that was such a horrible idea swept through me and left me shaking my head. "Uh-uh, no way am I going to agree to blindly serve the Cordova Family."

"I didn't say you'd owe the Family," he countered, an unsettling depth deepening his voice. "I said you'd owe me."

"You?" I choked out as my mind and body went to war. His clarification rattled the cage lurking in the deepest part of my hormone-driven psyche, releasing some of its down-and-dirty contents.

"Me," he confirmed.

"And what would this favor entail?" That damn cage rattled harder. I kicked it back into the corner.

"I'll know when I'm ready to call it in."

"And when would that be?" I pushed.

"When I'm ready."

Okay, that sounded like a threat... or maybe a promise.

God, I'm in trouble here. For an endless moment, I tried to decide if I was thrilled or terrified. Thrilled, because Zev fascinated me on a personal level I didn't like to admit to. Terrified, because continued contact with him would drag me into a volatile world I'd spent years avoiding. Injured pride wanted to call his bluff and dial Madeline to demand a meeting, but that wasn't just stupid. It was also reckless. Zev was right about one thing—if my professional future included dealing with the Families on something more than a superficial level, I needed allies. That meant there was no way to avoid the path looming before me. It would be a bitch to navigate, but I would do it. Not just because he'd invaded my dreams for months after we went our separate ways, but because I was willing to take whatever risks were necessary to find my best friend. Lena was one of the few things in my life that never buckled, never gave. For her, I would trudge through hell barefoot.

My silence must have gone on too long, because he said, "You're welcome to try calling Madeline and getting an appointment." He picked up his drink and sat back. "I'll wait."

Arrogant smartass. He and I both knew I wouldn't make it past the initial hello. Yeah, I had no doubt I was going to regret taking his offer, but it didn't stop me from saying, "Fine, I'll owe you, but only if you can get me in to see Madeline within the next twenty-four hours."

He gave me a wolfish grin, pulled out his phone, thumbed through his screen, hit a number, and brought it up to this ear. The entire time, he held my gaze captive, and I did my best not to squirm. "Hello, Debbie, this is Zev Aslanov. Any chance Madeline has time to meet with me to discuss some business?" He paused, his gaze unwavering. "Tomorrow works. Morning if possible." Another pause, and his grin morphed into a smirk.

I sighed and sipped my drink.

"Eight thirty, sure. I'll be there. Thanks." He hung up. Shifting on his hip, he pocketed his phone. "Your place is closer to Madeline's office than the Guild. How about I pick you up at eight? That work for you?"

Doing a mental review of my schedule, I shuffled a couple of items around. "Sure."

And just like that, I owed Zev a favor.

Joy.

CHAPTER SEVEN

ANXIOUS TO GET BACK to the Guild, I left Zev at the cafe. I had a long list for Evan to dig into and a boatload of fishing lines I wanted to straighten out. Before we went our separate ways, I didn't bother asking Zev what his plans were for the afternoon, nor did he ask what mine were, probably because his plans involved shadowing my ass. That would normally irritate me to no end, but I was more concerned about owing Zev an unspecified favor. Maybe I would get lucky and Sabella would need me to work over in Europe after all. If I wasn't here, he couldn't collect, right?

Safe in the confines of my Mustang, I could second-guess my decision to my heart's content. Hell, I was beyond second guesses and well into my fourth and fifth at this point. I didn't need the pit in my stomach or the bitter taste in my mouth to warn me that the ramifications of my choice would ripple far and wide on a personal level. Despite my initial knee-jerk refusal to Zev, the truth was, I would be less wound up about owing the favor to the Cordova Family instead of him. Yeah, it was dangerous to align with a Family when I was trying to keep my abilities quiet, but I'd been doing just fine for years. I had no doubt I could continue to do so.

But Zev was a different matter. On one level, being around him left me off balance and uncertain, two things I abhorred. But on a different, more intimate level, he fascinated me. It wasn't as superficial as his dark, good looks. Although I freely admitted I preferred the dark, dangerous rebel look he had going on, but it was worse than that. It was the lethally protective core he carried, the one I'd caught glimpses of when he rode to his nephew's rescue. Witnessing it had awakened an ache I hadn't even known I carried, one I didn't need a therapist to understand.

What would it be like to have one person willing to take on the world for you? It was an idealistic dream, which shouldn't have survived my childhood or the realities of adulthood. Bouncing in and out of an overworked social system and running the streets, I'd learned quickly to rely on myself. That wasn't a bad thing, but it could be lonely. Even now, those I called mine were few and far between. I knew if I asked, they would come to help, but it wasn't the same. And that was why prolonged contact with Zev was dangerous. At some point, I would try to reach out for what he offered others, only to get my hand slapped.

But it was too late to back out now. I'd made a promise, and I would see it through. In the meantime, I could appreciate the physical packaging and still keep things between us purely professional. Decision made, I ignored the dull ache it caused. Shifting gears, I aimed for the more troubling waters of finding Lena. Since Zev was clearly watching, I needed to appear as if I was heeding his advice and riding things out. "Appearing" being the keyword here, since my first step would be to sic Evan on uncovering the dirty details of the Thatchers, Cordovas, LanTech, and Origin. Information was power, and I needed every bit I could get, even if it rocked the boat.

Zev's involvement guaranteed there was a tie to the Cordovas, but other than Keith's connection to LanTech, the rest of the picture was murky.

Since I was stuck behind the wheel with time to kill, I went back through what I knew at this point.

Keith called in Lena to break a curse set by an unknown mage. Her first step was to identify the caster. While she managed to narrow it down to Madeline or Theo, Lena had once told me that curses came down to who was the most pissed at you. Curses were complex spells that required not only a focused intent, but also intimate knowledge of the victim. The more specific the curse, the more likely the caster was someone they knew. In this case, Keith's performance between the sheets had been targeted. That was a flashing neon sign that the caster was probably female and pissed, intent on humiliating the man. Female and pissed led me to Madeline. My assumption was biased as hell, but if the high-heeled shoe fit... Women were much more vindictive than men when it came to payback. A guy would sucker punch you or take a literal pound of flesh, but a woman? She'd make it so painful, you'd never forget.

Lena had to have made a similar connection. Just look at the timing. Keith's dead body shows up the same morning that Lena goes missing.

No, wait a second. That wasn't quite right.

Evan said Lena's phone went down around midafternoon the day before, so Keith's body actually dropped hours after Lena presumably went missing. So where did Lena go? We had narrowed her last known location to a rough ten-block radius in the West Valley. Zev indicated Madeline's office was close to my place, which was in the heart of downtown Phoenix, so that ruled Madeline's office out. Keith's place was in Scottsdale, on the east side. First on my to-do list for Evan, see if he could link anything in that area with the Thatchers or Cordovas. Maybe we'd get lucky. Not that I held out much hope. Movers and shakers were phenomenal at hiding their ass... ets.

The second item for Evan was to run a check on the names of known associates for both the Thatchers and the Cordovas. As dangerous as it was to poke around in a Family's business, Zev's involvement meant there was a connection somewhere. As an electro mage, Evan was the best suited for doing the poking. Plus, if Lena's presence was being blocked by a mage, then we needed to start running down mages with that kind of power. Considering our players, either one could afford that kind of talent, so it was best to start with their known associates.

With Lena's line untangled, I worked on Keith's.

Zev had mentioned he was following Keith. If that was true, then wouldn't he have an idea of who'd met Keith at his home? The scene at Keith's house made it clear someone had stopped by for a visit, someone Keith knew and felt comfortable enough to invite in for a drink. *Maybe someone like Zev?*

I shook that thought away. Nope, it didn't fit. Zev was many things—lethal, secretive, sexy as hell—but one thing he wasn't was sloppy. And whoever had fought with Keith at his house was just that. The lingering magic, the obvious destruction in the living room, hell, even the partially opened door. All of that spoke to either arrogance or incompetence. *Could it be the same mage that was blocking Lena?* Maybe. I made a mental note to pose that question to Evan, as well.

Back to Keith and the amount of residual magic flooding his place. Keith's meeting had obviously made a hard right into violence, and chances were high he was actually killed in his own home. But it didn't take much magic to kill, and what lingered behind hours later in the echo I'd stumbled across was a sure sign of seriously deep levels of expended magic. *Was it overkill? A miscalculation?* There was no way to know, not unless I could get my hands on the police report and description of Keith's body. *Hmm, I wonder if Evan would be up to hacking the police database?* Sylvia wouldn't be thrilled with my request, but I scratched it onto Evan's growing to-do list.

So if an argument went down at Keith's and things turned violent, why dump the body at my condo? Why not leave it at Keith's place? A private residence was a hell of a lot less public than a condo lobby. Not to mention it could be days before anyone swung by Keith's to find him. Dumping his body in a condo lobby was akin to sending a golden engraved invitation. Who was that invitation for, though? Lena? Or was it simply coincidence and whatever this was had been meant for someone else? Someone I hadn't identified yet. I let that thought rattle around for a second but couldn't shake it into place.

I turned into the Guild's garage and parked. While my trip to Keith's hadn't turned up any answers, it sure as hell gave me a bunch of new lines to pull. Zev's involvement added another layer to the mess. I couldn't see why the Cordova Family would have anything to do with a curse that screamed pissed-off lover. But if Keith, a former employee of LanTech, had anything to do with the aborted kidnapping attempt, then yeah, that could explain Zev's appearance. *Did that mean there were two separate issues here? The one Lena was investigating and whatever Zev was tracking?*

I deactivated the security ward on the glove box and grabbed the file. Caught up in my thoughts, I headed toward the elevators that would take me to the lobby. Maybe I was overthinking this. I could drive myself crazy with questions and possibilities. Setting Evan loose was a better use of my time. Getting on the elevator, I checked my watch and noted I had enough time to meet with Evan then head home and clean up. In fact, I might even be able to pull on one more string—Madeline's new boy toy, Theo. Despite Zev's little spiel about allies and name-dropping, Theo's name didn't carry the same weight as Madeline's, which made it worth a shot. With time tight, I scratched a phone call onto my to-do list.

The elevator doors slid open, spilling me onto the second floor. Still running through things in my head, I pulled open the door and came face-to-face with Detective Brenner.

"Whoa, Rory." He reached out with a hand to steady me as I stutter-stepped in surprise. Thankfully, he gripped the hand without the folder.

"Hey, Detective." My face heated, and my pulse raced. Hopefully, he would attribute it to the near collision instead of nerves. *Thank God the file carried no identifying labels.* Balance regained, I stepped back. With no way to hide the file, I decided to brazen it out and held it down by my thigh. "What're you doing here?"

"Doing my part to encourage interagency cooperation." Although he smiled, it didn't reach his eyes. He was obviously far from happy.

Behind him, Evan stood at the front desk, arms folded across his chest and a frown darkening his face. Light bounced off his lenses, but he caught my eye and gave a short shake of his head. Unsure of what that meant, I plastered a smile on my face and decided it was safe to play dumb. "I'm assuming it's about the dead body from this morning?"

The lines around Brenner's mouth deepened. "You'd guess correctly."

Playing my part, I asked the obvious. "Who was it?"

"You know we can't release that information until we notify the family." He recited the standard line. "Actually, I'm glad I ran into you."

And that didn't make me nervous. Nope, not at all. I prayed my smile didn't falter. "Yeah? Why's that?"

"I wanted to let you know the scene's been released, so

you're welcome to access your condo." He added a couple more inches of welcomed space between us and held the door open with a hand above my head.

Our positions meant we were blocking the doorway, so I shifted to the side. "That's good news, I guess, but you could've called, saved yourself the time and trouble."

"No trouble." His gaze tagged the file before he went back to studying me. "Have you seen your roommate today?"

A fissure of anxiety ripped through me, and my hand tightened on the file. *What did he know? Had he linked Keith and Lena already?* "Lena? No, why?"

"I was hoping to get her statement."

Utilizing my acting skills, I did my best to feign confusion. Frowning, I shifted my weight and tapped the file's edge against my leg. "I thought you couldn't release the scene until you got everyone's statement?"

His gaze didn't waver. "Seems your roomie wasn't home."

As hard as it was, I continued playing dumb. I bit my lip and winced. "Huh, we must have missed each other." I gave an apologetic wince. "Sorry."

"That happen a lot?"

I managed a small smile. "More than you'd think. I know she's been buried under work lately, and my caseload isn't much better."

"Yeah, the Guild seems to be hopping lately." His sarcastic tone matched the jaundiced glare he shot back toward a watching Evan. "Hard to get ahold of people around here."

With that one comment, he confirmed that no one from the Guild had shared about Lena's disappearance, and I decided to follow that example. "That's par for the course most days." I touched his arm, regaining his attention, and offered, "Hey, I've got to head home before a job tonight. You want me to leave her your number and a message to call?"

"Will it do any good?" There was a healthy dose of antagonism in his voice.

I was fairly sure it wasn't directed at me, since as far as I knew, we were on good terms, but I still dropped my hand and straightened my shoulders. "What am I missing here, Detective?"

A red tinge hit his cheekbones. The hand holding the door tightened; the other one rose to rub the back of his neck. "Nothing, Rory. I apologize." He moved back so he was no longer blocking the entrance. "It's been a long day."

On that, we could agree.

He continued, "I'd appreciate it if you could pass my request along."

Since outright lying to Brenner made me more nervous than lying by omission, I stuck with "Will do, but I can't promise or predict when she'll call back. Half the time, we barely see each other during the week. As soon as I see her, I'll have her call you."

He studied me for what felt like forever. It was hard to hold his gaze, but I managed. Finally, he said, "You do that."

"You got it. In the meantime, you take care." I went to step past him, but he called my name. I turned to look back.

"You remember what I said to you this morning?"

It took a second, but I found it. "Stay in town?"

He shook his head. "The second part."

My stomach clenched, because he wasn't just angry, but also worried. "Be careful?"

"That's the one. You call me if you see or hear anything out of the ordinary, okay?"

"Yes, sir."

He lifted his chin, shot one more disgruntled look at Evan, then left.

I watched the door close behind him before I turned to face Evan. "What the hell was that?"

Evan took off his glasses and squeezed the bridge of his nose. What he didn't do was answer.

I crossed the empty lobby and stopped in front of him. "Evan?"

He dropped his hand, resettled his glasses and grabbed my arm. "Come on, we'll talk in the back." He dragged me back, and as soon as we cleared the ward, he dropped my arm and paced a few steps away. He dragged his hand through his hair, leaving it standing on end. "The detective stopped by and demanded to see Sylvia."

"I'm sure that went over well."

"Don't know, don't care. I was in Sylvia's office, giving her a rundown on what we had so far, when Adele interrupted and informed us he was waiting in the lobby. Sylvia had me go and bring him back, so I did. The good detective informed her that they ID'd the dead body at your condo as Keith's."

"Okay."

He stopped mid-step, pivoted to face me, and narrowed his eyes. "You don't seem surprised."

"I'm not." But I was wondering how Evan managed to find out since a minute earlier Brenner refused to share that tidbit with me. "What'd you do, eavesdrop on their conversation?"

He shrugged.

A door to our right opened, releasing a team of Sentinels from a conference room. We got a couple of hand raises and chin lifts, but they were busy with their conversation.

Evan took my arm and pulled me away. "Come on." We headed toward the back of the office, and Evan kept his voice low. "Adele asked me to cover her desk while she went to check on something. The conversation inside appeared intense, and since I was sure it was tied in with Lena's situation, I might have accidentally triggered the computer's audio."

Accidentally, my ass. "If Sylvia finds out—"

He waved away my concern. "Remember who you're talking to here."

We came up on the empty break room. I followed him in, steering toward the coffee machine while he ducked into the refrigerator. I prepped the single-serve machine as he grabbed a soda. The thud of the refrigerator door closing had me turning to find Evan leaning against it, soda in hand, watching me.

"So how'd you find out the DB was Keith?" His voice was hard with suspicion.

Mimicking his stance, I leaned against the counter's edge, folded my arms, and raised my brows. "I'll tell you when you're finished with your story."

He managed to maintain his frustrated glare for a good three seconds before he shook his head and gave in. "Fine." He popped the soda's top and took a healthy swallow before continuing. "The detective told Sylvia that Keith had an appointment with Lena noted in his phone. Then Brenner requested access to Lena's case files."

"I'm sure that went over well."

"Like a lead balloon," he confirmed. "He was not happy to be told that the Guild would not share active case details without a warrant. He made a few more vague threats, Sylvia stone-walled, and then he stormed out. He was in her office for all of fifteen minutes. You caught him on the way out."

Remembering the visible resentment on Brenner's face, I winced. Sylvia took our NDAs very seriously. "He's going to request a warrant."

He raised his can. "That's my guess."

"How fast do you think he'll get it?"

"I don't know. Depends on how hard he's going to push and what else they have."

Considering how quickly they'd showed up at Keith's

house and knowing how dogged Brenner could be, I winced. "Dammit." Dodging Zev was bad enough, but throw in the Phoenix PD, and this was a cluster waiting to happen.

Evan opened his mouth but was cut off by Adele appearing in the doorway. "Rory, Evan, Sylvia would like you in her office."

Behind me, the coffee maker sputtered, dispensing liquid life into a cup. Unfortunately, it would have to wait. *When the director calls, you answer.* Evan and I shared a look, then followed in Adele's wake to Sylvia's office.

The director was standing in her doorway, waiting. "Costas, Fields." She waved us in. We settled into the chairs facing her while she took up a position in front of her desk and folded her arms. "Seems the dead body at your condo this morning belonged to Keith Thatcher." She eyed us both and correctly read our lack of response. "Something you two seem to already know."

Catching the slight movement as Evan tightened his grip on the chair's arm, I blurted, "I just found out. I was telling Evan when you called us in." My attempt to divert her attention worked.

Her eyes landed on me. "What did you find at Thatcher's place?"

I provided a concise recap of the scene at Keith's, including Zev's arrival. I shared most of my conversation with him at Haven's Corner. The only thing I left out was my promised favor. That was personal.

Hearing Zev's name, Sylvia raised her eyebrows, but she waited until I finished before asking, "Zev Aslanov was following Keith?"

"Yep."

Something worked behind her eyes. "Did he see Lena?"

I shook my head. "Not as far as I'm aware, but I didn't think to ask."

"Why?" she pressed.

I shrugged. "I kept details general when it came to Lena." When my answer got a quizzical look, I elaborated. "Zev's focus appeared to be Keith, which means his involvement and Lena's disappearance might be separate issues. Until we know if and how they tie together, I think it's safer to keep some things to ourselves."

Sylvia unfolded her arms and gripped the desk's edge on either side of her hips. "I agree, at least for now." She went quiet and gazed at her feet, clearly thinking things through. She came to some internal decision and raised her head, her gaze hard and unwavering. "If I told you I was turning this over to a Hunter—"

I didn't let her finish. "Your choice, but I'm not stopping until Lena's safe."

She studied me, her professional mask firmly in place. "If you were still a Guild employee, instead of a contractor, I could lock you down and ensure you didn't interfere."

Chalk up another reason to be grateful for my recent change in position. "You could try." It wasn't the most professional response, but it was honest. However, I knew that without her support, I wouldn't get far in this investigation, so I qualified my statement. "I understand why you'd prefer to put a Hunter on this."

"Do you?"

Refusing to look away, I said, "Yep, and you'd be right. Not only is this personal, but I'm not a trained investigator. However, I can't drop it."

A brief flare of resigned humor broke through before she quickly squashed it. "Can't, not won't?"

"Can't," I repeated, because it was the truth. If I had to work around the Guild, so be it. It wasn't like they could fire me.

She studied me for a long moment. "Investigations are not your forte."

Now wasn't the time for offended pride. I kept my voice even. "They aren't, but I've been with the Guild long enough to know how to ask questions."

"And if your questions set the powers that be against the Guild?" One of her fingers tapped the underside of her desk.

I held her gaze, my voice cold. "Plausible deniability. I'm not a Guild employee, which means you can deny any knowledge of my involvement and ensure my services are blacklisted should it be necessary."

A hard smile curved her lips. "Good to see you understand how it works."

Oh, I understood exactly how it worked. As a clearinghouse for magical mercenaries, the Guild had no issues hiring out to the Arcane Families for the right price, but they refused to take sides in the never-ending power plays. It was a tricky line to navigate, but the continued profitability of the Guild proved they were masters at the game. "I get it."

"Good." She pushed off the desk and walked around to her chair. "For now, I'll let you deal with it." She pulled out her chair and sat. "Well, you and Evan."

"I appreciate it." More than she knew. Relief drained some of the tension from my shoulders. I hadn't been looking forward to dodging the Guild.

"Now." Her voice took on a brusque tone. "What are your next steps?"

"I'd like to ask Evan to do some digging."

Speculation lit in her eyes. "How deep?"

"Deep."

She dipped her chin in agreement. "Is Aslanov going to interfere?"

Definitely. Before sharing my immediate reaction, which was more personal than professional, I thought it through.

No matter what happened between him and me, Zev's first, and probably only, loyalty was to the Cordova Family. Until he got the answers he wanted, he would be a pain in my ass. "So long as we don't bring trouble to the Cordovas, he'll stay clear."

"Then let's make sure we don't give him a reason to get involved." She turned to Evan. "What's your current caseload?"

"I can clear the deck," he said.

"Do that." She turned to me.

I answered before she could ask. "I've got the job tonight, but otherwise, I'm on this."

"If you need help—"

"I'll ask."

"Be sure you do." Those four simple words were proof that despite the potential firestorm, Sylvia had no intention of leaving one of her own twisting in the wind. She looked at Evan. "Watch your ass when you're mucking around. The last thing the Guild needs is the Phoenix PD and the Families displeased with us." After his nod, she continued, "I want regular status reports. No going solo, either of you. Watch each other's backs and get my Key back."

Evan and I answered at the same time, "Yes, ma'am."

CHAPTER EIGHT

CLOSE TO AN HOUR LATER, I left Evan in his office, working through his to-do list, and headed to the nearby stairs instead of backtracking to the elevators. I jogged down the steps, anxious to get home. Not just because I needed to get ready for tonight's job with Sabella Rossi, but because I wanted to go through my condo and see if I could find anything else that would help me track Lena while Evan ran his searches.

I pushed through the door and into the parking garage. Distracted, I approached my car as it sat alone in the assigned parking spaces meant for the tenants. The first faint touch of magic whispered across my skin, chafing against my power, which remained passively alert. Heeding the warning, I slowed my approach. I pulled my Glock from its concealed holster and held it barrel down and at the ready as I moved a few feet closer to my car. That feather-light touch of magic gained strength, taking on an irritating edge. My protective Prism blinked awake and stretched.

I stopped and scanned the shadowed garage for the unseen threat. When it came to a magical attack, bullets weren't the best option, but it was better than nothing.

Tension crawled along my spine and settled into my neck. I rode the rush of adrenaline as my ears strained to identify every sound and my eyes tried to pierce the gloom.

Nothing moved.

I waited, counting my breaths. The uncomfortable brush against my skin lessened and with it, my tension. The good news? The lingering magical echo was also fading. The bad news? It was centered on my car.

Oh, hell no!

If I found out who'd messed with my baby, I would make them regret it. It hurt, but I refrained from rushing forward to check that my Mustang was undamaged. I approached the car at an angle, scanning the ground around it. There were no marks on the ground to indicate a casting circle, and no strange objects lingered nearby for magical foci. There was one other area to visibly check. Cautiously, I moved closer, close enough to reach out and touch the door if I wanted, but that wasn't my objective. At least not yet.

Instead, I shifted my gun to my right hand and awkwardly pulled out my phone with my left. I thumbed the screen, activated the camera, slid it to video, and hit record. Then I dropped to a squat and aimed it under the car. It wasn't easy, as the Mustang sat low, but I did the best I could, running it from wheel to wheel. When I pulled it back, I stood up and rewound the recording. Before I could hit play, the faint ding of the elevator echoed. I shifted a few feet to the side until I could see the elevators, then I watched as a couple of business types continued their conversation while walking to their car on the far side. When they were out of sight, I went back to my phone. The video wasn't the greatest, but it was clear enough to relieve my mind that there was nothing in the undercarriage that shouldn't be there. I stopped the recording and dialed Evan.

He picked up on the first ring. "What's wrong now?"

"How fast can you access the parking garage security?"

"Why?" I could hear his fingers fly over the keys.

"Someone messed with my Mustang."

He let out a low whistle. "I'm in."

"Had to be recent, so just go back from now and see what pops."

I waited as he did his thing. The elevator pinged again. This time, a woman hustled out, engrossed in her phone.

"The angles aren't the greatest, but I'm not seeing anything," Evan said. "What did they do?"

"I'm not sure." I turned back to my car and frowned. "I'm picking up magical remnants, but nothing specific."

"Do you want me to send down a Hound?"

Utilizing an Arcane tracker wasn't a bad idea. If nothing else, they might be able to follow the caster's trail. "Is there one available?"

"Hang on, I'm checking to see if anyone is in house right now." Seconds ticked by, punctuated by the sound of typing. "Sorry, Rory, looks like they're all out on assignment."

And I had a job to get ready for. "Don't worry about. I'll handle it."

"You sure?" He didn't sound happy.

I couldn't blame him. "Yeah, but in case something goes boom, make sure your electronic eye is watching."

"That's reassuring."

It wasn't meant to be, but the longer I stood there, the more the skin-tingling indicator of expended magic faded. "I'm good, Evan. You'll be the second to know if I'm not."

"Not funny," he snapped.

Done with the conversation, I hung up and slid my phone back in my pocket. With nothing physical to fight, I re-holstered my gun. If something lay in wait, bullets wouldn't do a damn bit of good. That realization triggered an instant reaction from my magic, and the phantom sensation of invisible armor locking in place slid over my skin. I dug out my keys and deactivated the alarm. The one-two beep signaled the all-clear and unlocked the driver's side door with an audible click. Thankfully, the rest of my car remained intact.

Cautiously reaching for the door handle, I froze with my palm a hair's breadth above the metal. I braced then gripped the handle. Nothing happened. No searing pain. No bone-rattling jolt. Nothing. Air escaped on a shaky exhale. Staying to the side, I pulled open the door. The only thing that rushed out was the faint scent of leather and vanilla. *Okay, so maybe I was just being paranoid.*

I leaned down and peered inside, only to revise my opinion. Nope, I was definitely not being paranoid. In plain view on the passenger seat was a padded manila envelope.

I checked the passenger side of the car. The windows were intact, and the passenger lock was still engaged. *So how in the hell did that package get inside?*

Straightening, I did another scan of the garage, which was as pointless as the last one. No one lurked in the shadows watching. No strange cars lingered nearby. Everything was quiet with that particular sense of late-afternoon abandonment. With nothing for it, I slid into the driver's seat, keeping my left leg out and leaving the door open. Under the interior dome light, I studied the envelope. My name was neatly printed on the outside in artless block letters. Unsurprisingly, there was no return address or name.

I looked out the windshield, noting one of the security cameras aimed my way. Evan hadn't been lying about the angle. He could probably see me behind the wheel, but that would be all. *Good enough.*

I turned back to the package and considered a move that would have been dangerously stupid for anyone else. For me, as a Prism, not so much. Holding tight to the knowledge that if the package was magically booby-trapped, my ability would deflect the worst of it, I picked it up.

Nothing happened. As I held it, though, I could feel the last of the magical echoes fade, leaving behind an innocuous package. I tested the weight, and despite the interior layer of bubble wrap, the contents were easy to discern—a book, probably a paperback, based on the lack of rigidity. Confused and not a little bit curious, I turned it over. Clear packing tape sealed the flap, so I slid a key under the score line and tore it open, leaving the edges of the envelope a ragged mess.

I dropped the keys into the cup holder and upended the envelope, but the book remained wedged inside. I got my thumb and finger around the book and dragged it out. About two inches of worn leather cleared the envelope before it held fast. I adjusted my hold and tugged harder. It jerked free, and I hissed as the paper pages scored my knuckle. *Damn paper cuts.*

I dropped the envelope and the leather-bound book in my lap as I brought my stinging knuckle to my mouth. It was an automatic reaction to the small pain, and the faint tang of blood hit my tongue. I dropped my hand and examined the wound. On my middle finger, a thin beaded line of red marred the skin between my first and second knuckle.

I opened the glove box, grabbed a napkin from my stash, and wound it around my finger. First aid administered, I went back to the mysterious book. The leather covering was a worn brown, stained dark along the binding, indicating it was well used. I couldn't tell if it was authentically old or just made to look like it. There was no title embossed on the front, and when I turned it over, the back was equally blank. That changed my assessment from book to journal, as did the unlined pages. The first interior page was blank, but the ones after that were filled with what appeared to be childish drawings of lopsided flowers and weirdly formed animals, a theme that seemed to continue for the next few pages.

Confused, I shifted my hold so I could feather through the remaining pages quickly, and the napkin fell from my finger to land on the floor. Sighing, I shifted the book to one hand, sore finger caught between the pages to hold my place, and leaned down to pick up the napkin. I balled it up, tossed it in the cup holder, then went back to the book. My breath caught. The drawings had disappeared, and now neatly penned lines filled the page. A tiny smudge of red marred the edge of the page. As I watched, it began to fade, as if being absorbed by the paper. Understanding hit.

Holy shit! A blood key.

A mix of excitement and dread rushed through me. Blood key magic was old magic, stretching back to the founding Arcane Families. I knew that fact because of my obsession with Arcane history and fruitless hunts for information on Prisms. Once upon a time, a blood key was the preferred spell to send coded messages, especially when it involved Family-centered intrigue and machinations. They were the preferred security for covert communications during the World Wars, when the Families worked alongside the Allied Forces. It wasn't until the advent of communication technology that blood keys were altered to utilize a combination of electronic encryption and DNA, making them much more difficult to break. They were a cipher spell that could only be unlocked by the blood of a specific genetic profile. It didn't matter if the blood key was an older version or the more modern construct; either way, there was no fooling it. That this journal was spilling its secrets to me was mind-boggling and terrifying.

As far as I knew, I was no one. Just another forgotten kid from the street. *So why would my blood unlock this journal?* An ominous suspicion joined my confusion, but I scanned the page, the words hitting my brain but not sinking in. At least, not until I stumbled over the one word that explained everything. *Prisms*.

My pulse thundered in my ears as I grappled with the implications. Someone knew what I was. Not only that, they were able to deliver something that shouldn't exist to my car without leaving any usable trace behind. An approaching engine and the squeal of tires on pavement snapped my head up, and I watched a car hurtle around the turn to the next level. It served as a reminder that sitting in a parking garage was not the place to delve into this mystery.

I put the journal back into the envelope and set it on the seat. In a blur, I dug my keys out of the cup holder and put them into the ignition. My fingers tightened as I went to turn the ignition, but I froze for a long moment, thinking, *Final moment of truth*.

I closed my eyes and twisted my wrist. My baby woke with a soft rumble. As I was still in one piece, I blew out a breath, opened my eyes, sent Evan a thumbs-up, then pulled my leg into the car and closed the door. I backed out carefully and headed home.

CHAPTER NINE

THE TRIP HOME WAS UNEVENTFUL, and since my time was limited, I reviewed my priorities. Lena first, journal second. I parked in the condo's garage, grabbed the journal, and rode the elevator straight to my floor. Thankfully, it was a straight shot to the eighth floor. The doors opened, and I hustled to my door, where a business card was tucked into the frame. I pulled it free and noted that it belonged to Detective Brenner. Unlocking the door, I used my shoulder to push it open and stepped inside. Even knowing it was fruitless, I still called out, "Lena? You home?" as I cleared the entryway.

No surprise, but only silence answered. Well, silence and the hum of the air conditioner. I moved into the open space shared by the kitchen, dining, and living room, and tossed my keys and Brenner's card on the island counter. The layout of the apartment made it easy to see no one was home. Our bedrooms sat on either side: mine to the left and Lena's to the right, giving us a semblance of privacy. The blinds were pulled back on the glass doors leading to the balcony, and afternoon sunlight spilled across the light wood floors. I set the envelope and the journal on the island next to my keys

and headed for Lena's room. I knocked on the closed door
out of habit. "Hey, Lena? You in there?"

I pushed the door open and found what I expected—it
was empty. Standing in the doorway, I considered violating
my roommate's privacy. If I hadn't been so worried, I wouldn't
even consider going through her room. Not that she would be
able to tell. It wasn't that she was a slob, but in her personal
space, she tended to live in organized chaos. She swore she
knew where things were, and about once a month, she spent a
couple of hours restoring order. So long as that chaos didn't
spill into the shared areas, I couldn't care less. I wasn't OCD
organized, but I preferred to keep my stuff neat. All my
things had their assigned places. Hell, I made my bed every
day, even though Lena teased me about it relentlessly. In her
opinion, there was no reason to make something I was just
going to mess up again when I went to sleep.

I approached her unmade bed. The silky shorts and tank
she slept in were tossed in a chair in the far corner, along with
a pair of jeans and a shirt that looked like it was mine. I did a
slow turn. At a glance, nothing was out of place. Her dresser
stretched along the wall next to the door, the top covered in
the normal clutter. A mismatched collection of frames with
photos of friends and family sat next to a couple of paper-
backs and her Bluetooth speaker. A tangled mix of jewelry
spilled out of a couple of brightly colored stone bowls. Sticky
notes were interspersed with typical items that had migrated
from the en suite bathroom—nail files, nail polish, makeup,
hair clips, aspirin, and a couple perfume bottles. The nightstand next to her bed held an e-reader, an empty phone
charger, a bottle of electric-green nail polish, another nail file,
and a lone pendant earring, but nothing that screamed, "Clue
here!" Everything was just the typical female clutter.

I poked around and uncovered a small notebook with an
attached purple pen. Sitting on the foot of her bed, I flipped

through the pages, noting half-scrawled reminders and phone numbers with accompanied names. It looked like it was a catch-all scratchpad. I found a sticky note with an address stuck on a page. It was the only address she had with no name attached. Knowing it was a long shot, I sent it to Evan. I also included a couple of names and numbers I didn't recognize.

Setting it back on the dresser, I considered going through her drawers, but catching sight of the time, I decided it would have to wait until later. *Just like that damn journal.* I needed to get ready for the job with Sabella Rossi. *Thinking of the journal...*

I headed back to the kitchen and considered possible hiding spots. Best to keep it out of sight until I had more time to devote to it. The most-secure thing I had was a gun safe tucked in my nightstand drawer, but it was one of those that only had enough space for my Walther CCP. Since I was already carrying my backup Glock that I normally kept at the Guild, there was no room for the journal. When the ice maker dumped its contents into the refrigerator door, inspiration struck. I dug out a gallon-size resealable plastic bag. After folding the envelope around the journal, I was able to get it to fit. *Good enough.*

I opened the refrigerator, pulled out the veggie drawer, and found lettuce just starting to wilt, a trio of tomatoes, a couple of cucumbers, bell peppers, and avocados. I tucked the journal under the lettuce, where it wasn't readily visible. Not the greatest option, but I doubted anyone intent on tossing the place would do a run through my veggies.

Journal stashed, I jumped in the shower. Forty minutes later, I was locking my door, apprehension about Lena's situation perched solidly on my shoulders. Thank God I had a job to keep me occupied tonight. Otherwise, I would have been crawling the walls.

"Hey, Rory, looking ice, *chica*."

I turned to see my dog-walking neighbor's rainbow-hued head sticking out of her doorway. "Hey, Ang. I'm heading out for a job."

"I figured, considering the outfit."

I brushed a hand over the hip of my tailored slacks, a little self-conscious. My working wardrobe was upgraded to a mix of what Lena called "classy, aloof-sexy," and I still worried it might be a bit much.

Angie didn't miss the revealing move and grinned. "You look very chic, very professional." She looked back inside then back to me. "Can you hold the elevator for Martha?"

"Sure," I answered, but she had already stepped back inside her condo and disappeared. As I came up to the door, Martha stepped out, an empty plate in hand. We said our goodbyes to Angie and headed toward the elevator. We got on, and I indicated the plate Martha carried. "Cookies?"

Martha nodded. "After this morning, I went a little overboard with my baking." Her free hand fluttered, a faint pink rose under her cheeks. "I thought Angie would enjoy the extras."

I hit the button for the sixth floor. "Anyone would enjoy your extras, Martha." The doors slid closed.

She laughed. "Next time, I'll bring you and Lena a plate."

I gave her a smile. "I'll hold you to it."

She changed topics, her curiosity surging to the fore. "Have you heard anything more about what happened this morning?"

I shook my head. "Unfortunately, no, I've been at work since this morning. I just came home to shower and change before my next job. I did have a card for the detective on my door, though."

"Yes, I spoke to a nice officer earlier." She frowned down

at the plate she worried between her hands. "I just don't understand how something like that happens."

Trying to ease her worry, I teased, "What? You don't buy into Ang's Family soap opera theory?"

Martha's nervous movements stilled as she looked up, her lips twitching. "That girl just lives for drama."

"That, she does," I agreed.

The elevator stopped, and Martha stepped forward. "I hope they get to the bottom of what happened."

"Me too," I murmured, but I wasn't sure they would. Not if Zev and the Cordovas were involved. There was no way that Family would allow the police to take the lead on the investigation. Not to mention Families weren't keen about the local authorities messing around in their business. That attitude was one of the reasons I took Zev's deal. Besides, someone had to look out for Lena, and that someone was me.

Martha got off, gave me a small wave, and headed down the hall. The doors slid shut, and I leaned back against the wall as the elevator glided to the garage. Anxiety chased concern as I wondered how much Zev would interfere with my search despite his promise of cooperation. I was swimming in unknown waters, which left me uncomfortable and paranoid.

As soon as I stepped out, I couldn't help but scan my surroundings, wary about who or what might strike next. Luckily, I was unmolested, and so was my car. I made it back to the Guild without incident. This time, I parked my Mustang where I knew Evan's electronic eye could watch. No way did I want another unexpected gift, especially since I was still reeling from the first one.

Instead of poking my head into Evan's office, I sent him a text as I headed toward the far end of the garage. *I'm here. Anything?*

Still digging.

Watch my car?

He sent back a thumbs-up as I hit the well-lit, glass-enclosed office manned by one of the Guild's mechanics. I rapped my knuckles against the open door, gaining the attention of the cadaverously thin man dressed in olive coveralls. "Evening, Carl."

"Costas." My name came back in a smoker's rasp, which was strange, as I'd never seen him with a single cigarette. He swiveled in his office chair. "How's my beautiful girl?"

Knowing his question wasn't directed at me but at my ride, I grinned and answered with my standard, "Running hot and smooth." I stepped just inside the door, and the stale scent of coffee made my nose wrinkle. "What do you have for me tonight?"

"You're in luck," he drawled. "You have three thrilling options for tonight's task."

I refrained from rubbing my hands together in anticipation. The Guild kept a unique selection of vehicles on hand for their clientele's varied needs. It was an eclectic mix of luscious luxury and motley junkers that ranged from the four-wheel variety to the two-wheel, speed-demon versions. No matter the make or model, bike or car, each was outfitted with high-end security options, both mundane and magical, and housed a stunning amount of power. It was one of the best side benefits, in my opinion, of working with the Guild. "I'm ready. Hit me with 'em."

He stood up, amusement tugging at his mouth. "Option one, Cadillac CT6."

Nice. The Caddy was a blend of muscle and luxury powered by five hundred fifty horses that topped out at two hundred miles per hour. However, its biggest flaw was the high belt line that hampered my rear visibility and cut into my neck. "Next?"

Carl's eyes danced as he solemnly intoned, "Option two, BMW 7."

My fingers twitched because the BMW's cockpit was a driver's dream, not to mention decked out to the nines. Despite being a spacious full-size sedan, it was also built for speed of the Autobahn variety. "Tempting."

"Option three." Carl spread his hand out with a flourish. "The Audi A8."

Choices, choices, choices. Unfortunately, I would have to pass on the Audi. It had pretty lines, but its handling wasn't the greatest. In town, it tended to be bumpy, and at higher speeds, it went floaty. Considering who my package was, I needed smooth, responsive, and luxurious. Normally, I would have picked the Caddy, but it only clicked two of the three requirements. Considering my swanky package, luxury was a must, so with a touch of regret, I said, "Let's go with the BMW."

"Good choice." Carl slid a clipboard off the desk and handed it to me. "You know what to do. Standard clauses plus Section D for the Class 3 security package. Did you update your insurance info in the system?"

"Yep, last week." One of the drawbacks of being a contractor was the requirement to carry my own insurance that would ride alongside the Guild's. I began signing my life away, line by line.

"Good, that will make this faster." He turned to the metal box hanging on the wall and grabbed a key fob. He waited while I scribbled. When I was done, we switched items. "Stall eight." He double-checked the forms and set the clipboard aside. "It's due back tomorrow morning at the latest, with a full tank."

"Have I ever not filled up?" I pocketed the fob.

"You're one of the few," he muttered. He rubbed a hand

over his bald head. "I'm out at midnight, so if you're back after that, use the drop box."

"Got it." I pushed off the doorframe and turned to leave. "Have a good night, Carl."

"You too, Costas. Smooth roads."

I lifted a hand and headed to the elevator tucked behind Carl's office. It was used exclusively by the Guild and offered the only access to the garage's top floor, where the Guild vehicles were housed. I stepped inside, and years of familiarity made it easy to ignore the irritating flare of the active ward ensuring access to only authorized personnel. The doors opened and let me out on a floor that was miles away from the lower parking levels. Behind a wall of thick bullet- and magic-resistant glass, the top floor had been converted into a gearhead's wet dream. The floor was divided between what was affectionately called the showroom, which took up the first half, and the garage, which dominated the back half.

The showroom held gleaming works of automotive art to the left and a ragtag collection of vehicles meant to blend into the surroundings on the right. It didn't matter if you were making a splash in the uber-ritzy area of Desert View or if you were trying to stay low key in the outskirts of the eastern suburbs, the Guild had you covered.

I stopped short of the sliding glass doors as a computerized voice asked for my authorization code. "Mike, alpha, charlie, hotel, one, zero." I waited while the code and voice print was checked.

"Proceed."

I moved toward the doors, the fine hairs along my arms rising as I crossed through the multi-layered security ward. The door whooshed open, and I headed left. It didn't take long to find the BMW. Glistening like wet ink under the bright lights, it was parked in the second aisle toward the front. I pressed my fingers against the driver's-side door, and once it recognized my prints, the whisper of the releasing locks barely pierced the quiet. I took my time relearning the controls. Once I was comfortable, I entered Sabella's address into the GPS. Earlier, I'd prepped a quick navigation search, thinking it would send me to Scottsdale or Desert View, where most of the Arcane Families liked to call home. Instead, her address led to an exclusive neighborhood in Fountain Hills. With the GPS primed, I started up the car and hit the road.

Thirty-five minutes later, I turned off Sunridge Drive and into an exclusive neighborhood called Eagle's Nest. Luckily, the gate was still open, but the nearby signs warned the road was for residents only. No worries there. This ride would blend in just fine. I slowed to the required twenty-five miles per hour and cruised the last mile to Sabella's house. I wasn't familiar with this part of Fountain Hills, but it was clear the residents weren't hurting financially. Unlike many of the valley's planned neighborhoods, where space was at a premium, privacy reigned here. Driveways were unmarked openings off the street, and the few glimpses I could catch revealed custom-built beauties perched on regal lots with sizes measuring in acres. The sun had dipped behind the rugged hills, painting the sky in purples, pinks, and golds, while softening the streets in deepening shadows. This far out, there was no such thing as streetlights.

Not wanting to miss my turn, I split my attention between the street ahead and the GPS. I spotted the turn for Sabella's drive before the computerized voice could chirp up. I turned in, stopped at the gate, and input the gate code Sylvia had included in her directions. The gates slid back, and I nosed the BMW through and followed the uneven surface of the pavers as they curled around the rising hill and spilled into a courtyard surrounded by a three-car garage and a two-story masterpiece. Passing the stately saguaro cactus on the right, I was met with the exquisitely kept front yard of mature trees and sculpted desert flora, all artfully lit. The terraced landscape blended into the beautiful mix of stucco and river rock of the house, which was a tasteful blend of desert and mountain cabin. After stopping the car alongside the curving wall guarding the front, I got out. Brushing the creases from my slacks, I took a moment to savor the spectacular panoramic views. It was breathtaking and undoubtedly the real reason behind the hefty price tags.

Unfortunately, I wasn't here to bask in the desert's beauty, but to work. As I walked around the car, the sharp sound of my shoes against the pavers sounded overly loud in the peaceful quiet. I stopped in front of the distressed wooden doors set in the wall, pressed the intercom tucked into the stone pillar to my left, and waited.

It didn't take long for a woman's voice to answer. "Yes?"

"Hello, my name's Rory Costas. I'm here to drive Ms. Rossi this evening."

"Of course. Come on in."

There was a muted buzz, followed by a click, and then the wooden gate in front of me unlocked, opening a couple of inches in welcome. I pushed it wider so I could walk through. The calming sounds of falling water fell from a stone fountain to my left. The pavers morphed into smooth stone that led to the glass-paned door. Warm light spilled from inside, staining the entryway. Through the glass, I could make out a figure approaching, gliding over the tiled floor. I waited with a polite smile pasted on my face as I studied Sabella Rossi. Light haired, instead of the expected dark, she was tall and curvy, but then everyone tended to be taller than my five four. In her case, she had at least four inches on me.

She pulled open the door, her warm, welcoming smile adding depth to an ageless beauty. "Hello, Ms. Costas." She held her hand out to me. "It's lovely to meet you."

My polite smile thawed in response to her sincere greeting. "Rory, please." I shook her hand, repressing a shiver of reaction at the feel of magic she wore.

She let me go and stepped to the side, waving me in. "Please, come in. I'm just about ready."

Following her directions, I stepped inside, doing my best not to gawk. Oversized tiles that resembled marble stretched through the space. Thick trestle beams lined the high ceilings and disappeared into the living area to the right, where a glimpse of massive glass windows overlooked a pool lit with blue and purple lights. To my left, a staircase curled up to the second floor, and straight back, a wall of glass showcased the natural beauty beyond.

Sabella pivoted on a needle-thin heel that added an elegant touch to her deceptively simple but expensive slacks. She stepped around me, talking as she passed a settee and stopped by an accent table sitting under a mirror. "I got caught up in a phone call and lost track of time."

Moving to the side of the front door, I stood with my hands clasped casually in front of myself. "No apology needed, Ms. Rossi."

She paused in the midst of fastening an earring and met my gaze through the mirror. "Sabella, please. Ms. Rossi makes me feel my age."

"Sabella, then." I didn't think she had to worry about anyone making assumptions about her age. Despite a few fine lines, she was the epitome of timeless beauty, whether thanks to surgery or genetics. Sabella appeared to be in her late forties, early fifties at most. Considering her reputation and the stories about her family, I knew she had to be at least ten years older than that. Then there was the power that surrounded her like a well-worn cloak. It added another intimidating layer to the woman.

Earring in place, she brushed a hand over the cowl-neck

blouse that accented her curves. Not the dangerous center-fold kind, but the more voluptuous type. "I appreciate you coming all this way to pick me up. Normally, I'd be fine driving myself, but tonight, I fear I'll need to offset my socializing with a bit of alcohol."

There wasn't much I could say to that, except "I'm happy to be of service."

She laughed and turned, her face lit with humor. "So polite, Rory. Not at all what I expected."

Curious, I asked, "Dare I ask what you did expect?"

She grabbed a sleek clutch and shawl from the settee. "You could, but I think I'll wait until we know each other better."

As friendly as she was, something about her demeanor made me think she knew something I didn't, and that was going to drive me nuts. "Well, then I'll be sure to ask again soon."

She patted my arm. "You do that."

She headed to the door, and I followed her out, waiting as she locked up and activated a security ward. We walked across the patio. "Your home is lovely."

"Thank you." She swung her shawl around her shoulders, tossing the end over her shoulder. "I was lucky to find it. When it became clear I'd need a place here, I wanted something a bit different than the typical ranch style that seems to be prevalent." She held open the gate, and I stepped through then waited while she locked it.

"It's definitely unique." I moved ahead and held open the back door of the car for her.

She slid gracefully into the back seat. "It is that." She set her clutch on the seat next to her, and I waited until she had fastened her seatbelt before closing the door.

I rounded the car and got into the driver's seat. "Where would you like to go tonight, Sabella?"

"Estancia. Do you know it?"

"I do." I started the car and typed in the name of the exclusive restaurant into the GPS. "Do we need to make a specific reservation time?"

"No need to worry about time. The owner's an old friend."

The ETA came up on the GPS's screen. "We should be there in just under forty minutes then, traffic willing." I caught her gaze in the rearview mirror. "Would you like me to engage the privacy screen?"

She settled in her seat, crossing her legs. "Would you mind keeping me company?"

"Not at all."

Over the next twenty or so minutes, I discovered that Sabella Rossi possessed a dry sense of humor that was at odds with most in her social set. The casual conversation flowed easily, which didn't happen often for me, as professional distance was an ingrained concept. However, she refused to maintain that distance, and I found I enjoyed talking with her. I learned that she was a widow with three grown children scattered over the globe. She shared amusing stories of her family and friends and had no problem with poking fun at herself or the situations she faced.

It wasn't until there was a natural lull in the conversation that she shifted gears. "Sylvia mentioned you recently left the Guild."

A bit of wariness crept in at the topic switch. "I did."

"Do you mind if I ask why?" There was true curiosity in her voice.

When I glanced back in the mirror, that sincerity was reflected in her face. Instead of a glib answer, I stuck to the truth. "As much as I value the Guild's training, I prefer to work for myself."

"Admirable," she murmured. "But striking out on your own carries substantial risks."

I kept my attention on the road, even as my lips curled up in a grim smile. "So does working for the Guild, but at least this way, I choose which risks to take."

"Ah, so you like to be in control?"

I didn't quite smother my amused snort. "Control is an illusion."

"You're young to be so cynical, Rory." Amusement tinged her reprimand.

"Age is relative, Sabella."

At that, she laughed outright. "Oh so true."

I waited until her laughter faded then added, "Besides, I don't consider it cynical so much as being realistic."

"Comments like that make me think life has not been kind to you."

Feeling the weight of her attention, I shrugged. "Life didn't teach me that; people did."

Movement shimmered in the rearview mirror, and she leaned forward. "Sounds like there's a story behind that."

Not wanting to deepen the emotional quagmire, I tried to lighten the conversation. "Nothing too interesting, just a comment made by a teacher."

"Oh, don't leave me hanging. That's so unfair."

Her tone made me laugh, which made sharing easier. "It's nothing earth-shattering, I promise." I kept an eye on the road but could feel her sitting back and listening. "I ended up in detention after a rather heated disagreement with a classmate. I couldn't even tell you what we were arguing about now, but I do remember we weren't getting out of detention unless we explained what happened, took responsibility for our actions, and apologized to each other. There was no fooling Ms. Kelly with half-hearted apologies, and neither of us wanted to be the first to back down.

When she realized she was dealing with two equally stubborn kids, she decided to point out that we had a choice to make—let the situation control us or take control of the situation."

Sabella made a soft hum of agreement. "The familiar axiom of 'the only thing you can control is you.'"

"Exactly."

"Your Ms. Kelly sounds exceedingly intelligent."

"That, she was." I hadn't thought of that story in forever, but it really did sit at the core of who I was. As I grew up, life had reiterated Ms. Kelly's wisdom with frightening regularity. Whining about things I couldn't change wasn't just pointless; it was also a waste of time. It was easier to ensure I had my shit together than try to get everyone else's in line. I made the last turn to Estancia and could see the lights ahead. "We're here."

"Lovely." Sabella began digging through her clutch. "I'm not sure how long I'll be, but they have a delightful lounge."

Hearing her unspoken invitation, I offered, "I'm happy to wait with the car."

She paused with her lipstick in hand. "Do you mind waiting inside?"

There was a note in her voice that made my nape itch and nudged my sense of professional responsibility as I turned into the restaurant's parking lot. "If it makes you more comfortable, I'm happy to." Even though security wasn't my thing, I glanced to the mirror. "Are you expecting trouble?"

She did one last swipe of color over her lips and recapped the lipstick before dropping it back in her clutch. When her gaze met mine, her smile held a sharp edge. "Not at all, but trouble is trouble because it's not expected, yes?"

Fair point, but she didn't strike me as someone who would say something just to say it. If Sabella had concerns about what or who lay in wait, it was best not to tempt fate by providing an easy target like the car, so I bypassed the valet station.

"Apologies, Rory. If you'd prefer to wait, I'd understand."

I shook my head. "No apologies needed, Sabella. I'm happy to accompany you." I parked the car, stepped out, and opened Sabella's door.

She emerged, the picture of unconcerned elegance, and waited while I activated both the electronic alarm and pre-set security wards. I stepped back, taking in the faint shimmer of magic that now lay over the car, a visible deterrent to anyone with magic. *Good enough.* I turned to find her watching me with avid interest.

Instead of indulging her curiosity, she gave me another brilliant smile and asked, "Ready?"

I nodded and followed her to the restaurant.

CHAPTER TEN

WHATEVER TROUBLE SABELLA expected kept a low profile. From my vantage point at the end of the bar, I could see her on the patio, sitting at a round table across from a couple I didn't recognize, even though I thought I probably should. Especially if Sylvia was correct in her assumption that Sabella was evaluating me for a more permanent position. I committed their faces to memory, making a mental note to get their names later. Paranoid? Maybe, but I was having a hard time shaking the itch Sabella's earlier request created.

It wasn't the only thing keeping me from enjoying the experience. Feeling decidedly out of place, I continued to nurse my crystal-cut glass of ice and soda, letting the soft murmur of conversations punctuated by the occasional chimes of silver on china swirl around me in a score of unmistakable ambiance. Estancia was the type of place where heels and little black dresses reigned supreme. The one redeeming thing was the view. Not that much of it was visible with night in full bloom, but I had no doubt that during daylight hours, it was killer. Even though the restaurant sat away from the glow of the city, the night sky was filled with fairy lights of stars that normally hid behind the curtain of artificial light. Whoever had built the place knew what they were doing, because the main room flowed uninterrupted onto the patio, creating a stunning blend of warm welcome and open-air dining.

As Sabella visited, instead of squirming under hypothetical stares, I decided to indulge in my favorite pastime of people watching. Safely tucked at the far corner of the bar, I shifted on my padded seat, turning my attention to the other diners scattered throughout the room. Two firepits stretched along either side, and their warmth held off the nip of night-cooled air. Tables sat far enough apart to offer a semblance of privacy and so the servers could move like wraiths as they alternately whisked away plates and replaced them with new offerings. The patrons were a mix of couples and groups, but it was obvious the romantic atmosphere tilted more toward the couples' front.

My gaze drifted across the scene, faltering to a stop on a familiar face being seated at a table fitted into an intimate corner. Blood rushed under my cheeks as Zev's dark head bent close to his companion. His female companion. I looked away, fighting back the flare of unwelcome and inappropriate jealousy. *What the hell is wrong with me?* There was no reason to feel that pinch of hurt. No matter what absurd daydreams haunted me, I had no illusions there was anything more than curious animosity between Zev and me.

Shaking my head at my foolishness, I deliberately turned away from Zev's table, determined to ignore him. I managed to keep my gaze from straying back, but I couldn't do the same with my thoughts. *Who is she? Why are they here? Are they serious?* The stupid questions meant nothing and everything and proved that I really needed to get out more. I scratched that onto my to-do list for once Lena was home safe and sound.

Frustrated with myself, I shifted my position so I could watch the patio. Sabella and her companions were on coffee and dessert, which hopefully meant this night was close to being over. As I lifted my glass, movement near the entrance caught my attention. I turned to see the maître d' leading Madeline and Theodore Thatcher through the tables. Stunned by their unexpected appearance, I took an absent sip of my soda as I watched the couple make their way across the dining room. Seeing them reminded me I had forgotten to call and make an appointment with Theo. For a brief moment, I considered interrupting their plans for the evening, but when they drew close to Zev's table, I decided to stay out of it.

Zev lifted his head and caught sight of them. He said something, most likely calling out Madeline's name as she turned to greet him, forcing Theo to stop at her side. My position made it impossible to eavesdrop on their conversation, but it soon became clear that whatever conversation was happening was strictly between Zev and Madeline. Zev had risen from his chair to exchange hellos, and I couldn't help but note he looked hot in the black dress pants and silver-gray collared shirt. Hot and sexy. His female companion watched the interaction with a polite smile, waiting for Zev to introduce her before rising, as well. Theo did that over-the-top move of kissing the back of her hand in greeting. If I hadn't been watching so closely, I would've missed how her body went stiff. She was good, though, because she didn't give away any other signs of distaste.

I did my best to observe the tête-à-tête without being obvious as the two couples talked. Well, Zev and Madeline talked, while Theo and Mystery Woman listened. Interestingly, Theo's gaze swept over the room, clearly disinterested in whatever Madeline and Zev were discussing. He aimed a smile and lifted his chin in silent greeting toward a table with three men and two women. He touched the small of Madeline's back and leaned down to say something in her ear. She patted his arm but didn't let him go and turned back to Zev, which meant she missed the flash of annoyance on Theo's face before he smoothed it away.

Hmm, interesting reaction. I filed it away for later consideration.

A handful of moments passed, then Madeline and Theo left Zev and continued to the patio. Interestingly, they bypassed the table with Theo's friends with nothing more than wordless acknowledgement. I followed their progress, and when I turned back, my gaze collided with Zev's dark one. Despite the distance between us, I could see his jaw tighten. His annoyance amused the hell out of me. I tilted my head and lifted my cup slightly in acknowledgement before deliberately turning away. I figured I had about two minutes before I had company. I drained my drink and prayed Sabella would get to me first. No such luck. Zev's brooding presence hit my back like a looming storm.

"Fancy meeting you here." His voice smoothed down my spine like a brush of velvet as he nudged aside the empty barstool so he could stand at my side.

I could feel the weight of his gaze but refused to meet it. Instead, I caught the bartender's attention and nudged my glass forward with a smile. He came over, and I murmured, "Refill, please." He nodded and hustled off. Only then did I turn to look at Zev. "Hello, Zev."

He braced a hand on the bar as he studied me. "Why are you here, Rory?"

Not liking his tone, I held his gaze, my response carrying a bite. "Unlike you, I'm working."

Irritated speculation darkened his face. "Are you following the Thatchers?"

His arrogant assumption set my teeth on edge, but

instead of correcting him, I decided to see how deep a hole he could dig. "If I was?"

At my flippant response, his gaze narrowed. "I'd suggest you stop before you screw everything up."

Hmm, tempting. "And how would my being here do that, Zev?"

His gaze went beyond me to the patio, presumably to where the Thatchers were dining. "Madeline is not keen on public scenes." His attention came back to me, a whisper of disdain coloring his voice. "She'll have you removed before you finish your first question."

The bartender brought back my soda and turned to Zev. "Sir?"

Zev didn't look away as he ordered. "Two glasses, please. A Siduri and a Camins."

"Of course," the bartender murmured and left.

I waited until he was out of earshot before I said, "As much as I appreciate your advice, I don't need it." *Ever.* "I'm not here for them."

Instantly, I wished I had stopped before tacking on that last bit as his obvious frustration disappeared, to be replaced by an arrogant tilt of his lips. His tone shifted. "Are you following me, Ms. Costas?"

Heat rose under my skin at his unmistakable implication even as I rolled my eyes. "No, Mr. Aslanov, I'm not." I picked up my glass and, with a sweet smile, lied through my teeth. "You're not that interesting."

Instead of backing off, he leaned in, his voice dropping into an intimate rumble. "I could be."

I bet. It took everything I had to lock down the greedy cheer my hormones sent up, but I did it. Mirroring his lean and matching his tone, I purred, "And I bore easily." This close, I couldn't miss the spark of male interest that flickered to life at my challenge. Stubbornly holding his gaze and refusing to move back, I lifted my cup and took a sip.

"Sir, your reds." The bartender interrupted our silent battle.

Zev held my stare for a heartbeat, then he turned to murmur his thanks as he wrapped those long fingers around the slender stems of the wineglasses.

Taking advantage of the reprieve, I shifted my attention to the dining room, not really seeing it as I regathered my composure.

I didn't get far before we were interrupted by a welcomed voice as Sabella came up to my side. "Zev, what are you doing here?"

"Sabella, lovely to see you tonight." Zev set the wineglasses aside and stepped away to exchange cheek kisses with Sabella. "I didn't know you were in town."

Sabella gave a light laugh. "I had unexpected business on a potential acquisition to see to. How's Emilio and the family?"

I tuned out their small talk as I studied their interaction. It was clear Sabella knew and liked Zev, and her feeling was reciprocated. I wasn't sure why I was contradictorily both surprised and disappointed. The two ran in the same circles. The sound of Jeremy's name had me tuning back in to the conversation.

"And Jeremy? How's he doing?" Sabella's expression and voice held obvious concern. "My heart hurt when I heard. It was such a tragedy, him losing both of his parents so close together."

I wasn't sure losing his mom should be labeled a tragedy, considering Jeremy had paid a steep price of being kidnapped because of her poor life choices, but I kept my opinion to myself.

"Jeremy's doing as well as can be expected," Zev shared. "Emilio's doing his best to help him deal."

Sabella squeezed his arm briefly in sympathy. "Well, if you're in need of a name, do let me know. I have a couple I can recommend." She stepped back.

"I'll be sure to pass your offer along." He looked between Sabella and me, his speculation clear. "If you're in town for a bit, I'm sure Emilio would appreciate seeing you."

Sabella smiled. "Why don't you warn him I'll be giving him a call. That should give him time to clear his calendar for a lunch."

"I'll do that." The brief but genuine grin that cut through Zev's normally intractable mask stalled the air in my lungs. Without the normal weight of grimness, he looked years younger and infinitely more attractive.

"Good." Sabella glanced at the two glasses of wine waiting at the bar. "Well, I don't want to hijack you from your date. You best get back before she worries." She turned to me and straightened her shawl, leaving Zev to reclaim his drinks. "Shall we, Rory?"

"Of course." I stood up, ignoring the weight of Zev's gaze and doing my best not to let my smile turn smug. I dug some cash from my pocket and tucked it under my glass. I turned to find Zev giving Sabella another cheek brush as he held the two glasses aloft. "Sabella." His dark eyes came to mine, male amusement clear in the depths. "Ms. Costas."

"Mr. Aslanov," I returned as I took my place next to Sabella, and together we watched him walk away.

"If I was a younger woman..."

Sabella's low, appreciative comment surprised a laugh out of me. "I don't think he'd know what to do with a woman like you, Sabella."

She laughed as she touched her shoulder to mine with a gentle nudge. "Don't underestimate him."

Yeah, there was no danger of doing that.

Simple curiosity replaced her amusement. "How do you know Zev?"

For a moment, my brain stalled over an explanation that wouldn't require painful details. "We've crossed paths during a past assignment."

My casual response didn't discourage Sabella. "Sounds like there's a story there."

I managed a dismissive smile even as my heart rate ticked up. "Nope, no story."

She made a tching sound as she started walking. "You know, Rory, you really should indulge your elders when they're looking for juicy gossip."

I couldn't suppress my amused snort as I followed her. We wove our way through the diners. I swore I could feel eyes on me. Zev's or someone else's, I didn't know, but I refused to give in to the urge to turn and find out. We exited the restaurant and headed to the car. I offered to bring it around if she wanted to wait up front, but she brushed my suggestion aside with "My legs work just fine."

Remembering Sabella's earlier comment about trouble, I took comfort in the weight of my gun tucked against the small of my back and prodded my magic awake. It remained blessedly placid as we closed in on the sedan. The lack of reaction from my ability wasn't a foolproof warning system, but it eased my mind. It helped that the car's security ward appeared undisturbed. Deactivating the security, I opened the back door so Sabella could get in. I closed the door behind her and turned to the driver's door when a ripple whispered over my magic, like a phantom touch on a lake, causing me to pause. It was the same faint sensation I encountered when brushing against a lingering magical echo. Not unusual, just unexpected. It could easily be the remains of an old spell or simply an exceptionally strong magic user passing nearby. Regardless, I took a moment to scan my surroundings, just in case. Under the amber lights, the lot was quiet, with the exception of a man assisting a woman into a low-slung sportster. No lurking shadows or menacing cars lying in wait. On top of that, my magic was back to its unruffled normality.

Maybe I was just jumpy. I shook my head, opened my door, and got in the car.

"Is something wrong?"

At Sabella's unanticipated question, my gaze went to the rearview mirror to find her studying me. "No, why?"

She motioned with her hand toward the door. "You looked worried for a minute there."

I gave her a reassuring smile and thought fast. "Oh, I thought I saw something and wanted to ensure it wasn't the trouble you mentioned earlier." It was difficult to tell if she believed me or not. Her expression was hard to read, so I tacked on, "It was just another couple getting into their car."

She held my gaze for an interminable moment then looked away with a small, secretive smile. "You're extremely observant."

"Comes with the job." I started the car.

Within minutes, I was following the GPS directions back to Sabella's home. A comfortable quiet had settled in the car. Unable to shake off my earlier unease, I held my magic in place, just in case. Even though I kept my attention on the road and surrounding traffic, that part of my mind not involved with my job churned over Lena's situation. Knowing there was no way I was getting sleep tonight without some answers, I seriously considered taking the BMW back to the Guild just so I could pester Evan. I had a feeling he wouldn't be leaving his office anytime soon, either.

"You know you can't leave me dangling in curiosity."

Sabella's weird statement snapped my eyes up to the

rearview mirror to find her watching me with an unsettling intensity. Unsure of what she wanted, I asked, "Excuse me?"

"About what's between you and Zev."

Unable to hold her gaze, I turned my attention back to the road, hoping the heat rising under my skin wasn't noticeable in the dark confines of the car. "There's nothing between us."

"I may be old, but I'm not blind, dear. Whatever you two were discussing appeared intense."

"Not intense, just frustrating."

Sabella's burst of laughter surprised me. "Yes, I can see how Zev could frustrate a woman."

My face burned at her unmistakable, teasing implication, but I would have been stupid to deny the obvious impact he had on me. "Yeah, no doubt he's used to beating them off with sticks. Luckily for me, I'm not keen on being another notch for his ego."

"Then you're one of the few."

At her sardonic reply, my lips curved up in a grim smile. "I'm good with that."

"Are you sure?"

"Definitely." I was smart enough to understand how dangerous it would be to venture into Zev's world on either a personal or a professional level. As the Cordova Arbiter, he was the scarily efficient hunter feared by the other predators gliding through the unforgiving depths of the powerful. Personally, I would happily steer clear of him and his shark-infested waters. Unfortunately, professionally, I needed his help. Not just for cultivating those all-important allies to help secure my financial future, but because it looked as if I would have to wade into the blood-filled waters to save Lena. Better to do that with someone who knew what lay in wait than blundering around on my own.

"Would you mind some advice?" Sabella's question broke through my grim thoughts.

"Not at all."

"You may want to reconsider your current strategy."

Despite the lightness of her tone, her underlying warning had my fingers tightening on the wheel. "How so?"

There were sounds of her shifting in her seat, and I glanced in the mirror to see her looking out the passenger window. "If you present too much of a challenge, you'll become irresistible."

Amused by her assumption, I said, "I don't think I'll have to worry about that."

"Why's that?"

"Zev's made it clear that he considers me..." I searched for a polite way to rephrase "a pain in the ass" and came up with "An inconvenient obstacle."

"And that doesn't bother you?"

"Not in the slightest." *Liar, liar, pants on fire.* "Trust me, the extent of our 'relationship' is strictly professional, something I don't see changing anytime soon."

The weight of her stare threatened to set my hair on fire, but I managed to keep my attention on the road. It was a relief when she spoke. "You know, I'm not sure if I should be happy at your obvious practicality or miffed that I don't get a chance to indulge in my maternal side by offering unsolicited advice."

I checked my mirrors as a small smile escaped. "If it makes you feel better, advise away." I hit the turn signal and shifted lanes to pass a delivery truck.

"I think I will."

I laughed.

She kept up her light-hearted tone. "If you weren't so reasonable, I'd try to spare your feelings as I pointed out that Zev would be an exciting diversion for most, but a smart woman wouldn't get her expectations up for anything beyond that."

Playing along, I ignored the pinch in my chest. "And why's that?"

"Because no woman will ever replace his first love."

I hid my flinch at the unexpected hit. Thankfully, my voice remained steady. "Whoever that is must be someone special to deserve that kind of devotion."

"Oh, it's not a woman, dear." Sabella's voice lost its teasing hint and turned serious. "It's his family or, more to the point, the Cordova Family." Her sudden shift from teasing to serious had me glancing in the mirror. Her gaze caught mine, and the lingering traces of my humor disappeared under her steady gaze. "They will always come first." There was an unmistakable weight to her words.

"That's not news." I looked back to the road and swallowed against the sudden lump in my throat. "Zev's been very clear about his priorities."

"Interesting," she murmured, then continued before I could respond, although I wasn't exactly sure what to say. "Loyalty, much like alliances, are the core of Family relationships. It's not given lightly."

There was a patronizing edge to her comments that rubbed me the wrong way. "I don't believe that trait is specific to the Families, Sabella." It came out unintentionally sharp, but Families weren't the only ones who understood loyalty and commitment.

For a moment, I wondered if I'd gone too far, but a soft sigh preceded her apologetic "You're absolutely right, Rory. I'm sorry. That came out decidedly arrogant, and that was not my intent."

"Apology accepted." With our exit coming up quickly, I switched lanes. "There's nothing wrong with putting your family first." I hit the off ramp and began to slow, absently noting the headlights behind us. I gauged my speed as the driver following us seemed inclined to ride my bumper. I split my attention between the light at the end of the ramp and the headlights. Instincts blared in warning, igniting my magic. My power rose with anticipatory glee as adrenaline zipped through my veins, snapping my attention into sharp focus. Despite my spiking anxiety, my hands stayed rock steady on the wheel. "Sabella, are you belted in?"

"Of course."

"Good." Praying that I gauged the light change correctly, I hit the gas. At my unexpected move, the headlights behind me fell back. As we hit the top of the ramp, I angled the BMW into a smooth but fast left, blowing through the light just as it changed from red to green. In its holder on the dash, my phone rattled with an incoming text. Busy trying to avoid whoever was behind us, I ignored it.

"Rory?" Sabella's voice was tight with tension.

"It seems that your trouble has finally arrived." I kept my voice calm and level.

I could sense her moving and figured she was probably trying to see who was behind us. I did the same, using the rearview mirror. The streetlights pooled along the road and spilled over the dark sedan behind us. The light wasn't enough to tell if it was deep blue or black, but the light bounced off the tinted windows. There was no way to identify the driver or tell if there was more than one person inside. I looked back to the road ahead. At this time of night, traffic was quiet, which was both good and bad. Good, because it meant there weren't as many innocent bystanders to worry about. Bad, because shaking our tail would be difficult.

I increased our speed and began weaving in and out of the other cars. The last thing I wanted was to let them get close enough to be a real threat. Not to mention the insurance paperwork would be a massive bitch. Trying to figure out what exactly was breathing down our necks, I asked, "Does your trouble come with a name, Sabella?"

"Honestly, no. I'm as surprised as you that it showed up. I truly wasn't expecting it. The comment was just that—a comment."

Sure it was. Instead of calling her out, I snaked in and out of the cars, scanning for options. "We have two decisions. We can either lose them or find out who they are."

"How are those our choices?"

I swore there was amusement in her question, but I didn't dare take my eyes off the road to check. Instead, I explained, "As your driver, my goal is to ensure your safety. However, I'm also aware that someone in your position may prefer to discover who's decided to target them." Sabella was a power in her own right, and if someone was stupid enough to target her, I was sure she would be perfectly capable of handling it. Even though it wasn't my first option, I didn't want to continue to evade if she preferred an alternate option. That just wasn't good customer service. "What would you like to do?"

"If I said I wanted to confront them, would you really make that happen?"

"You *are* the customer." The sedan sped up, and I lowered my foot yet again. The BMW glided forward. The needle on the speedometer inched well into speeding-ticket territory. "However, I would point out that I may not be able to keep you safe should you choose to do so."

"Good to know."

Yep, that was definitely laughter in her voice.

"As I'd like to make it home in one piece, please feel free to evade," she said.

"Thank you." Permission granted, I muted the GPS and settled in for the best part of my job. Driving.

There was something exhilarating about being behind the wheel of a high-performance vehicle, especially one built for speed and so beautifully responsive. My world narrowed down to the feel of the steering wheel in my hands, the pedals under my feet, and the road under the wheels. I relaxed into my seat and, with a light touch, let the BMW fly. The street-lights blurred as we arrowed around the other cars. Soon, the street emptied and darkened as we sped into an unpopulated area that sat between Scottsdale and Fountain Hills—the perfect spot to lose our tailgaters. The street uncurled in front of me like a ribbon, stretching into the night, my head-lights illuminating the reflective paint on the road. I checked my mirrors and smiled when the sedan's headlights appeared well behind us.

Good enough. I checked the GPS one last time, cementing the road's path in my mind, and flicked off the BMW's lights, including the running lights. For anyone else, that would be an insanely dangerous move. For a Transporter, not so much.

I heard Sabella's quick inhale.

"We're fine," I reassured her as my eyes adjusted to the darkness. I brought up the mental image from the GPS and kept our speed steady. Transporters were a specialized Guild group for a reason. They were uniquely qualified for their job, thanks to an innate navigation ability that was paired with a preternatural reaction time. Much like any other mages, Transporters honed their skills through a mix of practical and magical training, but we also had a strangely symbiotic rela-tionship with vehicles. Lena laughingly called me a speed demon, and in a way, she was spot on.

Another check in the mirror showed the road behind us empty. Instead of letting up on the gas, I held steady and considered my mental map. The turn ahead would intersect with the road leading into Fountain Hills and should cut about ten minutes off our route. It had the added benefit of crossing through a subdivision. Headlights appeared ahead, and I shifted my gaze to avoid being blinded by the approaching car as they didn't have a chance to switch off their brights before we blew past them. I eased off the gas, knowing I needed to slow to take the turn without fishtailing or hitting the brakes. The road's incline helped, naturally decreasing the car's speed.

My world narrowed to the upcoming turn and the instinctual calculations whizzing through my brain. I let out a slow breath, relaxed my hands on the wheel as if gentling reins, and my motorized steed responded to my touch, gliding smoothly into the heart-stopping turn. As soon as the road straightened, so did we, our speed increasing as we put even more distance between us and our pursuers. When I was sure we couldn't be seen, I flicked on the headlights and eased off the gas, dropping to a more acceptable speed. As we slowed, the hypersensitive state that helped me navigate began to drift away.

"Well, that was exciting." Sabella's wry comment brushed aside the last clinging threads.

My lips twitched. "We should be clear, but I'm going to take an alternate return route, if you don't mind. It's a bit longer."

"Please, do whatever you feel necessary. I'm looking forward to a nice calming drink before bed."

In the dash holder, my phone rattled again. This time, I glanced at the screen and caught Evan's name as I unmuted the GPS. *Damn.* I wanted to see what he'd found, but it would have to wait until I got Sabella home. A loud sigh echoed through the car, and I shifted my attention to the mirror. "What?"

Sabella caught my eyes and gave a wry grimace. "I think I know who was chasing us." She lifted her phone. "It seems the local papers have caught wind I'm in town."

I went back to scanning our surroundings and followed the GPS directions as it led us into a winding path home. "You're thinking it was the paparazzi?"

"Possibly."

I wasn't sure I agreed, but it wasn't like I had any proof otherwise. Instead, I said soothingly, "Well, hopefully, they won't be camping out in front of your house."

That got a derisive snort from Sabella. "They won't make it past the gate, and those that try are in for a rather unpleasant surprise."

Since I had a good imagination, she didn't need to elaborate. It wouldn't do for anyone to forget this woman belonged to one of the oldest Arcane Families, including me. "I'll let you know if they decide to rejoin us."

She sat back with a quiet "Thanks."

I stayed alert for any more unwanted followers during the rest of our uneventful drive. When we pulled up to Sabella's gate, I was extremely grateful to find no one lying in wait. Though the oddity of it made me question, yet again, Sabella's assumption about our followers. I headed up the drive and watched my mirrors as the gate slid closed behind us. I parked, turned off the car, and got out to hold open Sabella's door.

Sabella stepped out and waited as I closed the door. Her hand curled around my arm, holding me in place. "Thank you, Rory."

I wasn't expecting her touch, and it sparked against my active magic, causing a small jerk. I covered my reaction with a smile. "My pleasure."

It must have worked, because her expression didn't change. She squeezed gently and let me go. "Perhaps Sylvia mentioned that I'm looking for a driver while I'm in town."

Excitement had my pulse leaping as I followed her to the

front door. I held it back as I confirmed in an even tone, "She did."

"Good." She unlocked her door and pushed it open. "I like you."

Instead of puzzling out why that simple statement sounded profound, I returned an honest "The feeling's mutual."

She stepped inside and turned around. It was hard to read her expression through the shadows thrown by the overhead porch, but I could feel her studying me. "Good." She gave a slight pause. "If I have my lawyer send over a contract, would you be willing to review it?"

I wanted to pump a victorious fist at her question, but instead I managed a courteous "Of course."

That earned me a knowing smile. "Then I'll be sure to have him do that first thing tomorrow."

I knew my grin revealed just how excited I was about her offer, but I couldn't help it. This was huge. "I'll keep an eye out for it then."

She laughed, not fooled by my casual comment. "I'm going to enjoy working with you, young lady. Be careful heading home, and I'll see you soon."

As the door shut, I turned and all but ran back to the car. Despite the mess currently tangling around me, I was buzzed. Unfortunately, as I sat in the car and read Evan's text, my buzz was quickly replaced by dread.

Possible location found.

CHAPTER ELEVEN

EVAN'S BRIEF, disquieting message had come in twenty minutes ago and included an address. I plugged it into the GPS, then knowing it was a long shot, I dialed him back. Sure enough, his phone rang and dumped into voicemail.

"Evan, I'm thirty minutes out. Call me."

The address was a familiar one. Situated near the university, it belonged to a defunct strip mall scheduled to be demolished. With one eye on the speed traps, I stayed within legal limits as I navigated out of Fountain Hills. Once clear of the residential area, I hit the gas. Taking advantage of the fact that the valley was veined with freeways, I took the first exit onto the 101 and raced south. It was late enough that avoiding cops wasn't likely to be a problem. As the miles disappeared under my tires, my promise to keep Zev updated on new developments, say like the possibility of finding Lena, tugged at my conscience. *But...*

Possible location, a small voice pointed out mercilessly.

Right, so maybe I would wait to update Zev. You know, once I actually confirmed I had something worth sharing. It had nothing to do with the fact he was out on a date. Not one damn thing. Besides, the last thing I wanted was to call Zev in, only to come up empty-handed. I was sure he would find a way to claim it was a bid for his attention. If Lena was there, Evan and I could handle things. Conscience appeased, I focused on cutting my drive time down significantly. I exited the freeway and hit the surface streets. With how late it was, the roads were quiet enough for me to ride the edge of reasonable speed.

With minutes to spare, I pulled into the parking lot of an apartment complex that sat across the street from the fenced-off remains of the mall. I knew I was in the right spot, because Evan's SUV was parked in a clearly marked visitor spot. Luckily for me, there was another open spot a couple of cars down. I pulled in, turned off the car, and undid my seat-belt. Leaning over, I popped open the Beemer's glove compartment and ran my fingers along the left-side seam, where the bottom and side met, until the faint uneven catch rasped against my touch. I pressed down, and a hidden latch released, revealing a small compartment. Inside lay what appeared to the untrained eye to be a couple of marble-sized river stones. I grabbed one, hit the latch to re-secure the hidden cache, then closed and locked the glove compartment.

I got out and set the BMW's electronic alarm. Since I wanted the car to blend in, not stick out, activating the wards I used with Sabella was out. Hence plan B. Taking a look around to ensure I was alone, I cupped the stone in my palm and sent out a tendril of magic as I whispered, "This old man, he played four. He played knickknack on my door."

Against my palm, the stone warmed as the warding magic activated. I crouched and tucked the ward into a customized niche on the underside of the wheel well. Once it was in place, I rested my hand on the warm hood and locked the ward into place. "Knickknack paddy whack."

Standing so close, I couldn't avoid the painful rush as the warding magic swept over the sedan, covering the car from bumper to bumper in a level-three security ward and changing the BMW to a mid-level sedan that matched the other cars. I wiped my hand against my hip and stepped back, confident that if anyone was stupid enough to mess with this car, they would soon find themselves spending quality time in an emergency room. The Guild was very possessive of its property.

As I walked away, I tried Evan again. *Voicemail. Dammit.* I pocketed the phone and touched the gun at my back, then I upped my pace, not slowing as I hit the sidewalk. I didn't bother crossing at the light. Instead, taking advantage of the lack of traffic, I dashed across the street, hoping to find a way past the fence surrounding the construction site. The last time I'd driven by here, maybe a couple weeks ago, they had just begun the demolition process. From what I could tell from the poorly lit structure huddled behind the fence, they were now about halfway through. There was no way Evan had entered from the edge near the street. That was too obvious if anyone was watching. Just because I couldn't see any cameras didn't mean they didn't exist. Granted, Evan could disable them with a thought, but again, if all the cameras blitzed at the same time, whoever was watching would come running. Stealth would be the name of the game.

Keeping my pace casual, I sauntered down the sidewalk that ran parallel with the fence. When the fence cornered and disappeared down a small side path, I slipped into the shadows and found myself in a narrow, unlit alley. The fence continued corralling the lot, and I hoped I wouldn't have to circle the whole damn block to find what I needed. Thankfully, it didn't take long to find what I was looking for—a section of the chain-link fence bent back just enough to squeeze through.

Nice.

I slipped through. Grateful nothing had snagged, I straightened then studied the dark structure in front of me. As expected, there were no obvious signs of life, no flickering lights or soft noises of movement to track where Evan was in this place. Not that I wanted, or needed, them since there was another way for me to find him. I dialed up my magic until it settled over my skin like invisible body armor. I locked down my emotions and focused on the task at hand. I pulled out my backup plan and held it in front of me in a two-handed grip. I crossed the lot to the building with the gun's reassuring weight in hand.

I crept along the building, using the shadows as much as possible, looking for an entry point. As I moved, I visualized my magic expanding outward like ripples in a pond, hoping to brush up against active magic. Splitting my attention between sneaking around in the dark and trying to pinpoint Evan's location without getting jumped wasn't easy. Sheets of plywood covered empty openings that had once held windows and doors. The need to hurry was riding my ass. I was seriously considering kicking my way in when I tripped and stumbled back into one of those plywood-covered openings. The wood shifted, scraping against the debris-strewn concrete with a sharp noise. I dropped to a crouch, my breath stalling and heart pounding, and put my back to the nearby wall. I waited for someone to come investigate. Interminable seconds ticked by, and when I was sure no one was coming, I slowly straightened. Shifting my gun to one hand, I used the other to carefully and awkwardly push the broken plywood wider so I could squeeze through.

Inside, I tugged the makeshift door back into place. No sense in making my entrance obvious. Darkness pressed in, leaving me blind. Without knowing who or what I would encounter, I didn't dare use any kind of light. Despite the underlying layer of dust in the air, it was breathable. I stayed close to the wall, waiting for my eyes to adjust. It took a bit, but eventually, the faint light was able to make it inside. The dim light layered the blackness in shades of gray, giving me enough visual clues to make out faint shapes in the shadowed interior. There was a sense of openness to the space—probably because, from what I could see, the main area was empty, except for scattered piles of what looked like debris. What appeared to be a half wall stretched along the far back of the space, and a pool of darkness waited behind that.

The skin-prickling sensation of magic nipped along the edge of my awareness, pulling me deeper inside. I narrowed my concentration and followed the lure of the faint touch leading me toward the shadowy pool at the back. Right, so whatever was happening, was back there. *Good to know.*

I crept forward and bit back an oath as my toe hit an unmovable object. I used my free hand to discover what lay in front of me as I shuffled around the pile and carefully made my way across the space. The farther back I went, the more the magical tug strengthened, and I had to consciously slow my pace to avoid tripping over obstacles.

I stopped at what I realized was a long counter, not a wall, and did my best to figure out what lay behind it. The counter separated the dining floor from the back kitchen, and now I could tell this had probably been a restaurant at some point in time. The only entrance to the kitchen area was a wide opening, the doors missing, gaping to my left. I considered calling out, but the same uncomfortable itch urging me to hurry kept me mute. I inched closer and stood at the side of the opening, every sense stretched taut. A faint sound reached my ears, like something brushing over the floor.

Muscles tight and spine lined with sweat, I put my back

to the doubtful protection of the wall and stepped into the inky depths of the kitchen. I only got a few steps in before my hip hit something hard enough to bruise. Feeling around with the cautiousness of the blind, I discovered the cool metal edge of what felt like a huge sink to my left. Keeping one hand on the sink's edge, I tried to make out the rest of the space. I was fairly sure a counter lined the wall to my right, while a long rectangular island divided the room. Just beyond that, against the far wall, large shapes hovered from the ceiling. The dull glint of metal made me think oven hoods, despite the blank spots sitting beneath them. Not terribly familiar with industrial kitchens, I figured the three lighter patches of darkness on the back walls probably belonged to walk-in compartments. The pull of magic was insistent now, and I had to consciously hold back from letting it pull me forward. Yet all I could see was shadows. Well, shadows and that island.

I shifted around the sink so I could see what lay on the other side of the island, then I blinked, wondering if my eyes were playing tricks. Nope. It was still there. A thin, faint ribbon of light trickled from under the doors of one of the walk-ins. Of course, it had to be the one in the far corner. A mix of anticipation and wariness hardened the magical shell covering my skin as I inched forward. With every step, the thread of magic tightened, confirming I was on the right track. As I got closer, the lighter shadows resolved into the dull gleam of a metal door. Swallowing the sour taste of dread, I tried not to think about what waited inside.

By the time I was close enough to touch the door, the magical pull was so strong, the pressure of it made my teeth ache. Unfortunately, I was also close enough to see the door wasn't fully closed, hence the escaping light. I wasn't sure if that was a good sign or a bad one, but I was about to find out.

Since the door opened out, I had no choice but to move away from the questionable protection of the wall and grab the handle. With the gun in one hand and the door in the other, I pulled it open. The luminescent flash was bright, leaving me blind.

CHAPTER TWELVE

AFTER BLINKING RAPIDLY to clear the starbursts from my vision, I stared at what hung in the middle of the damn walk-in. "Oh shit!" I breathed then rushed inside as I shoved my gun back in its holster so I could use both of my hands. "Evan!"

"Stop!"

At his guttural command, I jerked to halt. "What the hell happened?" Panic made my voice squeak.

"Tripped a fuckin' trap," he gritted out.

"Anyone else here?" Magic thrummed through the tight space and beat against my skull, but my concern about Evan pushed it aside.

"Did you run into anyone on your way in?" His voice was tight with pain.

"No."

"Then I'm guessing no."

Sarcasm meant he would be fine, right? Hoping he was right about our lack of company, I gave up stealth and got out my phone, activating the flashlight app to chase away the shadows. Whatever held him was more than a simple security ward. "Talk to me. What am I looking for?"

"I don't know." His answer was short. "I was trying to find a way inside when I got hit. Not sure how long I was out, but I woke up here."

My phone's light hit Evan, and I sucked in a sharp breath as I got my first clear look at him.

He jerked his head to the side, his eyes narrowing to slits to avoid the light, his breath escaping on a pained hiss. "Watch it, Rory."

"Sorry." I shifted the light away from his face but aimed it so I could see the rest of him.

He hung in midair like a living version of Da Vinci's Vitruvian Man. His face was etched with white lines of pain, and the cords of his neck were starkly evident. Blood stained the collar of his T-shirt, and his glasses were missing. "How long have you been awake?"

"Not long," he said. "Maybe ten minutes or so."

"Did you see anyone?"

"No, and no Lena, either."

Details on whatever had brought him here would have to wait, but since he hadn't answered my call when I left Sabella's, I figured whoever had strung him up had gotten him shortly after he arrived. I could hear him panting as I swept my light over the interior, looking for a way to get him out of this. "How bad is it?"

"Head's pounding like a bitch, but I'll live." His body twitched, and he grimaced. "Can't struggle, or this damn spell will pull me apart."

That explained why he was just hanging there. "But so long as you stay still..."

"It leaves me alone," he finished.

That didn't make me feel better. "So it's probably meant to hold you until they get back."

"That would be my guess, but it's getting worse, so it's a safe bet whoever's behind this doesn't care what condition I'm in when they return."

That meant we were probably racing against an unseen clock. "Then we should probably get your ass out of here."

"I'm down with that."

Finished with my visual inspection of the walk-in, I met his pissed-off gaze. "I'm not seeing anything that would act as a focus." Spelled traps came in various flavors. One of the most common used an inanimate object as a focal point, hence my search of the space. But other than dust, it was frustratingly empty of anything obvious. The second type involved channeling a spell through an Arcane circle, a combination of sigils and runes. I crouched and aimed my light at the floor as the magical pressure kicked against my skull. Taking that sign as evidence that I was missing something, I did my best to ignore the increasing ache and studied the grimy floor.

Above me, Evan gritted out, "No foci means they used a circle."

"That's what I'm thinking, but other than drag marks, which I assume are from you, there's nothing's here." That struck me as wrong. There should be something more, like, say, footprints from whoever had strung him up.

"Then they're using sub rosa runes." His voice was grim.

If that was the case, we were in deep shit. Not being able to identify which runes were used in the spell made breaking it a crapshoot. One wrong move, and Evan might end up a gory mess. I couldn't even risk using my ability, because while my magic might keep my ass intact, I couldn't promise the same for Evan. "We need a way to see the circle."

"I'm all out of fairy dust," Evan's response was dry.

Fairy dust? His words sparked an idea, albeit a crazy one, but it was better than nothing. "Have you tried accessing your magic?"

"In the middle of a metal box?" He sounded incredulous. "Do you know what happens when electricity meets metal? I guarantee it's not pretty."

The ticking of the invisible clock got louder, and I snapped, "Just answer the damn question, Evan."

"No, I haven't." His response was less than nice. "Why? What are you thinking?"

I studied the strange, mostly undisturbed layer of grime on the floor then straightened slowly. "A trap like this requires a complex set of runes, right?"

"To trap and torture your prey instead of outright killing it?" he mused. "Yeah."

I wasn't sure my ambiguous idea would work, and it must have shown, because he called my name. I looked up.

Whatever he saw on my face turned his voice hard. "Share."

I swallowed, praying I wasn't about to make a lethal mistake. "I think the dust layer is magically generated. It's too even, too clean. And if magic is a form of energy, like electricity, what happens if we reverse the direction of that energy?"

He studied the ground with narrowed eyes. "Like creating a magical magnet?"

The fact he could follow my half-formed idea made me hope it wasn't as crazy as I thought. "Can you do it?"

"Won't know until we try." He followed that dour statement with "Step back and get clear of the metal. Whatever you do, don't touch the door."

Nodding, I inched backward, keeping the light aimed at the floor, until I stood on the other side of the door.

Once I was clear, he warned, "Here goes nothing."

I held my breath as a faint luminescence burst into life,

outlining his distended form. The bluish light of his magic
fired along the previously invisible lines of power wrapped
around his neck, legs, and arms like phantom chains. Air
stalled in my lungs as a mix of dread and excitement rose. His
magic brightened, and the metallic stench of ozone filled my
nose. Invisible pressure slammed fists against my skull. Then
his magic appeared to stall, and I struggled to find a way to
speak around my clenched teeth. With a vicious slap, the
aching pressure in my head broke. Reeling back, I reached
behind me blindly, trying to avoid falling on my ass. Instead, I
stumbled against the island and fought to breathe through
the ricocheting pain. When my head stopped whirling and I
was fairly sure I wouldn't hurl, I was able to force open eyes I
didn't realize I had closed.

"Oh shit!" I staggered forward on unsteady legs and
dropped to my knees at the walk-in's threshold. My phone
tumbled out of my hand to land somewhere nearby, the flashlight flickering off. Not that it mattered, because the bluish
glow of Evan's magic filled the walk-in. In the unearthly light,
I could see Evan. His spine was bent in a painful arch, his face
a mask of agony, and his body frozen in a crucified pose.
"Evan!"

"Hurry." The one word was barely discernible.

I didn't need any further urging. I looked down and
almost sobbed in relief when the dizzying dips and curls of a
complex set of runes burned across the floor. My brain got
busy translating them even as I inched closer. Sure enough,
the spell's primary purpose appeared to be containment, but
there was a punitive layer to it, as well. Unfortunately, I wasn't
sure about the secondary set of symbols, nor did we have
time to Google the shit. But there was an hourglass rune that
really worried me.

Evan's agonized groan served as a brutal reminder that we

were running out of time. I shoved my panic aside, pushed to my feet, and snarled, "Fuck it."

Sinking into my magic, I deepened the protective layer until it was a heavy weight against my skin. An imperceptible hum filled my ears, and the fine hairs along my skin stood on end. Before I could think about it too much, I lunged forward, rushing the handful of feet from the door to Evan. Painful bolts seared through my shoes and up my legs, leaving a creeping numbness in their wake. I stumbled but miraculously stayed upright, even as the agonizing ache reverberated in my teeth. I hurt, but knowing the stakes, I forced my legs forward. Involuntary tears escaped, turning everything blurry and leaving me half blind. I reached out, and when I crashed into Evan, I wrapped my arms around his waist. With strangling intent, the trap's magic coiled around us, and our screams blended into one as I fought my way through the pain. Praying it would work, I visualized my Prism armor expanding and stretching to include Evan. My muscles quivered, and my vision gained tiny red dots.

With my arms locked around Evan, I twisted and yanked back at the same time. As we fell back, the magical web tore from its anchors. I landed on my ass with Evan's weight all but smothering me against the metal floor. The impact ensured I would carry a bruise in the shape of my gun at the base of my spine, but that was the least of my worries. Nerve-shredding shocks pierced my magic, whipping along my spine, through my shoulders, and down my legs, causing involuntary muscle spasms. My heart thundered, and there was a metallic taste in my mouth. Desperate to escape the electrified surface, I managed to shove Evan off and get into a wobbly crouch as my head spun sickeningly. Everything fucking hurt, but I got my arms under Evan's and dragged him out of the walk-in. It felt like forever but was more likely less than a minute before I cleared the metal threshold. The stinging electroshocks eased and began to fade as I lay on the gritty floor, staring up into the dark shadows, tears slipping down from the corners of my eyes to disappear into my hair. Next to me, I could hear Evan's panting breaths. Finally, I managed to croak, "You alive?"

He coughed. "I think so."

"Good." I kept my eyes closed and concentrated on breathing through the receding waves of pain. I could hear ominous noises as the echoes of broken magical waves washed through the structure. "We need to get out of here."

"Yeah." But he didn't move.

I considered staying where I was, but those noises combined with that relentless dread had me rolling to my side. I couldn't quite stifle my whimper as my body protested, but I managed to get up on all fours. "Get up, Evan."

"Not sure I can." But he rolled over, swearing a blue streak the entire time.

I looked around and saw my phone off to the side where I'd dropped it. I locked my muscles and hoped my balance would hold as I reached out and snagged it. With it gripped tightly in hand, I faced a new dilemma. Realizing I would need both hands to get up, I clumsily shoved the phone in my pocket. Then I used the edge of the island to haul myself up. My body swayed, and my head spun. I drew in a couple of deep breaths until everything steadied.

Off to the side, deep in the shadows, something heavy fell to the floor with a loud bang. "Hurry," I hissed to Evan and reached down to help drag him up.

He got to his feet and stumbled into me, almost sending us both back to the floor. I kept him upright by bracing my shoulder against his chest. "Dammit, Evan."

"Sorry." His voice slurred.

I was close enough that I didn't need light to see his pale

face above me. "Please tell me you can make it out." There was no way I could lug him out on my own.

"Yeah," he grunted. "Give me a minute."

"Not sure we're going to get that." But I inched back, slowly letting him go when I was sure he wouldn't collapse. His head hung down as he white-knuckled the edge of the island. I dug out my phone, and it took a couple of swipes across my cracked screen to activate the flashlight. I aimed it at the walk-in. The interior was shadowed, but from the corner of my eye, I caught the sheen of lingering magic coating walls that now appeared to be buckling. On the edges, flickering light danced with shadows, like magical floating ash. The phone's light didn't reach far, but it was enough to make out a mix of scorch marks and jagged tears marring the floor. I debated getting closer but decided against it. Whatever spell had been laid was well and truly gone, thanks to my hammer-like approach. I turned to Evan. "Ready?"

Instead of answering, he grunted and pushed off the island with a lurch.

Worried he was about to faceplant, I lunged forward and wrapped an arm around his waist. "Careful."

He slung his arm over my shoulders, his added weight threatening to drop me to my knees. Forgetting the phone in my hand, I reached for his wrist, dangling in front of my shoulder, and fumbled. "Here, hold this."

I held my phone out, the light dancing over his face and making him squint.

He managed to grab it and hold it in his free hand. "Got it," he mumbled.

"All right then." Considering his dazed state, I was grateful he could at least hold my phone. It would have been better if he were steady enough to handle my gun, in case we ran into trouble, but I didn't trust him with something that could leave lethal holes in its wake. I gripped his wrist and locked it against my shoulder, then I used my arm around his waist for counterbalance. Together, we did a drunken stumble through the kitchen, careening off counters and doorjambs like a pair of human pinballs. Behind us, disconcerting moans and groans of the collapsing metal unit chased us out of the kitchen. We hit the open space, both of us breathing hard. I peered into the gloom, praying we wouldn't run into whoever set the trap. The feeling of impending doom nipped at our heels until finally, we were in front of where I'd entered. "I've got to let you go."

Evan shifted, widening his stance as he slowly let me go. The light from the phone steadied and fell over the plywood sheet. "I'm good."

Taking him at his word, I didn't waste time dragging the plywood back. I couldn't do shit about the noise it made. All I could do was pray no one was around to hear it. As soon as I had enough room for us to squeeze through, I turned to Evan, taking in the mask of dust and blood streaking his drawn face. "Can you tell if there's any active security out there?"

"Give me a second." He handed me back my phone. As soon as I took it, his magic flared.

I winced as it reawakened irritated nerve endings. I turned off my phone's light and shoved it back in my pocket. By the time I was done, so was Evan.

"They're down. We're clear."

Taking him at his word, I slipped through the narrow opening and moved aside so he could follow. I scanned our surroundings even as the night's light breeze left a chill on my overheated skin. Everything stayed still and quiet. As soon as Evan was out, I waited until he was steady, then I backtracked to the gap in the fence. The sense of urgency grew claws, and I was all but dancing in place as I waited for

Evan to crawl through. Worried, I kept an eye on the street at the end of the narrow alley. This late, the street should stay quiet, but hearing a car approaching, I hissed at Evan, "Move it!"

A car zipped by, and I caught the impression of a dark sedan. Evan bumped into me as he cleared the opening, and I reached out a hand to steady him. The sound of the car's engine downshifting had me all but dragging Evan down the narrow space. Just before it opened to the sidewalk, I motioned for him to stop then peeked around the corner. Half a block up, the passing car was in the left turn lane, waiting for the light. It was the only car on the road, but the distance made it impossible to make out the license plate. I waited for it to complete its left turn before I grabbed Evan's wrist, did a quick check to make sure there was no other traffic approaching, and pulled him with me as I dashed across the street. "Come on."

We made it to the other side just in time. Headlights flashed from the north as we hustled down the walkway arrowing through the apartment complex. I gave silent thanks that the apartment's parking lot was tucked behind a wall of tall oleander bushes. As soon as I knew we couldn't be seen from the street, I told Evan, "Let the cameras go."

The scrape of magic faded, and I shuddered at the relief. Evan dug into his pocket as he stumbled along at my side. When I heard the faint chime of keys, I grabbed his arm, bringing him to a stop. "Uh-uh, you're not getting behind a wheel."

"I'm fine," he said.

Instead of wasting time we didn't have arguing, I let his arm go and shoved my palm against his chest.

Predictably, he stumbled back as if I had sucker punched him. Only luck kept him from landing on his ass. Once he regained his balance, he glared at me as he rubbed his chest.

I held out one hand, palm up, and curled my fingers. "Hand them over."

He grumbled under his breath but shuffled forward and slapped his keys into my palm.

"Thank you." As my point had been successfully made, there was no reason for both of us to be pissy. "Your ride should be fine here until morning."

He didn't answer but muttered something I refused to acknowledge. We made it to our cars, and I directed Evan toward the illusionary ward that hid the familiar lines of the BMW. As we approached, we split—me to the driver's side and Evan to the passenger's side. I warned, "Don't open the door until I say so."

As I moved to the front wheel well, the warm edge of the ward recognized me. My hand hovered over the warding stone, and I whispered, "Knickknack paddywhack, give a dog a bone, this old man came rolling home." The ward dropped, revealing the BMW. I grabbed the stone, straightened, and told Evan, "You're good."

"Nice ride." Evan opened his door and got in.

I took one last look around before I joined him and got us the hell out of there.

◆

Evan sat in the passenger seat, his head back, eyes closed as I got us clear of the apartment complex. I let him have his moment of peace and quiet while I stayed vigilant, constantly monitoring my mirrors and the road. The itchy sense of dread began to fade as things stayed quiet, but it wasn't until we approached the freeway exit that I relaxed enough to ask, "Do you want to go to the office or home?"

We both knew a hospital was out of the question, but if he needed medical help, our chances of finding someone was higher at the Guild, even at—I snuck a look at the dash clock —just after midnight.

Without bothering to lift his head, he simply rolled it until I could feel him looking at me. "Home."

"Address?"

He lifted his hand, his fingertips brushing the dash, and the GPS's electronic voice said, "Starting route to 2384 East Camelback."

"Nifty trick."

His response was a grunt.

As the GPS corrected our course and began routing through surface streets, I made a series of lefts and put the freeway in my rearview mirror. "You up to telling me what the hell happened?" Evan stayed quiet long enough to make me uneasy, and I snapped, "What?"

He blew out a noisy breath. "Did you know Lena's related to the Clarke Family?"

"Bullshit." It was a knee-jerk response.

"Nope, not bullshit."

The certainty in his voice cut through me like a knife. My grip tightened on the wheel, and I refused to look at him. Focusing on the road, I shot back, "I've known Lena for years. There's no way she's tied to an Arcane Family."

"Why?" he asked. "Because she didn't tell you?"

Yes. No. Gah, I didn't know. Not that I had any right to feel betrayed, but the bitter taste lingered. So what if she kept this from me? How was it different from me keeping my Prism ability from her? We all had secrets, right? Instead of sharing the mess in my head, I grasped at fragile straws. "No, because if a Family could claim someone with her level of talent and skill, they would. There's no way they'd let her work for the Guild without serious pushback."

In contrast to my heated tone, Evan's was eerily calm. "They would if the Family in question refuted her existence."

"Did they?"

"Yeah, they did." There was a hint of pity in his voice. If he ever spoke to Lena like that, she would kick his ass. Oblivious to my thoughts, he kept talking. "When the Guild vetted Lena's initial application, they sent an official query to the Clarkes."

"How do you know?"

"Because I hacked Lena's personnel files."

That had me glancing at him. "You could lose your job."

He looked away. "Rather lose my job than lose Lena."

The depth of emotion in his statement resonated since I felt the same. "Let's make sure we don't do either, okay?"

"That's the plan." After an awkward moment, he said, "She's going to be pissed we found out."

"Probably," I agreed without correcting him on the "we" part of his statement. It wasn't like I was going to open that can of worms with Lena. Not unless there was a damn good reason to do so. *Like, maybe it had something to do with Lena's current situation?* I was tired enough that it took a second for that question to click. "Wait. Do you think the Clarke Family had something to do with her disappearance?"

"I don't know." His frustration came through loud and clear.

"Then why bring it up?"

"Because to find her, we need to know everything." He turned to look out the passenger window. "Even things she doesn't want us to know."

Hearing his mix of hurt and frustration, I slid him a glance. "If Lena didn't want to share, that's her right."

"I know."

I hoped he did, because I was willing to bet anything there were damn good reasons for Lena not to share. As curious as I was about those reasons, right now, we needed to focus on solid leads to her whereabouts. "What did you find on the information I sent you?"

"Jack and shit." He ran his hands through his hair. "The phone numbers were dead ends, either past clients or known contacts. The address was a private residence with no ties to anyone of significance. And don't get me started on those names. Do you know how hard it is to link a first name with any usable information?"

I was starting to remember why working with Evan left me pulling out my hair. "Then how did you end up hanging in an abandoned freezer?"

"Because Lena's phone came back online and started pinging from this area."

I jerked the wheel at his unexpected answer, then quickly corrected. He really needed to warn me before dropping bombs like that. "What? I thought the signal was blocked by magic."

"It was." He shifted in his seat. "And probably still is."

I frowned. "I'm not following."

"I think someone knows we're poking around," he explained. "And they decided to spoof her signal."

If he was right, that meant... "They deliberately drew you in."

"Maybe not me specifically." He fisted his hand on his bouncing knee. "But whoever was trying to find her."

"And you weren't able to tell they were tracking you?" I glanced at him, eyebrows raised. "How did that happen?"

"If I was to guess, one of my searches hit a cloaked trip wire." His disgruntled tone made it clear he took that very personally.

Maybe I should be a better person, but... Nah, I was going to push it. "Aren't you the equivalent of a cyber ninja? Able to get into anything without being noticed?" I caught his one-finger response and snorted. "All right, then. Whose interest did you catch?"

"That's the bitch of it," he said. "I don't know. I had searches going on both sides—the Thatchers and the Clarkes."

"What about the Cordovas?" I asked.

"They were up next," he mumbled.

Since his night had been far from a barrel of monkeys, I let that go. The GPS interrupted and led us into an older neighborhood. "Could there be a connection between the two?" When he blinked at me, I clarified, "The Thatchers and the Clarkes?"

"Haven't had time to find out," he admitted with an embarrassed shrug. "I'd just broken through on the background info when I was notified about her signal. I need to dig a hell of a lot deeper and start some serious cross checks before I can confirm or deny." He shifted in his seat, touched the dash to silence the GPS, then pointed. "Make a right at the stop sign."

I did as directed. "Considering who all is on the board, you know someone has to connect somewhere. All those Arcane Families do in one way or the other." I paused, the worry from earlier creeping back in. "You need to be careful."

"I've been at this awhile, Rory. I know that better than you."

I'm sure he did, but the deeper we went, the messier things got.

"Third house on the right," he said.

I turned in to a short drive in front of a mid-century cinderblock home. I put the car in park and shut it down, including the lights. For a moment, we sat there in the dark interior, quiet. When my thoughts kept spinning like a hamster on a wheel, I rubbed my burning eyes. "We need to find her."

"We will." His words carried the weight of a vow. "Once I get in, I'll call the Guild, see if I can't get a Hound back over there to track who set that spell."

"You think they'll get anything?" I asked. "The walk-in was all but crumbling into rubble when we left."

He shrugged then winced. "Don't know, but if it gets us any closer to Lena, it's worth following through."

Can't argue that. The amorphous suspicion that had been lurking in my brain since Nat's casual comment—*Was that only this morning?*—about Lena's mystery man solidified, and I nudged, "Have you looked into the rumors flying around the Guild?"

Evan stiffened. "Which rumors?"

"The ones that claim Lena had a mystery man." When he didn't so much as blink, I asked, "Is it you?"

"Does it matter?"

Hmm, that wasn't a denial. "It does if it's not you."

He looked away, obviously considering his response. Then, in a low voice, he said, "Yeah, it's me."

I wasn't upset. In fact, I was happy, because that was one less thread to tug on. "Good."

A rough laugh escaped, and he shook his head. "You're so weird."

"Yep," I agreed.

He reached for the handle then stopped. "Will you be okay getting home?"

I nodded. "I'm good. I'll head back to the Guild and drop this off."

"Good idea." He stared out over the dash. "I think I caught all the cameras, but you never know. And this ride, as sweet as it is, is memorable."

"That she is," I said as he opened the door.

"Get some rest, Rory." He got out and moved to shut the door.

"I will," I promised. "You do the same."

He managed a weak smile. "I'll get on that."

Neither one of us sounded convincing. We exchanged good nights, despite the fact it was technically morning. Then I watched as he let himself into his house. Only when he was locked inside did I put the car in reverse and head to the Guild.

CHAPTER THIRTEEN

AFTER DROPPING off the BMW and reclaiming my baby, I managed to stumble through the door of my empty condo around two. My body protested with a series of complaining aches and pains as I kicked off my shoes and toed them to the side of the door. Barefoot, I walked to my room, where I stripped off my clothes and tossed them into the dry-cleaning pile, hoping they could be salvaged. I went with a brief, luke-warm shower instead of the long, hot soak my body wanted. Despite the fatigue nipping at my heels, I was too jittery to give in to exhaustion. Ten minutes later, dressed in comfy sleep pants and a tank, I hit the fridge and retrieved the mystery journal, a sharp knife, and some ice water. Then I sank onto my couch. I set the water and knife aside, unsealed the plastic bag, and dumped the journal into my lap.

For a moment, I sat there, staring at the stained leather cover, and wondered what the hell I was thinking. For all I knew, this was some sick hoax meant to keep me distracted. Considering the timing of its appearance and the face that Lena was missing, it was an option. Yet that explanation didn't quite fit. Still, the whole situation was dodgy. Not dodgy enough for me to ignore my unexpected gift, especially since pacing the floor or worrying about Lena would be a waste of time. Sleep was out of the equation, as well, so it was time for some nighttime reading.

I ran a finger over the cover and thought about families and magic. When it came to families, I didn't have much to go on. I grew up splitting my time between shelters and group homes—a typical story for street orphans. I don't remember ever having a real family, the kind I could tap for information about who I was and where I came from, much less get the details about inherited magic. It wasn't a horrific way to grow up, but it was as lonely as hell, and trust didn't come cheap. Up until the day I accidentally rebuffed an attack from a bully who happened to be a low-level fire mage, the only magical talent I'd displayed was an emerging trend of quick reaction times and an innate sense of locations. After giving the bully second-degree burns, I started to wonder how I'd done it, but there was no one to ask.

Even spending hours in the library researching Arcane history hadn't helped. There was no mention of an ability that could repel magic. I'd spent months thinking I was some kind of weird mutant, then I met Alvin, an old, schizophrenic street tramp. I was cutting through an alley from class, trying to beat the shelter's curfew, when I interrupted Alvin being hassled for his recently acquired cart. The two-on-one odds just struck me as unfair, and since Alvin had always been nice to me, I'd figured it was my turn to return the favor. During the intense "discussion," one of the demanding biddies used her connection to animals to call in rat reinforcements. Riding on a wave of panicked fear, I'd turned the tide and sent the nasty rodents chasing after the dastardly duo. To this day, I abhorred rats, with their beady eyes and twitchy bodies. Afterward, Alvin had called me a Prism.

Relieved to have an actual identification, I started digging through old documents and piecing together old wives' tales in a quest for more. There wasn't much out there. It was as if any and all information regarding Prisms had been wiped away, which only served to deepen the mystery. In fact, all these years later, I still knew next to nothing about what it meant to be a Prism. From experimenting, I knew it could act like a magic-repellant armor, for lack of a better term. It wasn't impenetrable—a purely physical attack could breach it —but when facing another mage, it gave me enough time to react and escape, which was preferable to ending up dead. Normally, my ability stayed inert, but when flight-or-fight kicked in, so did my magic. Under extreme circumstances, which until recently were rare for me, it shifted from defense to offense, redirecting a magical attack back to the originator. Unfortunately, that was instinctive, and I still hadn't figured out how to replicate that response on demand. Eventually, I gave up my research and concentrated on other things, like excelling at being a Transporter. I was more concerned with creating a solid reputation so I could be my own boss.

The Guild had been my first stop on that road, mainly because it catered to those with magic but no Family ties. A perfect fit. The Guild had actually sprung up around the same time the Arcane Families stepped into the public spotlight, which was right in the midst of the decades-long World War when countries fought over resources and borders, decimating their own in the process. According to the history books, when the end of the world shimmered on the horizon, the Arcane Families came together and stepped up to shift the tide and restore order. Governments had been so grateful that when things finally calmed down, they had no problem welcoming the Arcane Council to their sides, and the Families became a power in their own right. Almost a hundred years later, magic existed in various forms and degrees, but the strongest belonged to the Families.

Yet as far as I knew, I had no Family to claim. That meant, whether this book was real or not, I would feed the blood key and see if it could satisfy my curiosity. Decided, I opened the cover and flipped through the pages covered in sketches and nonsensical phrases. If it hadn't been for that unexpected paper cut, I would've thought it belonged to a kid at some point. Just a book for them to jot down thoughts or use as a sketchpad. But a kid wouldn't use a blood key to lock up their doodles. Because I had a Key as a best friend, I knew more than my fair share about what went into laying wards, keys, and curses. A blood key, while straightforward in usage, was complex to set. Like most magic, it came down to the caster's intent, which in this case, included an additional layer of blood ties. There was a sense of age to it, and... I was procrastinating.

After taking a bracing gulp of cold water, I picked up the knife. If the minute amount from the paper cut had worked, I shouldn't have to open a vein to read it. I pricked my finger and touched the first page. The ink blurred, faded, and reformed into neat, feminine handwriting. It didn't take long to get engrossed in the author's story, and it was a doozy. Even having to re-prick my fingers every handful of pages couldn't make me stop reading.

The author was clearly a Prism, but she never mentioned her name. That made sense when I realized she and her partner, an illusion mage she called M, were on a covert assignment posing as a wealthy Arcane couple to infiltrate a suspected Axis organization. The organization included a high-powered mix of scientific and magical minds focused on furthering the Axis's goals. The more I read, the more Angie's belief that a shadowy Cabal still existed gained weight. That kind of hunger to push the boundaries of science and magic wouldn't just disappear. Not unless everyone involved was erased. And that was an ugly thought.

The author's entries ranged from personal impressions of the people she and M interacted with, to recounted conversations that ignited potential problems, to her innermost thoughts about her evolving relationship with M. She mentioned that she'd initially been assigned as M's personal guard, a position Prisms were naturally adept at. Unfortunately, she didn't go into how she wielded the power that allowed a Prism to shield another mage. That would've been extremely helpful. Instead, she worried that the longer they worked together, the closer they got, and the closer they got, the more she worried about keeping M safe. Reading between the lines, she was falling hard for M, and it was messing with her impartiality. Not a good thing while deep undercover in enemy territory.

There were a couple of troubling entries after she and M had argued, where she wondered if his Family had deliberately pulled strings on their assignment. Specifically, to get her to be M's shield, a position that made her question the truth of his feelings for her. I might have chalked her rants up to jealous, wannabe-girlfriend paranoia, if not for the other entries. They recounted interactions with M where he said little things that would make a cynical person go "hmm." Then there were the other entries detailing the suspicious deaths of other Prisms she knew, and it wasn't until the third such entry that I realized why she was so upset. Families on both sides of the war were being targeted for assassination at such an alarming rate that they were willing to do anything to keep their precious genetic heirs safe—even if it meant sacrificing a Prism or two. To that end, Prisms were in high demand, and that demand made them primary targets to both sides. Wiping out the Prisms would give them a clearer shot at taking out the target and eventually erasing those genetic one-offs from the bloodlines. That sentiment walked over my skin, leaving chills in its wake.

If the journal and the conclusions I was drawing were real, there might be an even bigger reason for me to avoid Zev, Sabella, and any other Arcane Family. Especially considering that Arcane history hadn't become part of the public awareness until close to the end of the World Wars, and as everyone knew, history was written by the victors. If those victors wanted to exclude something like, say, the existence of a talent that was immune to most magic, it wouldn't be hard to accomplish. Not if said talent was hunted to, or near to, extinction. Families were notorious for hoarding secrets, and a secret like this was definitely not for public consumption.

As terrifying as it was, I had to consider that possibility when dealing with the Families and anyone connected to them. The book was in good shape for being close to a hundred years old, which meant it had spent considerable time being locked away under ideal conditions. That would be easy enough if it had been part of someone's personal collection, and with no way to verify how it was delivered or by whom, it was in my best interests to keep its existence quiet. Besides, the information it contained was bound to stir up trouble I not only didn't want but didn't need.

Time ticked by as I continued reading through the Prism's entries, and I managed to make it about halfway through the journal before the day's cluster caught up with me, and I zonked out.

CHAPTER FOURTEEN

MY PHONE'S alarm ripped me out of an uneasy doze and left me blinking into the bright morning light spilling through my patio doors. Groaning, I uncurled from my slouched position on the couch. The journal tumbled from my lap to the floor. Rubbing at the persistent ache in my shoulder, I reached for my phone dancing over the coffee table. My sore fingertips found the phone. A stinging hiss escaped as I touched the screen to shut off the annoying sound. As soon as it went quiet, I put my aching fingers to my mouth. It was amazing how the tiniest pricks hurt worse than deep cuts.

The last time I remembered checking the time, it had been close to three, and my alarm had been set for six, so I'd managed a whopping three hours of sleep. *Good enough, I guess.*

I checked my texts for any updates from Evan, but my screen was frustratingly blank. Wiping my fingers against the thin material of my pajama pants, I leaned over and grabbed the book, the knife, a notebook I had used for notes, and my glass before shoving awkwardly out of the couch. My body vigorously protested my change in position, and I did a couple of spine twists to release the kinks, then moved to the kitchen.

I set the journal and notebook on the counter, dumped the glass and knife in the sink, then headed to the coffee maker on the counter. I stared into the empty cupboard where the magical beans lived and remembered how my morning had started the day before. *Was that only yesterday?*

"Dammit." It appeared that the coffee bean fairy was on strike because no bag of beans graced my cabinet. Grumbling under my breath, I headed to my bedroom. If there was no coffee on hand, I needed to wake up enough to make a quick run before Zev showed up to take me to Madeline's office.

I walked through my room, pulling off my tank, and tossed it on my bed. A few minutes in a hot shower should ease most of my body's complaints. I stepped into the bathroom, not bothering to look in the mirror. Last night's glimpse had revealed a newly acquired collection of scrapes and bruises, some I'd discovered when washing my hair. It hadn't been pretty then, and after a few hours of marinating, there was no way it was any better.

After flicking on the shower, I waited for the water to heat and stripped. I stood inside the tiled enclosure and leaned against the wall, using my arm to cushion my forehead as the hot water did its thing. The muscles in my back slowly loosened as steam rose, turning the air opaque. I might have fallen asleep again, but when the water pressure hitched then cooled against my overheated spine, I blinked blearily awake. I wiped away the misty drops from my face and, with a sigh, shut off the water. I grabbed a towel and dried off, being careful of my more tender spots.

With the towel wrapped around me, I flicked on the fan to chase out the steam then headed to my walk-in closet. Since we were meeting with Madeline, jeans and a T-shirt were a no-go. Instead, I pulled on a pair of linen pants and a lightweight blouse. Barefoot, I left the closet, draped the damp towel on a rack, and moved to the sink to stare into the mirror. The steam was no more than a thin ribbon at the top of the mirror, so it was easy to see the dark circles under my eyes from lack of sleep. I gingerly touched the lighter bruise skating along my cheek and wondered when that had happened. *Maybe when Evan all but crushed me to the floor? Probably.*

There were a couple of red marks—one along my jaw and one by my temple—and my lower lip looked a little puffy. Thanks to the heat of the shower, my hair held a hint of curl as damp ends brushed under my jaw. I combed it out then used my fingers to tousle it. The faint ache in my skull warned that if I pulled it up, I would regret it later, so I left it alone. Then I dealt with the mess from last night. It took a bit longer than normal to disguise the array of marks and scrapes under makeup, but when I was done, I looked almost normal. *Yay me!*

Carrying a pair of pumps out of the bathroom, I flicked off the fan as I left. I reached for my bedroom door and froze at a noise from the kitchen. It wasn't overly loud, and for a second, I wondered if I was so tired, I was hearing things. With my eyes aimed at my mostly closed bedroom door, I watched the sliver of space for any revealing movement. My ears strained as I slowly crouched and set my pumps on the floor. I rose and, on quiet feet, angled toward the nightstand where I kept my guns. I inched out the drawer, wincing at the soft scrape of wood against wood. My backup Glock lay on top of the Walther's safe. I lifted the Glock out and carried it in a two-handed grip, finger to the side of the trigger, as I crept back to my door. By the time I reached the door, my magic was locked in place.

I took a position to the side and used the Glock's barrel to edge the door open on silent hinges. When nothing and no one swept in, I rushed the entry with the gun up.

"Easy."

"Dammit, Zev!" For a second, I considered pulling the trigger just on principle. "What the hell are you doing here, besides practicing your B&E skills?"

Dressed in what I was beginning to think was his standard go-to black cargo pants, paired with a well-fitted iron-gray T-shirt, he leaned against my counter, a paper cup stamped with a familiar logo held halfway to his mouth. He pushed a second cup toward me. "Is that any way to greet the man who brought you coffee?"

Despite the luscious aroma of dark beans tempting me closer, I held my position for a long moment before lowering my gun. "You're early."

"Figured we could talk." He swept his dark gaze over me, and I refused to acknowledge the goosebumps erupting over my skin. "Nice outfit."

"Thanks." I set my gun down on the counter next to the barely hidden journal lying under the spiral notebook. For a moment, my mind stumbled as anxiety tripped my pulse. *Did he see it? Look through it?* No way was I up to explaining what it was or how it ended up in my hands. From under my lashes, I studied his expression, unable to tell. I reached for the coffee, grateful my hand didn't shake. "What did you want to talk about?"

He sipped and set his cup down, then pulled out one of the barstools. "Do you mind?"

I shook my head then chased back my nerves with a fortifying mouthful of the hot caffeinated brew.

He sat then curled his hands around his cup. "Yesterday, you asked why the Cordova Family was interested in Keith Thatcher."

His opening gambit caught me off guard, but I cautiously prodded, "And you tried to play me off with some bullshit about your Family being interested in me." However, considering my early-morning reading, that claim might not be bullshit after all.

In an eerie coincidence that mimicked mind-reading, he cocked his head. "Why would that be bullshit?"

For a moment, I froze, dread tightening its greedy hands on my throat. I swallowed hard, escaping its grasp. "I'm not doing this dance again, Zev. Just say what you want to say." I took another sip and set my cup down.

"Fine, we'll come back to that."

No, we won't. Not if I had anything to say about it.

Zev drummed his fingers against the counter. "We have reason to believe that Keith Thatcher is in possession of an encrypted drive that may contain proprietary Family information."

Yep, that would definitely put Keith on the Cordovas' radar, but that alone wouldn't be enough to justify Zev's involvement. I did a quick run-through of what I knew of the Cordovas and the even less I knew of Zev for another plausible explanation. Only after I added in his insistence that we work together did I find a conclusion that left my stomach in knots. "Is this proprietary information connected to the research that led to Jeremy's kidnapping?"

His gaze remained disconcertingly steady. "It's possible."

Not the answer I wanted to hear. "How possible?" I pushed.

His mouth tightened. "Highly possible. When we retrieved Lara's initial research for LanTech, we found evidence that she stored a copy of her test results on a secured company file."

Bet that burned Emilio Cordova's ass. The head of the Cordova Family was a control freak, a trait exposed by his single-minded campaign to punish LanTech. I was beginning to suspect Zev shared that trait. As he spoke, I casually gathered the notebook and journal, turned, and went to the counter by the fridge. I opened a drawer filled with takeout menus and other odds and ends, and dropped the books inside. With my back to him, I said, "And you think that copy is on the hard drive Keith stole."

"Pretty much," he confirmed.

I turned and leaned against the counter, folding my arms over my chest. "How did he get ahold of it?"

Zev frowned. "Does it matter?"

Maybe not, but something about the situation niggled at the back of my mind. "Humor me."

He all but rolled his eyes. "It seems that as a financial manager, Keith had access to sensitive company files. When LanTech kicked him to the curb, he decided to supplement his forced retirement through alternate means."

It wasn't hard to put two and two together. One pissed-off ex-employee with access to the company's financials and a bunch of proprietary information... "Like selling LanTech's trade secrets to its competitors?"

"Competitor," Zev corrected, a reminder that Origin was the other player in this convoluted mess. "That was probably his initial intent—to sell Origin the information Lara promised them."

"But?" I prompted when he paused.

"But based on his behavior, it's possible he had no idea of what exactly he had in his possession."

I wandered back and picked up my coffee. "Why do you think that?"

"Because if he knew, he would've approached Emilio first." When I aimed a silent question his way, he explained, "Not only did Keith know about Lara's research, he helped draft her contract with LanTech. A contract that stipulated her research belonged solely to her, and if something should happen to her, it would go to her heir."

"Her heir being Jeremy," I finished, finally following his trail of breadcrumbs. "And because Jeremy is a minor, that means that research belongs to his guardian." That poor kid could not catch a break. Not only had he lost his mom, but his dad, Emilio's younger brother, had died some time before that. *Funny the things you find out when you're stumbling through a botched kidnapping.*

Zev lifted his cup. "To Emilio, yes."

And Emilio would pay to ensure that information stayed away from Origin. "I'm guessing Emilio never heard from Keith?"

"Not a peep." He continued to watch me with a disconcerting intensity completely at odds with his casual tone. "Yesterday, the head of Origin's research received an anonymous email that offered a copy of the test results for an undisclosed amount of money."

"Yesterday?"

"Yesterday," he confirmed.

I frowned. "Why didn't you tell me that when we were at the café?"

"Because," he said with maddeningly patience, "I didn't find out until after our meet."

"And here I thought we were going to share information." I wanted to choke those words back as soon as they escaped, because I'd failed to share a few things of my own.

"Like how you're going to share why you were at Estancia last night with Sabella?" The deceptive nonchalance of his question didn't quite hide the order buried within.

"That has nothing to do with this," I snapped, unwilling to revisit last night's events or my unwelcome reminder of my reaction to his date. "If the email came in after Keith's death, either he delayed the delivery or—"

"He's working with someone," Zev finished.

I was betting on option number two. "So who's Keith's partner?"

His gaze didn't waver. "Where's your roommate, Rory?"

And with that, I knew exactly why Zev was dogging my heels. My temper rose to a low boil. "Lena is not Keith's partner."

Proving he didn't know me at all, he ignored the warning signs of my temper and blithely continued down his twisted path of logic. "Keith stole a magically encrypted hard drive, then he contracted a Guild Key, likely to unlock it. Now, Keith is dead, the drive is nowhere to be found, the Key is missing in action, and someone has made Origin an offer they can't refuse. Do you see where I'm going here?"

I shoved my coffee aside hard enough that it wobbled a second before regaining its balance. I braced both hands on the counter and leaned in, my voice a low, vicious whip. "I know exactly what you're insinuating, but you're wrong."

"Am I?" His sardonic demeanor disappeared, leaving behind the merciless Arbiter. "Lena Davis is an unacknowledged offspring of an excised daughter of the Clarke Family and a First Nation Shaman. As a child, she was used as a negotiating tool for her parents' constant power plays and guilt trips. When she was thirteen, she joined the Guild as a Key and voided any claim she had to the Clarke Family or to the First Nation Tribes. Essentially, she made herself an orphan. At thirteen." He leaned forward, closing the space between us. "She has grown up knowing her heritage and the advantages it offered, but with a singular youthful choice, she reinforced a Family edict and ensured she'd never get to claim any of it. You don't think that might breed a fair amount of resentment?"

"Not for Lena." That was more information than I wanted to hear from someone who wasn't Lena, but I would be damned if I let Zev know that. It also didn't help my ragged temper to hear the hint of contempt in Zev's voice as he laid out his faulty logic. "Not everyone ties their self-worth into whether or not they share blood with an Arcane Family," I sneered. "The fact that you feel being renounced by a Family is reason enough to betray everything you are says more about you than Lena." It also meant that Lena was now on a Family radar, another thing to add to my growing "worry about it later" list. I straightened and stepped back, my hands fisting as I fought back my rising resentment. My voice went arctic as I held his gaze. "Lena is not Keith's partner, nor is she the one extorting Origin." And if he continued down this path, our little arrangement was going to go straight to hell.

His blank expression and empty voice made it difficult to determine if what I said made any impact. "If that's the case, then where is she?"

"If I were to guess, probably being held hostage by Keith's partner."

My snide tone bounced off his titanium hide. "What are you basing that conclusion on?"

Mimicking his derisive tone, I shot back, "The facts."

Completely unfazed, he demanded, "What facts?"

If the situation weren't so dire, I would have kicked him out of my home in a heartbeat. But the truth was, I needed him and his contacts to get Lena back, because the more he shared, the more worried I became that Lena's trouble ended and began with an unknown power player. And to fight that kind of clout, I needed a heavyweight, which left me with no choice but to continue working with his pretentious ass. "Lena disappeared the day before yesterday. We were able to track her until earlier that afternoon before losing her signal." No sense in getting into the fact that the Guild tagged their people with *loci* spells; better to let him think we relied on technology.

"We, being the Guild?" Settling into his interrogation, he sat back.

I nodded. "An electro mage conducted a search of the area where her signal was lost and confirmed that her location was being blocked by a spell, which meant someone was deliberately keeping her off the radar." Even knowing it was a long shot, I tossed out the bait—my implication being that the mage behind the spell was strong enough to block electronic signals or any other undisclosed tracking techniques. I waited for any betraying flicks of emotion from Zev. Unsurprisingly, he didn't oblige, even though we both knew a mage of that caliber would be connected to a Family. Moving on, I said, "Then there's the fact that sometime between yesterday morning when Keith's body showed up at my condo and when Lena disappeared, Keith had a violent struggle with someone in his home. My guess: it's probably the same someone who sent Origin the extortion email."

"She could've easily disabled whatever your electro mage was tracking and gone after Keith herself, retrieved the drive, and sent the email." His tone was one used when pointing out the obvious.

The fact that Zev hadn't considered the Guild would use more than one technique to track its employees was telling. It was also confirmation that the Guild could be just as secretive as the Families. "That's one option," I conceded, "but it's not realistic. Not only was Keith Lena's client—something that was easily traced—but the minute she deactivated the tracking, she put the Guild on alert. Then there's the spelled trap from last night."

That got a reaction. Zev's spine snapped straight, and his expression shifted to lethal menace. "Start explaining."

"Per protocol," I said with the same condescending tone

Zev had used earlier, "the Guild kept an eye on Lena's signal, in case it reactivated. Late last night, after I left Estancia, it did just that. I was notified the Guild was heading in to investigate." Okay, so I was taking a few liberties with the retelling, whatever. Having Lena twisted up in this was bad enough; I wasn't sure I wanted Evan on Zev's radar, as well. "As soon as I completed my job, I headed over to help. Instead, I found the investigator strung up in a complex holding spell."

"Alive?" Skepticism was loud and clear in his question.

"Yep."

His eyes narrowed. "That means whoever set it was probably planning on coming back to find out who it caught."

I barely refrained from rolling my eyes. *Gee, thanks, Captain Obvious.* "That was our assumption, but we didn't stick around to find out."

"Why not?" His sharp question needled my temper.

"Because," I snapped back, "the spell did not react kindly to being broken and neither one of us were in any shape to stick around and deal with the fallout."

His hand fisted on the counter, and his eyes narrowed. "Tell me you called in a Hound."

Pompous jackass. His statement inferred I didn't know how to do my job. Instead of answering, I folded my arms over my chest and glared. A silent staring contest ensued. Damned if I was going to blink first.

After a few tense seconds, he broke first. "Fine." His lips quirked, an indication he'd gotten my silent point. He backed off. "Have you heard back from them?"

That I was willing to share. "Not yet."

He studied me, his thoughts hidden, but something was working in that thick skull. Eventually, he put the pieces together. "Someone didn't like you poking around."

"No, they didn't." I dropped my arms and braced my hands on the counter. "But it also tells me Lena's still alive."

There was something in his expression—pity or compassion, I couldn't tell which—but the confrontational edge in his voice disappeared. "You sure about that?"

Refusing to admit how deep his question sliced, I answered, "Very, because if they wanted the Guild off their ass, they would have already dumped her body. Probably at Keith's so it would appear as if the two had argued and killed each other. It would be the easiest way to redirect the Guild's attention and have them chasing their tail long enough for Keith's real partner to get away clean." Not that I would have bought that scenario.

We held each other's gaze as a somber quiet crouched between us. Who knew what he was thinking? But I wouldn't give up on Lena until there was indisputable proof she was gone. Even then, I would tear my way through any- and everyone to find out the who and why, then I would make them pay.

Zev looked to his cup and idly moved it around on the counter. "You told me yesterday, you ended up at Keith's on Guild business."

I nodded. "When we researched Lena's active cases, Keith's name came up, along with a note that she had scheduled a meeting with him for yesterday at his house."

When I didn't elaborate, he prompted, "Any idea of why she wanted to meet with him?"

"No," I lied without a qualm. I didn't mind sharing actual facts about Lena's contract, but my assumptions about her meeting with Keith could be twisted to add weight to Zev's suspicions.

His eyes narrowed, and he flexed his fingers around his cup, clearly on the fence about whether or not to believe me.

I waited him out. Finally, he asked, "What *do* you know about Keith's contract?"

"It was initiated by his medical provider." Was it nice to take a mean sort of pleasure in his confused expression? Probably not, but I did. However, the sooner we got our shit on the table, the faster this unholy partnership would be done. So before he could ask, I said, "Dr. Oliver Martin, a urologist at the Reid Clinic, requested assistance from a Guild Key for a magical contagion."

My answer didn't erase his frown. If anything, it deepened. "A what?"

My lips curved, but considering how I felt, there was nothing nice about it. "Keith's dick had been cursed."

Zev blinked. "You're shitting me?"

I shook my head. "Can't prove it, but if it involves a urologist and a curse..."

He grimaced and downed the rest of his coffee. "Who the hell does that?"

"Oh, I don't know," I drawled, heavy on the sarcasm. "Perhaps he pissed off a woman by fucking around on her?"

He looked away, but not fast enough to hide a purely masculine wince. He tried to cover it by running a hand through his hair. "That would make sense, I guess."

I grabbed my coffee and took a sip, grimacing at the now-lukewarm liquid. "Keith had quite the reputation." I carried the cup to the sink. "According to Lena's documented interviews of known associates, infidelity was just one of the reasons he split with Madeline. Something the gossip rags had a field day with." I popped off the lid and dumped the contents down the drain.

"You can't believe everything you read in those," he muttered.

"And the interviews are what? Sour grapes?" When he didn't say anything, I slid him a glance as I rinsed out the sink. "You really think he was faithful?" When he remained silent, I shook my head. "Ever hear that adage about where there's smoke, there's fire?"

"You think Madeline set the curse." There was a note of incredibility in Zev's voice that rubbed me the wrong way.

I shut off the water. "Do you have someone else in mind?"

Instead of answering, he said, "She's his ex."

"Exactly."

"And when she denies it?" Zev asked. "What's your next move?"

I dried off my hands and shrugged. "I'm sure she'll be happy to share the name or names of whoever it is that is... was," I corrected, "keeping Keith company. If anyone knows the dirty details of Keith's love life, I can guarantee it will be Madeline."

"That makes no sense," he grumbled.

"Only because you're a guy," I shot back. "Women have long memories, especially when it comes to men who screw them over. A woman like Madeline, who's made a lifelong career based upon her social status and public image, is not going to leave herself open to being blindsided by an ex with an ax to grind. They were married for what? Twenty-eight years, right?"

Zev gave a short nod.

"That's a long time to store up hurt feelings, and signing divorce papers won't erase those. She not only knows Keith better than anyone else, but she'll know all his tucked-away love nests, or who was the latest body keeping his sheets warm. Once I have a name—"

"We," Zev interrupted. "Once *we* have a name."

I waved off his correction. "Fine, we have a name. We have another thread to pull on."

He still didn't look convinced. "That's a hell of a lot of assumptions."

"If you have something more solid, please share. I'm all ears." I waited, knowing he had nothing. Otherwise, he wouldn't have been in my damn kitchen.

"Fine." He lifted his cup, drained it, and straightened from his seat. "Let's go ask Madeline if she cursed her ex's dick."

CHAPTER FIFTEEN

MADELINE THATCHER'S office was one of multiple suites taking up the top floor in a downtown high-rise. We stepped out of the elevator and into a hall, where a surprisingly bright reception area waited on the other side of a glass wall. We crossed the hall to the door, which Zev reached around me to hold open. As I walked through, the heat of his palm rested lightly against the base of my spine. The courteous gesture set off an unexpected but purely feminine reaction that I did my best to ignore. From behind me, Zev's deep voice said, "Good morning, Debbie."

We crossed the ash-tone wood floors and stopped at the elegant desk created from an artistic blend of wood and marble.

Debbie, the stylish forty-something woman at the desk, matched the office's refined air, and her greeting held a wealth of sincerity. "Zev, good morning to you too." Her gaze shifted to include me, and her welcome dimmed just a tad. "I'll let Madeline know you and your guest are here."

Zev tapped the counter and murmured, "Thank you." Then he angled toward me as Debbie murmured into the discreet headset hidden by her hair. His gaze caught mine and held it. I had no idea what he was thinking, but it felt like a silent dare of sorts. Of what, I wasn't sure, but I wouldn't be the first one to look away.

It wasn't long before Debbie broke our silent contest with "Ms. Thatcher's ready for you." She waited until Zev turned his attention to her to add, "Since you know where you're going, go on in."

Zev's grin sideswiped me with its charisma, which made me grateful it was aimed at the helpful Debbie instead of me. "I appreciate the trust."

Debbie's brows rose over the thin edge of her glasses. "I never said I trusted you, young man."

Zev put his hand over his heart in mock offense. "That hurt."

She laughed. A light blush colored her skin, proof that being charmed by an attractive male didn't lessen with age and wisdom. "Go on and leave me to work."

I followed Zev through the entryway and to the right as he stopped at a wide door and rapped his knuckles twice. "Madeline."

"Zev," a strong but husky voice answered. "Come on in."

Zev stepped back and waved me forward. "Thank you so much for agreeing to see me and my business associate."

I entered a large office. A couch sat to my right while an L-shaped desk and two comfortable blue chairs dominated the rest of the space. The entire far wall was glass, showcasing a breathtaking view of Phoenix's skyline, while flooding the space with natural light.

A woman came from behind the desk. She paused mid-step, her smile taking on puzzled twist, her attention on me.

My first up-close impression was that Madeline was as striking in reality as she was photogenic. I managed a polite smile as Zev stepped around me and moved toward her.

Madeline's attention shifted to him, and her smile steadied as she continued to move out from behind her desk.

She took the hand Zev offered, her smile deepening as he covered their hands with his other one. "I apologize for springing an unexpected guest on you."

"It's fine. My morning doesn't ramp up until nine." She patted his hand, and he took the hint and let her go. She turned and waved us toward the chairs. "Please, have a seat." She rounded the desk and settled into her chair. "Can I get either one of you a coffee or water?"

We both demurred and took our seats. Once everyone was in place, Zev spoke. "To be honest, I wasn't sure if you'd be in today. I heard the news about Keith this morning. My condolences on your loss."

Madeline's smile faded. "Thank you." There was the slightest tightening around her eyes, and her shoulders stiffened. "It was quite unexpected."

I didn't doubt that, but if her tone was anything to go by, she wasn't all that torn up over it. In fact, she sounded almost annoyed by Keith's death.

She turned to me, and I swallowed hard under her relentless gaze. "And you are? My assistant didn't mention your name."

"Madeline," Zev interrupted smoothly. "May I introduce Ms. Costas. As I mentioned earlier, a business associate. I asked her to accompany me this morning at the last minute."

If his intention was to appease her, I figured he failed. A calculating light joined the hardness in her brown eyes, and there was nothing welcoming in her return smile or her murmured "Ms. Costas."

Yeah, getting in to see Madeline on my own would have never worked. Tapping into the same skills I utilized with difficult customers, I held on to my polite demeanor and kept my voice unremarkable. "Rory, please."

"Rory," she repeated. Only then did she turn to Zev, all but dismissing me. "What brings you here?"

Zev laced his fingers over his abdomen and stretched out his legs, crossing them at the ankle. "Have you been paying attention to the fallout of LanTech's closure?"

Instead of answering right away, she studied him for a long moment. Finally, she said, "It's my understanding there were quite a few ramifications from that. Do you have a specific one in mind?"

"The unfulfilled-military-contracts fiasco," he clarified, making the initial move in the polite game of verbal chess with masterful ease.

"Ah, yes." She picked up a pen and began to play with it absently. "Didn't one of your Family's companies pick up most of those?"

Zev's casual demeanor didn't change. "Yes, Cazador Innovations was able to renegotiate favorable terms to complete most of them."

"How fortunate for Emilio." If I'd been paying less attention, her slight snide undertone would have slipped by without notice.

"Yes, it was quite unexpected," Zev echoed her earlier sentiment. "Unfortunately, now that the dust is settling, the true depth of LanTech's questionable business practices are coming to light. The repercussions of which may prove to be damaging to various parties."

I'd witnessed plenty of barbed conversations in my time, thanks to Sylvia and the myriad of clientele the Guild served. This one, though, was inching up toward my top ten, and we were barely getting started.

Madeline's pen stilled, and I didn't think it was possible, but her spine got straighter. "There were rumors, of course, but we all know how those play out."

"This is not one of those times," Zev warned.

I sat in my chair, doing everything I could to stay invisible
while the two circled each other. Normally, having Zev take
control of the conversation would frustrate me to no end, but
since this was clearly way out of my league, he was welcome
to it. I would do my part and file away the bits and pieces for
later evaluation.

Madeline shifted her chair until she was staring out the
window. I didn't think she was taking in the scenery. "I'm
assuming you being here, saying this, I am one of those
parties?"

Zev waited until she turned back to him. "I'm here to find
out."

Bracing her elbows on the desk, she steepled her fingers
and leaned forward, a frown marring her forehead. "And how
do I go about helping you with that?"

"I wish there was another way to go about this, Madeline." It was difficult to tell if the sympathy snaking through
Zev's cool mask and into his voice was real or not, but the
older woman seemingly bought it. Some of her wary stiffness
eased. Then he added, "I need to ask you some delicate questions about Keith."

Her shoulders twitched. Obviously, she hadn't been
expecting that particular move. She sat back, trying to hide
her reaction. "Keith?" Astonishment disappeared as realization seeped in, leaving her mouth tight and anger flashing in
her eyes. "Please don't tell me you have evidence he played
some part in LanTech's downfall?" She shoved back from the
desk and got to her feet. I caught the red flush welling under
her skin before she turned and paced over to the window. She
stood there, staring out, her arms crossed over her chest, her
shoulders moving with her agitated breaths. "That would be
so like him," she all but hissed. She looked over her shoulder
at Zev, temper and disgust clearly evident. "He always wanted
to be more important than he really was." Her chin lifted

mutinously. "Whatever he's done, I had nothing to do with it."

Yep, someone harbored a shit ton of emotional baggage about her ex. I could easily see her ensuring Keith's carnal performance remained uninspiring, but if that were the case, how had she crossed paths with Lena?

In an attempt to soothe ruffled feathers, Zev lifted his hands, palms out. "I'm not here to accuse you of anything, Madeline. I was hoping you could answer some questions about him. It would help us"—he motioned toward me, dragging me into the conversation—"to get a better idea of what, if any, part he may have played in this mess."

Looking unconvinced, Madeline angled her back to the window and propped a hand on her hip as she switched her attention to me. "Who is it you work for?"

I caught Zev's slight nod out of the corner of my eye and answered, "The Guild."

Perfectly groomed eyebrows rose, and Madeline's gaze moved to Zev. "Why is the Guild involved in a Family business matter?"

Even I couldn't miss the insinuation layering her question, but Zev checked her move with ease. "My investigation crossed paths with Ms. Costas's, and we felt it would be best if we worked together." His "for now" was loud and unspoken.

Madeline considered his answer, her thoughts veiled behind a coldly professional mask. "What business does the Guild have with Keith?" She directed her question to me as she reclaimed her chair.

As Zev and I were juggling too many bits and pieces to risk tripping over our own feet, we had decided earlier to stick as close to the truth as possible. "Dr. Oliver Martin at the Reid Clinic contacted the Guild on behalf of Mr. Thatcher," I said.

That was as far as she let me get before she cut in sharply, "For what? Was Keith sick?" She didn't wait for my answer. "He never said anything." Her mouth turned down with either disapproval or disgust; I wasn't sure which. "Not that he would. Heaven forbid he admitted to feeling his age."

"Ms. Thatcher," I interrupted as politely as possible, not wanting to get lost in the rabbit holes of what was obviously a highly toxic relationship. "Your ex-husband was recently diagnosed with a magical contagion that impeded his sexual performance."

Madeline's expression blanked before she threw her head back and laughed. "Oh my God, so he really was cursed. That's priceless."

Zev and I waited the few minutes it took her to regain her composure.

With one last chuckle, she wiped a hand over her face. "I apologize. I know it's not nice to laugh, especially at the dead." She sat back in her chair and, for the first time that morning, looked relaxed. Humor still played around her mouth. "But if you knew him at all, you would understand how perfectly fitting that is. When you find out who set it, will you let me know? I owe them a drink, at least."

A couple of responses flew through my head, but I kept my mouth shut, because any one of them would probably offend her. Especially coming from me.

But since she considered Zev an equal of sorts, he didn't have the same problem. "Is it safe to assume you didn't curse him?"

"I wish I had," she answered, her amusement fading slowly. "But, as I mentioned to the young woman who was asking questions before, since I'd be the first one he'd accuse, it wouldn't be worth my time." Her gaze landed on me and went sharp. "Ah, you thought it was me."

I tightened my grip on my professionalism and kept my

tone pleasantly neutral. "It was a consideration that needed to be explored."

"I'm sure," she agreed. "But as much as I would like to take credit for such a brilliantly devious idea, I can't." She sounded surprisingly sincere.

Zev shifted in his chair. "Can you think of anyone else who would pursue that particular avenue?"

She absently tapped a glossy nail against her armrest and gave his question serious consideration. Eventually, she said, "I haven't really paid much attention to who was decorating his arm in the last few months. I've been a bit busy with finalizing the divorce and my upcoming engagement. The last name I can safely recall is Dori Aimsworth, and only because she made quite the scene at the mayor's Spring Gala. Whatever upset her probably had to do with the young brunette that showed up on his arm at a charity thing a couple weeks back."

I committed Dori's name to memory so I could share it with Evan at my first opportunity.

"And the mayor's Gala was..." Zev prompted.

"About a month and a half ago." She shook her head and went to say something more but was interrupted by the buzzing of her phone. She was reaching for it even as she said, "I'm so sorry. Do you mind?"

Zev shook his head, but Madeline had already answered. "Yes... Oh." Her gaze went to her computer, and a small frown crossed her face. "Please send him back."

It sounded as if our time was coming to an end. Taking care to be discreet, I dug my phone out of my pocket and held it in my lap, screen up. I swiped the screen, brought up Evan's name in my text and sent Dori's name off while Madeline concluded her call. My phone was back in my pocket by the time Madeline hung up and turned to Zev. "I hope you don't mind, but Theo's here." She got up and began to round her desk. "I thought we might as well have him join us. Maybe he'll have heard or seen something that might help."

I wasn't quite sure that logic worked, but what did I know? When it came to exes, my friends tended to avoid them like the plague, but maybe Theo didn't have that luxury.

Zev rose and moved to stand next to me, freeing up a chair. Madeline crossed the office to the door, and I twisted in my seat to watch as she met Theo at the door. "Darling, I wasn't expecting you until later." She stepped into the younger man's arms.

He pulled her close and brushed her cheek with a chaste kiss. "I just heard about Keith and was worried about you." He looked up and caught sight of Zev and me. He dropped his arms and stepped back. "I'm sorry, Maddie. I'm interrupting. Should I come back later?"

"No, you're fine, Theo." She led him into the office and went through a round of introductions. Hands were shaken, greetings were exchanged, and then everyone settled in. Theo perched in the seat Zev had abandoned, Zev leaned a hip against the back of my chair, and Madeline reclaimed her spot behind her desk. She then brought Theo up to speed in record time, explaining that Keith had been cursed and we were trying to identify the who and why. Gauging his reaction was difficult. His blank face was as adept as Madeline's and Zev's, but he held himself with a curious tension I didn't understand.

When Madeline finished, Theo said, "That would explain a few things."

Zev asked, "Like?"

Theo shared a look with Madeline before answering. "His behavior at our engagement party."

Madeline waved her hand. "He was just being a jealous bastard."

"There's a difference between vindictive and certifiable,

and he was closing in on the second before we had him escorted out." Without waiting for Madeline's response, Theo turned to Zev and elaborated, "Keith showed up to the engagement party, uninvited, with his latest girlfriend, in an ugly mood. It didn't get any better after he made serious headway through the open bar. Maddie and I managed to steer clear of him for the most part, but eventually, our luck ran out. He started in on Maddie with his usual round of accusations and innuendos, doing his best to make everyone uncomfortable."

"He was an ass," Madeline muttered.

"He was drunk," Theo chastised. "A mean drunk. I had security escort him and his date out as soon as I could." He laced the word *date* with a hefty amount of disgust.

Uh, wonder why that didn't make it into the gossip rags?

As if reading my mind, Madeline said, "Thankfully, it was a private get-together, so we didn't have the added headache of dealing with the press." She flattened her hands against the top of her desk. "It was difficult enough trying to downplay his paranoid delusions to our friends, much less such unsavory behavior. Most of them are aware he's been a bit... off lately."

Theo shifted in his chair, looking as if he wanted to say something, but a sharp look from Madeline had him looking away, his jaw clenched.

Zev caught the revealing exchange and turned to Theo. "You don't agree?"

Theo looked to his fiancée, and a silent conversation ensued. When it finished, Theo turned to Zev and in a hard voice said, "Maddie's being polite. Keith's always been a dick, it's just that since he was fired from LanTech he's been an even bigger dick." He shrugged. "Or maybe he was being a bigger dick because finally someone was screwing with his."

"Theo." Madeline's reprimand was soft, but it carried a clear warning.

The angry lines in Theo's face softened. "Maddie, he's dead. What does it matter? As soon as they talk to the others, they'll find more than just me with that opinion. Hell, all his dirty little secrets will come out."

"And what dirty little secrets are those?" Zev asked.

Theo and Madeline exchanged another long, silent look before Madeline sighed and answered, "As a financial manager, Keith could read the writing on the wall about his future at LanTech, so he began negotiating with the company for a large severance package. They had settled on an amount, and the papers were drawn up. The morning Keith went in to sign them was the same morning the news broke that LanTech was all but broke and closing its doors. Keith called me and railed endlessly about being cheated of his money. He bounced from one wild claim to another."

"He accused Maddie of screwing him out of his severance package," Theo all but spat. "He claimed that she conspired with Stephen Trask to bankrupt LanTech, which left him, Keith, with nothing."

I wasn't sure, but that seemed like quite the logic jump to me, but I wasn't a paranoid ex. What, if any, influence did Madeline hold with the CEO of Origin? Zev obviously had the same problem, because he said, "That doesn't make sense."

"It didn't have to," Madeline said. "During the last few years, Keith was always convinced someone was out to get him or what he considered his." Her expression was wry, but worn. "That depth of paranoia is not only exhausting, but it never follows logic."

I was betting it also played a big part in her divorce, along with the accusations of embezzlement and affairs. *Yeah, Keith's looking like a real winner.*

"Stephen and I have been friends for years," she explained. "But Stephen never really got along with Keith, and vice versa. Add in the intense business competition between Origin and LanTech, and Keith managed to piece together some warped version of reality that made me the villain and him the victim."

"Everyone knew it was all bullshit and that Keith was the one stealing from LanTech," Theo cut in. "I never understood why the company didn't charge him."

Probably because LanTech didn't have a dime to spare on taking Keith to court once the Cordovas were done with them.

Theo wasn't done. "If you ask me, he just wanted out of paying you alimony."

She inclined her head. "Maybe, or maybe between the divorce and losing his job, he just finally broke. Whatever the case may be, when the situation with LanTech came to light, Keith did not handle the whispers well. In fact, he burned quite a few bridges with his rather vehement denials of wrongdoing and erratic accusations. Many of our friends and acquaintances found it best to cut ties until the dust settled."

The image of rats and a sinking ship came to mind.

"It would be the smart thing," Zev said. "Were there any specific someones that he burned more than others?"

"You mean besides me?" She shook her head. "Not that comes to mind."

Theo turned to Zev, and whatever he saw on Zev's face had the younger man's eyes narrowing as he rose to his feet. "You don't actually think Maddie had anything to do with Keith's death, do you?" When Zev didn't answer, an angry flush swept through Theo's face. "Maddie didn't have anything to do with that bastard's death."

Something about the vehemence of Theo's reaction struck me as being off, but I didn't know him enough to pinpoint why. I couldn't look to Zev for clues, either, as he stood behind my chair, but there was no missing the tension emanating from him as it crouched at my back. The last place I wanted to be was between the two men, but I was stuck.

"Calm down, Theo," Madeline intervened, rising from her chair. She rushed around her desk and got a hand on Theo's arm, as if to hold him in check. "Zev is simply asking questions for the Cordova Family."

If she thought that would be enough to rein in Theo, she was wrong. If anything, it made him edgier. "What's the Cordovas' interest in Keith's death?"

Zev's presence behind me shifted, and his knuckles brushed against the back of my shoulders as he gripped the top of my chair. Would he tell them the truth? And if he did, would it help or harm us in finding Lena? I wasn't sure which way I wanted him to go at this point.

"As I explained to Madeline before your arrival, Cazador Innovations is in the midst of completing contracts that were initiated with LanTech." In contrast to Theo's edgy temper, Zev was cool and collected, simply sharing the facts. "Unfortunately, we've recently realized there were some financial discrepancies, and we were hoping to discuss those with Keith. While I was trying to corner Keith, I crossed paths with the Guild's investigation into his curse. As Keith was dodging both of us, we thought we'd join forces, hence the call to Madeline yesterday for a meeting on the off chance she could help us hunt him down. His unexpected death raises even more questions, and now we're simply following the trail in hopes of finding answers."

Theo's agitation bled away, taking the heavy pressure in the air with it. He wrapped an arm around Madeline's waist and brought her into his side. "I wish you luck, then." He pressed his lips against Madeline's temple. "I know you have a meeting coming up, but will you call me after?"

She gave him a wan smile. "Of course."

He turned to Zev, his hand extended. "Despite the circumstances, it was nice to meet you."

Zev shook his hand. "Same."

Theo gave me a nod then headed out, taking the remaining tension with him.

In my pocket, my phone vibrated. I must have jerked or something because Zev shot me a look. I gave a small shake of my head, indicating it was nothing.

He turned back to Madeline, his polite mask firmly in place. "Madeline, I know you're busy, so we won't keep you. Thank you for making the time to talk to us."

She folded her arms over her chest, a small frown marring her brow. "I'm not sure I was all that helpful. Keith is... was," she corrected, rubbing her forehead, "a difficult man to understand." She looked up, and for the first time, I caught the hint of buried grief in her face. "I truly hope you find out who killed him."

Zev gave her a careful hug, and I almost missed his low "I'll do my best."

I rose and waited until they had stepped apart before I offered my condolences. "I'm truly sorry for your loss, Ms. Thatcher."

"Thank you," she returned in such a way that I knew I was being dismissed.

Unoffended, I moved toward the door, leaving Zev to follow after finishing his low-voiced goodbyes. Something about this whole discussion bothered me, but I couldn't pin it down. My head was stuffed with half-formed impressions and questions that required Zev's insight to piece together. It left me frustrated and worried that this whole meeting had been a waste of time. *Time Lena doesn't have.*

CHAPTER SIXTEEN

ZEV and I didn't say anything as we left Madeline's office, each of us lost in our thoughts. I had no idea what Zev was thinking, but I was stuck stumbling over Theo's reactions. They struck me as insincere, as if he were playing to expectations. It wasn't his deep anger at Keith, because that rang true. Not a surprise since dealing with a jealous, bitter ex could reduce anyone to a red-faced, fire-breathing maniac. But there were a few times Theo's frustration and anger at Keith oozed over to Madeline, adding a hint of mean. Maybe I was wrong. Maybe I was just looking for things that weren't there. But I couldn't shake my suspicions that something else was at play in that relationship.

I was getting into Zev's SUV when my phone vibrated again, reminding me I had a text waiting. While Zev started the car, I pulled out the phone, fastened my seat belt, then read Evan's text. My spine snapped straight, jerking me against the seat belt. "Holy..." I re-read the words as excitement coursed through me.

"What?"

At Zev's sharp question, I shared, "Evan narrowed down a

possible address of where we lost Lena on Monday." I sent Evan a response even as the three dots popped up, indicating he was already typing on his end.

"Where?" Zev hit a button on his steering wheel, activating the GPS system.

Reading through Evan's incoming texts, I missed the car's voice prompt.

"Rory?" Zev said with a hint of impatience.

"Sorry. What?"

"Address?" he repeated.

"Right." I rattled off the address as I continued my text conversation with Evan.

As the GPS shared route specifics, Zev demanded, "How'd he find it?"

My answer was short and distracted as I continued texting Evan. "Dori Aimsworth."

"Dori?" Zev pulled out of the parking lot and followed the GPS prompts. "How in the hell is Dori tied to Lena?"

I finished my latest text and hit Send. "I don't think she is. I mean, not directly." I looked up as he calmly wove his way through morning traffic.

He shot me a look. "Then what makes this address so special?"

My phone vibrated with another incoming text, and I went back to reading my screen. "I don't know, but we can find out," I muttered, fingers flying over my screen. Question sent, I squirmed in my seat as we waited for Evan's response. I couldn't quash the rising hope that this lead would be the one to finally pan out. The seconds stretched by, turning terminal. The bubble indicating Evan was typing stared back. I was about to send my own nudge when the first text popped up. "Okay..." I read it out loud. "According to Evan, they added Dori's name to the search parameters."

"What search?"

Zev's question reminded me that we hadn't shared specifics on the Guild's search for Lena. It was time to change that. "Evan's team of electrogeeks have been combing through all the electronic records attached to anything located near where Lena's phone signal disappeared. They've been working their way through a maze of names and businesses, using Keith and any known connections for possible ties."

"Seriously?" There was something I couldn't interpret in Zev's one-word question.

"Seriously," I shot back, unable to tell if I'd heard suspicion or skepticism. Another text snagged my attention.

He gave a low whistle. "Damn, I'm impressed."

My head jerked up. "Why?"

Unmoved by my sharp question, he said, "Because that's like searching for a needle in a haystack. The fact they have an address a whole, what? Twenty minutes after you sent Dori's name? That's either luck or skill."

"I'm thinking it's both." I didn't understand his surprise. The Families weren't the only ones with access to skilled mages. "Not that it matters."

"How so?" He made a rolling right at the stop sign. A horn sounded from the irate driver he cut off.

Since I was anxious to get to the address, I refrained from commenting on his rude driving. "Lena belongs to the Guild, and the Guild takes care of its own."

"Seems a little above and beyond to me," he muttered under his breath as he checked his mirrors.

Since I wasn't sure if I was supposed to have caught that or not, I decided to ignore it and get us back on track. "With Dori's name, the search got a hit. It seems she has a penchant for Chinese takeout." Zev gave a disbelieving snort, but I kept summarizing. "They managed to link Dori's delivery app to an address in the target area."

Keeping his attention on the road, Zev shook his head. "So what are we looking at with the address? Business? Residential?"

I pulled up the satellite image Evan had sent me. "Looks residential."

"Good, less hassle trying to explain why we're there." He paused. "Is it Dori's or just somewhere she's visiting?"

"Hang on." Instead of continuing the flurry of back-and-forth texts, I hit Evan's number and activated my phone's speaker. As soon as he picked up, I started talking. "Who does the house belong to?"

"Not Dori, but we're still unraveling those knots," Evan answered, unaffected by my lack of greeting. "Two years ago, the house was bought by an LLC in a foreclosure auction. We're trying to trace the LLC to an owner, but so far, we've only managed to find a possible connection to a defunct subsidiary of LanTech."

My pulse sped up, and excitement seared under my skin. "Are Keith's fingerprints on any of it?"

I could hear him typing and knew he was probably hunched over his computer in the cave that was his office. "Not to the LLC, but I do have Keith's signature on the closing documents as a witness."

"Zev, is that typical?" I directed my question to the man who was more familiar with how things worked in Keith's world. When he shot me a puzzled look, I clarified, "For a financial manager to witness the corporate purchase of a property?" I paused then added, "Actually, why would a corporation buy a residential property in the first place?"

"Cheaper than reimbursing for long-term stays at hotels or depending on local rentals. Not to mention the tax write-off," he answered my last question first. Then his brow furrowed. "Having Keith involved wouldn't send up any red flags. LanTech could easily have sent him in as a financial rep for that transaction."

"If it helps any," Evan interrupted, "the property deed was transferred a year ago from the purchasing LLC to a Signature Enterprises."

Zev's frown deepened. "I've heard that name somewhere recently."

"Give me a second," Evan muttered. "Okay, they're a property investment firm that was funded by a bunch of angel investors."

My hand tightened on the phone as I shuffled the bits and pieces around. They were disjointed enough to hurt my brain, and my shallow knowledge of corporate financial shenanigans didn't help. "How likely is it that Madeline and or Keith were one of those angels?" I threw out.

Zev shot me a look. "I think it's a safe bet."

"It'll take me time to find out," Evan said.

I was shaking my head, even though Evan couldn't see me. "Wait!" I felt like we were slipping down a rabbit hole and farther away from what was relevant. "Evan, can you track down who was making the mortgage payments on that house?"

A tension-filled minute passed before he spoke, frustration clear in his voice. "It was paid in full."

Of course it was, because that would be too easy. I tried another route. "Okay, what about the utilities?"

I could hear him typing, and this time, his voice was triumphant. "Looks like those were being paid by a corporate card tied to LanTech."

"Gotcha." I shared a fierce smile with Zev. "Thanks, Evan!"

"I'll keep digging, see what other connections I can unearth," the electro mage offered. "In the meantime, Rory, be careful and let me know what you find."

"Will do." With that, I hung up and turned to Zev. "How much you want to bet that Keith was using company funds and resources to create his love nest?"

"Not worth the odds." Zev's lips curled, disgust sweeping over his face. "What a sneaky shit."

Elated by finally catching a damn break, I didn't check my filter. "Yeah, well, fucking his employer and his girlfriend at the same time sounds exactly like something Keith would get a kick out of doing."

Unoffended by my blunt observation, Zev said, "Got to agree with you on that."

Our best bet was to get to the house and hope we found Lena somewhere inside. I wanted to urge Zev to drive faster, but a glance at the dash confirmed he was already exceeding the posted limits. Needing something other than the myriad of possible scenarios awaiting us to think about, I turned my phone facedown against my thigh and drummed my fingers against the case. Staring blankly through the windshield, I mulled over what we had so far, including our interview with Madeline and Theo. "Madeline doesn't strike me as a woman who's easily fooled."

"She's not." Zev didn't elaborate, clearly waiting to see where I was going.

Happy to take the lead, I wondered, "Then how did Keith manage to keep her at his side for so long?"

"Money, influence, power—pick one." Zev's voice was dry. "Their marriage was more a business arrangement than a love affair."

That sounded downright horrific to me. I shuddered. "That's just... yuck."

His mouth curled up in mocking amusement, and a rusty chuckle followed. "Are you a romantic, Ms. Costas?"

Refusing to dignify that with a response, I resolutely stayed on track. "If that's true, then Madeline had to have known about all of Keith's..." I searched for a polite word for "screw-ups" and came up with "Indiscretions, both personal and professional."

"More than likely," he agreed. "I can attest that professionally, she prefers to keep the upper hand in negotiations. She doesn't react well to being blindsided."

His statement made me curious. "What do you mean? She doesn't react well?"

Instead of answering right away, he choose his words with care. "She approached Emilio with a business venture, which appeared solid on paper. His team went to work and thoroughly researched the opportunity. When they turned up disturbing discrepancies, Emilio politely turned Madeline down. When she pressed for an explanation, he shared what the investigation uncovered. She was obviously shocked by the findings, and embarrassed. Two days later, her entire investigation team was fired with no references. Then she went out of her way to ensure that particular business venture never got a chance to get off the ground. It disappeared within weeks."

I winced. "Yikes."

"Yep." Zev slowed and turned off the main road into a neighborhood.

"Okay, so Madeline is definitely someone you don't want to cross," I said, thinking aloud. "I hope Theo knows that."

At that, Zev shot me a look. "Why?"

I shrugged, trying to find a way to put my vague feelings into words. "It's nothing I can put my finger on, but there's something about him that seems... off. Then there's his reaction to Keith. It just feels as if there's something more to it than a pissing match between an ex and his younger replacement."

Rather than blow off my impression, Zev asked with what

sounded like sincere curiosity, "If someone was making your life miserable, embarrassing you every chance he could get, wouldn't you be pissed?"

"Yeah, but…" Frustrated at not finding the right words to articulate what was bothering me, I trailed off.

Thankfully, Zev didn't press. Instead, he made one last turn and rolled to a stop in the shade provided by an old-growth Palo Verde tree that sat between two older, neatly kept cinder-block homes. "For now, let's concentrate on Keith. Maybe we'll get lucky, and you'll find something that will help you figure out what's bothering you." He leaned an arm over the steering wheel, peering through the window at the house. He indicated the house on the left. "Doesn't look like anyone's home."

I turned to study the house. The postage-stamp front yard was done in rock and desert plants, while the neighbor's equally small lawn was cut short and patched in greens and yellows. This was one of the older neighborhoods that dated back to the mid-century. The one-story brick and stucco homes ranged from boxy to arched facades guarded by narrow front porches and sported carports instead of garages. Despite the age, it was clear those who lived here took pride in their homes, because it was like stepping back in time. Neat yards, flags, tall trees, and plant boxes abounded.

The one we wanted looked newly painted. The slate-gray accents unmarred by sun and dust were dark against the light-beige paint. The carport was empty, and the blinds were drawn on the large front window. "What's the plan?"

"Let's knock first and take it from there." Zev opened his door and got out.

I did the same and waited for him to come around the car. As I stood there, I studied the nearby homes. To the right, an older-model sedan with a light layer of dust sat in the neighbor's carport. Across the street, one of the homes held a minivan with one of those annoying "My student..." sticker collections. The house next to it was guarded by an older import with flashy tires. Add in the flag with the university logo in the bedroom window, and it was safe to assume college students were tucked inside.

I turned back as Zev came up to me, and together, we walked up the drive. I did a quick scan of the house's exterior, looking for any cameras. It seemed everyone had them nowadays. Thankfully, this appeared to be one of the few who didn't.

As we got closer to the door painted in a burnt sierra, my skin prickled in warning. Zev raised his hand, but before he could knock, I stopped him with a hand on his arm. "Hold up."

He looked at me. "What?"

I opened my mouth to warn him that some sort of magical security lay in wait, then realized that would create questions I didn't want to answer. So I shook my head and changed what I was going to say. "Let me knock." He arched a brow, so I talked fast. "If anyone is home, I'm less intimidating. They look out and see you, they'll call the cops before they open the door."

Those dark eyes focused on me with uncomfortable intensity, but he finally nodded and stepped back, making room for me. I took his spot and waited until he stood between the door and the window, out of sight of anyone inside. Tugging on my magic, I drew it close, dragged in a bracing breath, lifted my left hand, and knocked. When a jolt of magic shocked my knuckles, I bit the inside of my lip in an effort to squelch my reaction. Pinpricks of pain raced along my muscles, making them jump under my skin. I couldn't tell what spell I'd tripped, but it was clear someone wasn't keen about visitors. I dropped my hand to my side, hoping Zev wouldn't see me curling and uncurling my fingers as I rode out the painful tingling in my arm.

We waited for a response, and when I looked to Zev, his brows lifted in question. I shrugged.

He tilted his head toward the door.

Damn, he wants me to knock again. Now that I knew what lay in store, I held my breath and did three sharp knocks. The jolt wasn't nearly as bad this time. When no one came and nothing stirred inside, I lifted my hand. Holding it just above the doorknob, making sure not to make contact, I looked to Zev in silent inquiry.

He hadn't missed my hesitation. He looked at the knob then back at me, a frown I couldn't read on his face. This time, his nod was slower, more reluctant.

I didn't draw it out. Either this would hurt like a bitch, or it wouldn't. I grabbed the metal and twisted. Whatever spell guarded the door snapped around my wrist like an invisible vine seeded with thorns, and I must have made a noise, because Zev closed in. It was clear he didn't know what was happening, just that something was, and he didn't like it. I raised my free hand, palm up, holding him in place. "Don't." I did my best to keep the pain out of my voice. My magic hardened, lessening the pressure of the painful grip. "I'm good. I think I tripped a spell, though."

"How bad?"

"It's fine."

While my response didn't appear to reassure him, he appeared to accept it. "Is it open?"

I twisted my wrist, but the knob didn't move. My magic shoved against the spell's grip, and with a silent pop that echoed in my skull, I felt the magic shatter and fall away, but the door remained stubbornly locked. "Nope. Locked tight." I pulled my hand back and shook it out as a dull throb set up shop behind my temples. "But if someone's monitoring this spell, they know someone's here."

Zev closed in and caught my arm, bringing it up. His fingers brushed over my skin as he examined my wrist. The spell's hold had left no visible marks, but his featherlight touch set off a series of goosebumps I couldn't control. As he continued to stroke my arm from wrist to elbow, my pulse raced. He was so close, his scent seeped into my lungs with every shallow breath. "You okay?"

"Yeah, I'm good." My voice was husky. I cleared my throat and tried again. "I'm good, it just stung. I don't think anyone's home."

"Doesn't look like it." He lowered my arm, his fingers tangling with mine before he let me go. "Wait over there." He gave me a gentle nudge.

I took his spot and watched as he pulled out two thin pieces of metal from one of his many pockets and went to work on the lock. Before long, the last tumbler released with a dull thunk. He pocketed the picks, shifted to the side, and grabbed the knob. "Ready?"

I nodded.

He opened the door a couple of inches. When nothing rushed out, he used the flat of his hand to push the door until it hit the wall behind it. Silence and cool air greeted us. He looked at me in silent question.

After dealing with the magic guarding the door, I was perfectly fine letting him stand between me and whatever might lurk inside. I tilted my head in a "go ahead" motion. He smirked and stepped inside, leaving me to follow. I stopped at the threshold and braced one hand on the doorjamb, uncertain about testing whatever magical security remained. Something lingered, but it was fragmented and wispy, like phantom fingers brushing over my skin.

Zev hadn't gone far. He stood in the tiled entryway, hand on the door, and eyed me. "What? You need an invite?"

Instead of answering, I gingerly stepped inside and braced. Nothing struck out and tried to kill me, but the discomforting sensation of walking through magical cobwebs remained. Zev waited until I cleared the door before pushing it closed behind me, shutting us inside and away from curious neighbors.

Disappointment cruised through me. The house wasn't overly large, but the interior had undergone a recent upgrade. The open space didn't provide much by way of hiding spots, especially if Keith was holding Lena captive. The floors were done in a slate tile, and the few intact walls were coated a bright white broken by an occasional canvas splattered with color. The furniture was clearly staged; everything was picture-perfect, right down to the place settings with cloth napkins on the table to our left. From the entryway, I could see the kitchen to the right, complete with high-end appliances and a small island. Two chairs sat with a couch in the main living space that stretched along the left side of the house, ending at a river-rock fireplace. I'd never understood the need for a fireplace in the desert, but it seemed to be a thing nowadays. To the right, just beyond the kitchen and before patio doors leading off the open living space, was a doorway. Another one broke up the left wall, closer to the fireplace. My guess was the bedrooms were to the left, a bathroom or utility room to the right.

"Not what I was expecting," I said as I went to step around Zev.

His arm shot out, blocking my way and pulling me up short. "Uh-uh, not yet." He dug into one of his many pockets. "Let's make sure we don't trip any more wards, shall we?" He opened his hand. On his palm lay a yellowish shard that, at first glance, appeared to be some kind of wood.

Without thinking, I grabbed his wrist, holding his hand steady as I peered closer. "What is that?"

"A wolf tooth."

Now that he said it, I could see it. The slight curvature that ended in a point, the discoloration from dark at the thicker end to light at the pointed end. I looked up and frowned. "Why?"

In the depths of his dark eyes, a feral light kindled. "Natural material holds magic better." Before I could ask what kind of magic, he added, "It's a sniffer spell." His long fingers closed around the tooth, the move shifting his tendons under my touch.

Without warning, power sparked, ripping against my magical skin like striking flint. Unprepared, I flinched and let go of his arm. "A little warning next time," I groused, wiping my stinging palm against my thigh.

Zev gave me a sharp look, but since a sniffer spell was will based and required the caster's attention, his focus returned to the charm in his hand. Despite the fact he was holding perfectly still, the charm quivered and wobbled. His lips moved, but no sound escaped, and the trembling object steadied. Slowly, it rose to hover in the air above his palm. His hand drifted down, leaving the tooth floating in place. "You know how this works?"

"Yeah." I caught the faintest shimmer of blue surrounding the charm like a water globe. I tore my gaze away and looked to Zev. "It's like a magical dowsing rod." Much like the name implied, a sniffer spell basically sniffed out a magical scent trail. To avoid running all over hell and back chasing down false trails, the spell had to be keyed to a specific person's unique magical "scent." *So who did Zev key this spell to?* "Is that keyed to Keith?"

My question earned an impatient glance. "Who else would I use?" He stepped back, giving the charm room. We both watched as it twisted like a leaf in a gentle wind. First one way, then the other. "If he's the one blocking your Key, this should tell us."

As the tooth inched in my direction, I couldn't stop my heart from picking up speed. "Why's it doing that?"

"If I were to guess? I'd say it's picking up whatever traces you're carrying of the ward you tripped. The sniffer analyzes all residual magic scents in an area then locks on to the unique scent it was given. Much like actual scents, residual magic is layered. The more recent the use, the stronger the trail. Even though it's a targeted search, it still has to shift through all existing traces before locking on to the one it wants."

A warning went off in my head, and before I could put together why, I tamped my magic down tight. The charm stilled for a breathless moment then resumed its movements. This time, it shifted away from me and slowly began drifting farther into the house. I stayed put as Zev followed it past the kitchen and into the living space.

"How reliable is it?" When he turned back at me with a frown, I continued, "I'm just saying, it's not like there are a ton of hiding places here. Everything's open. There's no base-ment. The bedrooms are within hearing distance, which means if Lena was here, we'd already know." When he didn't say anything, I ran a hand through my hair, fighting back my urge to leave him here and just clear the damn house myself. "It's just that a sniffer spell seems like overkill, and you're being awfully cautious."

He turned so he could see me, and he closed his fist. The charm stilled in the middle of the living room, like a dog on a leash. "You sure about that? What if your friend is trapped in an occlusion spell? You'd rather trigger a complex conceal-ment spell that could kill your friend outright if she is here?"

Since there was no way to respond without appearing

childish, I locked my response behind my teeth and glared at him.

Unmoved, he hammered his point home. "You know that expression, 'hide in plain sight'? It's not that hard to get your hands on an occlusion spell if you can afford it."

I winced at his scathing comment, and an embarrassed heat washed over the back of my neck. *Dammit, I should've thought of that.* If Keith had gotten his grubby hands on something as complex as an occlusion spell, it would explain why the Guild couldn't track Lena. I scrambled to regain my footing. "We know Keith wasn't hurting for money."

"Nope, he had plenty of pockets to pick," Zev said, letting me off the hook. "Not to mention his position at LanTech gave him ample opportunity to develop a wide network of contacts. If he was holding your friend hostage, he wouldn't have many places he could use that wouldn't garner attention. This place, though…"

"Would work," I finished, finally following his logic. "Especially since he's been using it to hook up with his girlfriends for years and no one's caught him."

Zev studied me for a long minute, then he turned back to the sniffer and unclenched his fist, like dropping a leash. The sniffer resumed its hunt. We followed its slow path as it cleared first one bedroom, then the next.

My frustration grew as we retraced our steps back through the hall into the living room. Some instinct whispered Lena was somewhere close, which left me antsy and impatient. Not a good combination. "You're sure that thing's working, Zev?"

He leaned against the wall and folded his arms, his attention on the sniffer as it crisscrossed the room. "I'm sure."

I gave a loud sigh and took up a position next to him.

He shot me a look. "Patience is not your forte, Costas."

"I feel like we're wasting time, chasing shadows. It's

obvious she's not inside." I fought back the urge to leave Zev and his stupid sniffer here. "Maybe I can head outside while you finish in here." There had to be something I was missing.

My bitching was cut short when the sniffer gave an odd jerk then darted to the patio door, where it stopped a hair's breadth from the glass and vibrated in tiny jerks.

CHAPTER SEVENTEEN

THE SNIFFER'S unexpected behavior brought both of us to attention, and we were moving in seconds. Zev hit the door first, unlocking and then sliding it open. The sniffer sprang forward, zipping into the backyard. I followed in Zev's wake as we dodged the patio furniture, bypassed the sparkling pool, and rushed over the crushed-gravel path leading to what appeared to be a well-kept office shed. The charm hovered in front of the glass-paned double doors, but the in-glass blinds were shut tight, making it impossible to see inside.

Zev rocked to a stop, blocking the way. Impatience warred with caution and won. I went to step around him, only to be brought up short by his outstretched arm. "Wait."

I bit back my not-so-nice comment and grabbed his arm, my nails digging in unconsciously as I resisted the urge to shove him out of the way and break down the doors. "Hurry the hell up."

He shot me an exasperated look as he dropped his arm. "Rushing in could kill us or your friend, especially since we don't know what kind of protections are in place." He caught the sniffer and deactivated it with a soft word before dropping it in a pocket.

"You have some other nifty charm that will tell us what's in there?" It came out snarky because my instincts were all but yelling that Lena was on the other side of the damn doors. If Zev hadn't been there, I would have already broken in, magic be damned. It wasn't like it could touch me—much.

Zev ignored me, his attention on the shed. I danced from foot to foot as the seconds ticked by with agonizing slowness. Just when my patience hit its end, a rush of power stole my voice as Zev raised his hands a few inches from the doors. Whatever he did caused the air in front of him to shimmer with a hint of blue flame. A spark of white flashed like a lightning strike, leaving me blinking away faint shadows. When my vision cleared, I found myself staring at a circle of runes illuminated by an icy-blue flame. They writhed in mesmerizing beauty as if alive, but there was something about them that set the hairs at the back of my neck on end.

My jaw dropped, and I breathed out an incredulous "Holy shit, what is that?" Because the best I could tell, this was way more than a simple, straightforward casting.

Zev's face was drawn tight in frustration and what looked like anger as his hands dropped to his sides. "That is a double-layered occlusion spell."

That didn't sound good at all. There was a note in his voice that made me swallow hard. "Can you break it?"

He curled and uncurled his fists. "Yes, but it'll take time, and we have no idea who or what is on the other side."

"But—" I snapped my mouth shut on what sounded suspiciously close to a whine. I took a deep breath and studied the spell. Not that it helped much. This was more Lena's specialty than mine. My mind spun uselessly before teetering on the edge of a dangerous decision. Even though I suspected the answer, I had to ask, "How long will it take you?"

Zev avoided my gaze and ran a hand over the back of his neck. His response was almost too low to hear. "Too long."

Yeah, that's what I thought. Guess I wasn't the only one feeling the weight of a proverbial clock ticking down. I closed my eyes in resignation, my decision all but made. Magic was powered one of two ways—through either the mage's will or the complex ritual of casting. My ability landed smack dab in the depths of will power. When a stubborn mage was pitted against a complex spell, the winner tended to be the one with the most brute strength. In this case, with Lena's life in the balance, pitting my secrets against an unknown caster's spell was a no-brainer.

Resolute, my magic wrapped around me with diamond-hard intent. When I opened my eyes, I didn't look at Zev, didn't dare clue him in to what would happen next. I slipped by him, my goal to breach the spell and access the locked door. As I stepped through the floating runes, tendrils of the spell curled around me as power hit with breath-stealing force that made my vision shimmer. Zev's shout sounded dim and muffled, as if my ears were stuffed with cotton. Dismissing him, I concentrated on staying upright under the unrelenting pressure of magic trying to squash me like a bug. The remaining couple of feet to the door stretched endlessly before me. I shuffled forward, each inch a hard-won conquest.

Every breath hurt. Every move zapped agony along my nerves, seizing muscles and electrifying tendons. Holding fast to why I was willingly suffering this hell, I gritted my teeth and kept going. To avoid the nauseating visual spin as the magic battered me, I closed my eyes even as I reached out. My palm brushed the cool metal of the knob, and I gripped the unforgiving surface. The magic whipped around me like invisible flames, searing my skin until I wanted to scream. As my grip tightened, invisible spikes tore through my hands. I bore down, refusing to give in, and even though it felt as if I were breaking my own wrist, I twisted the knob. The door swept open with unexpected ease, and I tumbled inside, my knees hitting the threshold with bruising force. Like taffy, the occlusion spell, and whatever else was layered into it, tore apart. Remnants of power clung to me, avidly searching for a chink in my magical armor, only to come up empty.

Struggling through the unforgiving magic, I blinked away the tiny white explosions in my vision. A shadow fell over me, making me wince, but it was only Zev. He crouched just out of reach, his hands up as if afraid to touch me. I barely managed to shake my head to keep him from making physical contact before another brutal wave of magic hit. This time, it reverberated down my spine and wrapped cruel chains around my ribs. I forced myself forward, and my palms slapped the floor—hard. My head hung down, and my world narrowed to getting air into my aching lungs. The inexorable pressure continued to batter me, and I fought my way through with each wave, determined to get past the spell and reach Lena.

There was no sense of time passing, but it was getting harder and harder to push through. Frustration boiled under the strain, joining with the fear and worry that had been my constant companions since Lena disappeared. Anger and resentment at risking exposure of my secrets to Zev, of all people, joined the volatile mix. It all came to a violent head and smashed against the incessant spell with agonizing force. My spine arched as pain lit up every nerve ending, and a scream was locked in my throat. My vision went dark with streaks of color that bled to white. For an infinite second, it felt as if vicious claws shredded my body, one agonizing inch at a time. Then, as if a switch flipped, it was gone, leaving me a gasping heap on the floor, with tears drying on my face.

"Dammit, Rory, can you hear me?" Zev's voice rushed and receded.

I didn't want to open my eyes, because everything hurt. Everything. Even my damn hair. Cheek pressed against the floor, eyes closed, I tried to answer, but my voice didn't work. I swallowed against my dry throat and winced. Then I tried again. This time, I managed one word. "Yes."

Hands brushed over my shoulder, and despite the light touch, it set off more aches and pains.

"Stop." That came out on a croak, but the touch disappeared. After a couple of deep breaths, the pain subsided enough to risk movement. I opened my eyes first, happy when the world stayed steady. I gingerly rolled over, and every muscle protested. At least my bones no longer felt like water. I pushed up to my hands and knees.

Kneeling, I blinked my spotty vision clear, and Zev's dark features swam into focus. The only thing keeping me from collapsing back to the floor was his grip on my arms as he pulled me up to my knees. "Ow."

"What the hell was that?" Anger and what looked like worry turned his dark gaze turbulent.

With my balance shot to hell, I braced my palms against his chest. "What was what?" My question came out jumbled as my thick tongue stumbled over the words.

But he translated just fine as he shifted his grip, helping me to sit. "Are you trying to kill yourself, Rory?" In contrast to his harsh question, his touch was careful. "Because strong-arming your way through a spell like that is the fastest way to a casket."

"We didn't have time to screw around." For some odd reason, I was talking to his chest. It made me feel... vulnerable, so I straightened my spine and inched back so I could see his face. "We needed inside. I got us inside."

A muscle flexed in his jaw, and his fingers tightened on my arms. Temper, exasperation, and something else moved through his face. "Swear to me you won't do that again."

I gave him honesty. "I can't."

His face darkened. "You won't."

I held his gaze and bit my lip because it wasn't a promise I could make. He muttered a foul word under his breath and looked away. Before I even understood why, I reached up, cupped his jaw, and brought his attention back to me. I gave him the only explanation I could, and one I knew he would understand. "Lena's family. My family."

"Fine." It was reluctantly given, but I would take it. Zev's grip shifted. "If I let you go, you going to collapse?"

"Nope, I'm good." And to make sure, I braced my hands against the floor and finally looked around. Unfortunately, Zev was blocking my view. I leaned to look around him and gasped. "Lena!" I scrambled to my feet and lunged forward. I didn't get far.

Zev's arm wrapped around my waist and pulled me up short, hauling me against him as we both faced Lena. "Hold up, Rory!"

"Let me go, dammit." I tried to pry my way out of his arms, barely noting the bloody scratches I left along his forearms. Just beyond Zev, Lena was slumped in a chair that sat in the middle of a complex ring of sigils and runes. I couldn't tell if she was breathing, and what little of her I could see didn't look good.

He tightened his hold and growled, "Dammit. Calm down!"

I forced my body to still and curled my fingers into his arm. "What's wrong with her?"

His answer came out harsh. "She's trapped in a Drainer's Circle."

Shock sent a chill arrowing into my soul, and my voice shook. "Can you get her out?"

A Drainer's Circle, according to urban legends, was a corrupted spell supposedly created by the twisted minds of the Cabal who'd mixed science and magic with disastrous results. It was designed to slowly drain a mage of their power, but it didn't stop there. When there was no more magic to draw on, the spell would shift focus and attach to the unprotected mage's soul, snuffing it out piece by piece until only a soulless wraith remained. Or so the whispers claimed.

The muscles in Zev's arm flexed under my hands. "It depends on you," he muttered darkly, his arm at my waist tightening before falling away. Before I could shift back, he caught my arm and turned me from Lena.

"Me?" It came out in an undignified squeak.

He studied me, his thoughts hidden. "There are two ways to break this spell. One is to unravel it." His gaze flickered to Lena and came back to me, a grim darkness swirling in the depths, and he finished with brutal honesty. "Which, considering the state of your friend, I don't think we have time to do."

When he didn't continue, I nudged, "The other?"

The cords along his neck tightened, and his jaw flexed. He pinned me with a piercing intensity, and his harsh words carried unspoken implications. "We do exactly whatever it was you did with the occlusion spell—we overpower it."

"We?"

"Yes, we," he shot back. "A spell of this level requires more than one mage to break."

"Spellwork isn't my thing, Zev." My pulse raced, and a clammy sweat coated my spine.

His lips curved, but it wasn't with amusement. "Then it's a damn good thing you have me, isn't it?"

Trusting him with Lena's life left me sick with fear and worry, but I swallowed my panic. "Swear to me you can do this."

His answer was immediate. "We can do this."

If he was lying, he was damn good at it. But for Lena's

sake, I would take him at his word. "All right, what do you need from me?"

He studied me for a second then asked carefully, "Your magic, is it Elemental or Mystic in nature?"

It was a deceptively simple question, one not normally asked in polite company. But this was far from polite company, and my answer was far from simple. With the clock ticking on Lena's wellbeing, I shoved aside my paranoia and answered, "Mystic. Navigators are Mystic." It wasn't a lie, because the abilities that made me a Transporter originated in the psychic realm, just like those of a Prism.

"Good." He stepped around me to crouch next to the circle. "That'll make this a hell of a lot simpler."

"How so?" Uncertain, I stood there watching him.

"Combining sympathetic magic is easier, and we need easy where we can get it." He touched his fingers to a sigil etched on the tile floor. Magic rushed over my raw nerves, and I bit back a groan as the miserable sensation reawakened echoes from my earlier ordeal. The blue fire I was beginning to associate with Zev crawled over the floor, sliding into curves and lines, illuminating the complex collection of sigils and runes etched around Lena. Instead of stopping once the circle was complete, the blue fire doubled back, leaving a secondary layer of symbols and lines hovering inches above the first. The magical ropes radiating from the circle to Lena and locking her in magical chains left a sickening sense of dread in its wake.

A low curse erupted from Zev. "Whoever set this wasn't fucking around," he all but growled. "See this?" He pointed to the second layer that appeared to be a mess of knots. "It's a secondary spell set to act like a magical dead man's switch."

I mimicked Zev's crouch. Magical theory wasn't my strong suit, but I knew enough for the basics of a dead man's switch. I tried to unravel the sigils and runes into something familiar. "Is that a death curse?"

"A modified version of one, yeah. This pattern here"—he gestured to a set of runes interspersed with a wavy symbol—"implies the intent of the spell and curse are woven together." Lines marred his forehead as he studied the casting. "If I'm reading this right, any interruption on the draining lines"—he pointed to the ethereal chains attached to Lena—"will shift the speed of the drain from slow and constant to immediate and lethal."

I looked at Lena. Her face carried a gray cast under the tangle of hair, and her chest rose and fell with each shallow breath. There was no blood and no marks on her skin, but the press of bone under pasty skin was evidence that the Drainer's Circle was currently taking more than magic with it. "It's done a hell of a job so far, but she's still hanging in there."

"Yeah, she is," Zev agreed as he continued to study the circle. "Although maybe it's a good thing she's out."

Considering what we were about to attempt, I had to agree, but something in his voice made me wonder aloud, "Would it help if she was awake?"

"Maybe." He rose to his feet and offered me his hand. "Up."

I took it and straightened. "I can try to get through to her."

He walked me around the circle. "We'll give it a shot; it can't hurt. If nothing else, she can make sure we don't step wrong." He let me go once we stood at the south point of the circle. "Stand here and do what I say, when I say it, okay? I'm going to use you as a mirror to boost my energy."

As I faced Lena, my mouth was dry as a damn desert, but I managed a nod.

He retraced our steps and took up a position at the north

point, putting the three of us in a straight line. He looked at me over Lena's bowed head and raised his hands in a familiar casting position, arms extended at waist height with palms facing forward. "You ready?"

I mirrored his stance and braced. "Ready."

He took me at my word, and the swell of magic swept through the room. It pressed against my palms like a hot wind and then rushed back to Zev. He met my gaze, his dark eyes blazing with power. "See if you can rouse her while I work on this."

I did my best to ignore the discomfort and focus on my friend. "Lena, can you hear me? I need you to wake up for me." The pressure of Zev's power grew, then it washed through me, mixing with mine before sweeping back out in a bigger wave. I could feel our combined abilities, like an invisible current trying to squeeze through a tight opening, as it seeped into the circle. "Lena? Can you hear me?"

As Zev's power spilled into the power lines, it left behind a brilliant blue. The otherworldly glow crawled toward the first quarter of the circle, and the blue inched into the chains, snaking their way toward Lena. When the first drop touched her skin, she gave a soft groan.

Tamping down my excitement, I hardened my voice and demanded, "Dammit, Lena, open your eyes." I caught the faint movement as she curled one hand into a weak fist. Her head lolled. I glanced at Zev, and at his sharp nod, I barked out, "Lena Davis, get your ass up right now!"

"Lemme alone, Ror," she mumbled. "Tired."

"Get up, Lena," I snapped, forcing back my shaky relief at hearing her voice. Magic swirled through me, hollowing me out. I bore down, determined to give Zev and Lena whatever I could.

Her head bobbed then lifted, her lashes rising sluggishly.

"Rory?" She winced and shifted against the restraints. "What the hell is wrong with me?"

"You're in deep shit, Lena, so pay attention." My voice came out a little rough, but at least it was steady. "Look at me."

She did her best to focus on me. I kept an eye on the signature blue fire that inched its way around the circle toward where I stood. "Talk to me, Lena."

"Shit, shit, shit," she muttered as she lifted her head and looked around blearily. I could tell when her brain came back online, because she twisted hard in her chair, her gaze darting around. "Where is he?" Despite both the physical and magical restraints, her movements were harsh enough to make the chair wobble and to worry me she might tip over, chair and all.

"Where's who?" I asked, knowing it was better if I kept her talking and distracted.

Her jerky movements stilled, and she glared at me. "Theodore Mahon, the slimy sack of pus."

Although I was relieved to hear Lena's normal testiness in her shaky voice, that was not the name I thought she'd give. "Theo did this? Not Keith?"

Lena's lips twisted into a grimace, her hands fisting against the chair arms. "They're working together. Assholes." Anger saturated that last word. She shook her hair out of her face, winced, and took a deep breath. When she spoke again, she was all business. Her attention shifted to the circle and the blue flame that was just about to hit the halfway mark right at my feet. Her eyes met mine, and despite her visible panic, her voice was level. "What's happening?"

Zev's power struck the center mark, bleeding into the lines at my feet. I felt the impact in my teeth, and a coppery taste coated my mouth. I sucked in a breath and managed a sickly smile. "We're trying to get you out of this Drainer's Circle."

"Who's 'we'?" She twisted in her chair, trying to see behind her. A red undertone flashed under the blue along the chains holding Lena in place.

"Stop!" Heart racing, I leaned forward, barely remembering not to move my hands and hold my position. If I stepped into the circle before Zev was ready, we would all be dead. "Don't struggle, okay? Just stay still. Please."

Lena stilled, except for the occasional tremor. Her hazel eyes locked on to mine. "Who's behind me?"

Zev answered without looking away from the spell he was crafting. "My name's Zev Aslanov."

"Zev Aslanov?" Lena repeated even as fever-bright color rode under her ashen cheeks. Her eyes narrowed on me. "As in the same one that works with the Cordova Family?"

I didn't get a chance to say anything before Zev confirmed, "The one and the same. Nice to know my reputation precedes me."

"Oh, it certainly does," she muttered without looking away from me. Now it was my turn to blush under her stare. "What's going on, Rory?"

"Long story short, you went missing, I went searching. When my investigation crossed with Zev's, we teamed up." The mystical pull from my center went from teeth-gritting to butt-clenching. I checked the progress of Zev's magic. The blue fire was closing in on the three-quarter mark. Unfortunately, its approach appeared to be slowing the closer it got to Zev.

"That's too short," Lena snapped.

"Keith stole a file that belongs to my Family," Zev bit out. "I was tracking him when his body dropped at your condo."

The first circle snapped closed with a harsh rasp of magic that left me stifling my painful groan. The magic deepened and grew teeth as it flicked up to the second layer of the circle and started to bleed through the symbols.

"I knew it would work." Fierce satisfaction filled Lena's face before she winced and hissed. The layer of blue in her restraints darkened to indigo as Zev's magic rode the spell lines. This time, it was visibly faster as it wound its way through the secondary circle.

I kept track of its progress from the corner of my eye. Then, in an effort to distract both Lena and myself, I asked, "Knew what would work?"

"Explain after we get you out of this." Zev's voice was tight and dark.

I met his gaze above Lena's head and sucked in a shocked breath. His arms were steady, but the tendons in his neck popped with obvious strain. His eyes blazed with an unearthly light, and a thin layer of magic outlined his body in a ghostly flame. Fear forced his name out on a breath, "Zev?"

He grimaced and bit out, "You ready?"

I nodded and braced, despite the little voice in my head screaming, "Not really!"

The secondary circle snapped closed, and an invisible wind whipped my hair back and left me squinting so my eyeballs wouldn't dry out. A heartbeat, then two, passed before the brutal power eased back. An itchy line of sweat trailed down my temple.

Between us, Lena stiffened, her gaze dropping to her arms, where the blue now mixed with the red, creating a purple so deep, it was closer to black. Her hands curled, and welts rose on her arms. She shuddered once and looked at me, her eyes wide, but her voice held no evidence of the panic creeping into her gaze. "What do you need from me?"

"You're a Key, right?" Zev waited for Lena's nod. "Do you see that hex to your left at about ten o'clock?"

She turned to her right.

He corrected, "Your other right."

She looked the other way and froze. "That twisted little shit. He used an amplifier rune."

"If you attempt to disarm it with your power, you'll trigger it." Despite the situation, Zev's voice stayed calm.

"You use yours, and we risk the same thing," Lena shot back, anxiety clear in her voice.

Completely unruffled, Zev said, "Not if we hit it hard and fast enough. I need you to make sure I don't take a wrong turn."

Lena couldn't see Zev, but she could see me. Her worry and fear were barely held in check. "Rory, are you sure about this?"

Zev stood behind her, like some avenging angel—or demon, the glow of his power adding a sinister cast to his features. He met my gaze and waited for my answer. Without looking away, I told Lena, "Yes, I'm sure." A flicker of relief swept through his face, so fast that if I hadn't been watching, I would have missed it. I switched my attention to Lena. "Trust me?"

She didn't hesitate. "Always."

"Good." I managed to fake a confident grin. "Then let's get you out of here so we can go kick some ass, shall we?"

CHAPTER EIGHTEEN

"ONCE WE START, we can't stop," Zev warned. "If either of us falters, we all die."

"That's cheery," I muttered under my breath. "Let me guess—this is going to hurt?"

"Like a bitch," he confirmed.

Knowing it would just prolong my agony, I gritted out, "Bring it."

Taking me at my word, Zev shoved power into the circle, his muscles visibly straining, teeth bared, eyes narrowed. His power barreled through the lines and hit me like a tidal wave. I grunted under the impact and locked my knees to keep from crumpling. Around us, the magical rings began to rotate with Lena as their center. The first one remained at waist level, but the second drifted higher then shifted until it was perpendicular to the first. The power snapped and snarled, whipping clothes and hair in its wake. The pressure deepened until I swore I could hear my bones creak. My Prism ability quivered in distress, wanting to rise to fight it back, but if I let it loose, it would screw up everything. Caught in the dual fight, the only thing that kept me on point was the threat of killing us all if I faltered.

An invisible tether latched on to me, just under my ribs, and gave a painful jerk. I almost missed Zev's voice under the rush of white noise. "Rory, on two, I need you to step forward into the circle. You need to let the magic flow through one hand to the other, like you're keeping a merry-go-round spinning. When I give the order, we're going to reverse the circle. Ready?"

Afraid I would be reduced to a screaming mess if I unlocked my teeth, I stuck with nodding.

Zev counted down, his voice echoing hollowly. "One... two."

We stepped forward in tandem.

My breath caught as a fierce wave of power seared the soles of my feet to sweep up my legs like a forest fire. It snaked up my spine then exploded at the base of my skull, whiting out my vision. The constant circuit of magic hurt, but I held my position. It was like riding lightning. It spread out, tearing through my palms. The painful ache crawled down my arms like some vicious insect burrowing through my veins. I scrambled for a metaphysical handhold, using Zev's imagery to keep the magical merry-go-round spinning. Lost under the magical deluge, all I could do was endure.

I caught the faint sound of Lena's voice then Zev's deeper response, but it was just noise. The magical current split, threatening to tear me wide open. Caught in its ruthless grip, I could do nothing but hold and wait for Zev's next move. I blinked, feeling the damp traces of tears chilling against my overheated skin. I locked eyes with Zev.

Even through the glow of power, the signs of his struggle were apparent. Lines of strain radiated from his eyes. His lips were pulled back in a snarl; his cheeks were pressed so tight to his skin that the bone threatened to cut through. But I hung on to the steely resolve flickering deep in his dark eyes. It was the only thing keeping me from collapsing into a sobbing ball of pain. The ache grew, slipping like acid into my bones.

Caught up in the agony, I almost missed Zev's "Rory, now!"

That invisible tether tightened, and together, we paced the circle counterclockwise. Each step felt like trudging through burning quicksand while dragging a boulder. I was covered in sweat by the time Zev reached my initial position and stopped. I stood at the north point, worried my legs would fold, and forced air through the tight bands around my chest. I swore my ears were bleeding and razors were scraping against my bones. Numb acceptance began to dull the sharp edge of pain. My brain went foggy, but jumbled though it was, I heard Zev's warning. "Lena, brace."

From my position behind her, I couldn't see much. In fact, the only thing I could focus on was Zev's face—fierce, determined, and washed in a field of icy blue. Everything else had been reduced to a mass of shifting shadows. Caught in the storm of magic, I missed whatever he did, but I sure as hell felt it. Like a tsunami, magic crested to a towering behemoth and hovered over us. Between one breath and the next, it broke, thundering down with inescapable force. Bowel-loosening fear held me in a merciless grip and triggered my magic. I didn't get a chance to stop it before it snapped into place with bone-jarring intensity. I heard Zev's pained grunt, but I was scrambling to rein in my power so it wouldn't screw up whatever the hell Zev was doing.

I almost missed Zev's snarled "Rory, stop!"

"I can't—" I snapped my mouth closed as desperation powered by panic wrestled my magic into obedience. For a breathless moment, everything seemed to pause. Fear that I would kill us all choked me, but then a high-pitched whine started. It grew in strength until the urge to scream was almost undeniable. Just when I was going to give in, the illuminated circle shattered in a silent explosion. The staggering release of pressure sent me stumbling forward. I landed on my bruised knees, barely managing not to knock myself unconscious against the back of Lena's chair. Not that it mattered because my head felt like someone buried a hatchet in it. There was a metallic taste in my mouth, and everything, every inch of skin, every hair follicle, everything fucking hurt.

I took precious moments relearning to breathe. When I was fairly sure movement wouldn't turn my bones to dust, I managed to crawl around Lena's chair. My shuffling movements smudged the now-dulled sigil marks marred with jagged lines. A dusting of ash drifted down, but I couldn't see where it was coming from. I swatted a few flakes from my face, and my hands left black smears against the smooth floor. When I was close enough, I used the back of Lena's chair to keep myself upright. I reached out and felt for a pulse. A harsh sob of relief escaped when a steady beat raced under my touch. "Lena?"

"I'm okay." It came out croaky and was followed by a hollow groan. "Oh my God, that hurt." She lifted her head, blinked at me owlishly, and said with a note of stunned surprise, "You look like shit, Rory."

I swayed on my knees but didn't fall over. "Have you looked in a mirror?"

"Been a little busy." She managed a shaky grin.

Relief swept through me, pushing everything else aside as a giggle escaped. I clamped a hand over my mouth. "Sorry."

"What the hell was that?" Zev growled as he stumbled closer, his features stark in his bone-white face. He dropped to his knees on Lena's other side.

There was no avoiding his eyes in their bruised sockets, and I didn't have the energy to try. I even ignored Lena's wide-eyed, silent "oh shit" look. Instead, I played dumb. "What was that?"

Before he could respond, Lena interrupted. "Think maybe you can get these ropes off me?"

I went to work on the knotted rope wrapped around her wrist, grateful when Zev did the same on the other side and didn't pursue his question. When neither Zev nor I appeared to be making any progress against the stubborn rope restraints, I stopped. "We need something to cut through this."

Looking around, for the first time, I took in the interior. From the outside, the shed might fool most into thinking it held the normal yard implements, but this was definitely a mage's casting space. The only things on the unbroken floor were the marks of the shattered circle and the chair holding Lena. The walls were lined with open shelves cluttered with bottles, herbs, yellowed bones, candles, and various other artifacts required for Arcane works. If we were lucky, there would be a blade or two somewhere in the jumble of objects.

With a groan, I pushed to my feet and stumbled over to the shelves. I caught my balance against the narrow table under the small window, the impact sending a few animal bones rattling across the surface. I spotted the familiar shape of a hilt and pulled it down. It was a short blade, like a paring knife, but based on the dried mud and brown bits, it was used on herbs instead of veggies. "Good enough."

I brought it back to Zev, and since my vision was washing in and out, I handed it over. "You do it. I'm not sure I can."

As he worked on sawing through the rope at Lena's wrists and ankles, I sank to the floor beside him. I braced my elbows on my thighs, dropped my head into my hands, and closed my eyes. The magical hangover was worse than one induced by a night of drinking. Even with my eyes shut, the darkness still dipped and swirled with nauseating frequency. "This sucks," I groaned.

"Whatever you do, don't puke on me," Zev said.

"Wouldn't dream of it." I let myself drift as my aches and pains settled into a dull throb. There was the sense of movement around me, but it wasn't enough to drag me all the way back. I had no idea how much time had passed, and it wasn't until I heard Zev say, "That's the last one," that I opened my eyes.

Zev pulled the last pieces of rope from Lena's ankle, straightened, then held out a hand to her. "Can you walk?"

She nodded.

I blearily got to my feet and moved to her other side, shoving out a hand to help. Between Zev and me, we were able to get her upright. She used our hands to find her balance. Her wrists were a raw mess where she'd struggled against the ropes, and I bet under her wrinkled slacks, her ankles were in the same boat. With Zev on one side of Lena and me on the other, we did an awkward three-person shuffle and escaped the shed. It was a good thing it was a quiet neighborhood and no one seemed to be watching, because heaven only knew what we looked like as we stumbled out of the house and into Zev's SUV. I helped Lena get strapped in then climbed into the back-passenger seat next to her. Zev was at the wheel with the engine started and the AC on full blast by the time I clicked my seatbelt into place.

"Guild or hospital?" He looked at me through the rearview mirror.

"Hospital," I decided before Lena could interrupt. I pulled out my phone and brought up my text string with Evan.

"Dammit, Rory, I just want to go home," Lena groused without opening her eyes.

"And I want to win the damn lottery, but we're both

bound for disappointment," I shot back absently as I started typing. "You know the Guild rules. If you sustain an injury on the job, first stop is medical services."

"Well, the rules suck," she whined.

"Yep," I agreed without looking up. "And stop pouting."

She huffed then grabbed my wrist. "Who are you texting?"

I raised my head and took in the ugly circles under her eyes that matched the bluish-purple bruise spanning from the corner of one bloodshot eye down toward her cracked lips. "Evan."

Her hand fell away, and a flash of surprise swept over her face. It was replaced by a mix of emotions I couldn't untangle before she turned to look out the window.

Before I could poke and prod, Zev said, "There's a Guild Mercy about ten minutes away."

I sent the text and held the phone in my lap. "That works."

The electronic voice of the GPS began its route, and Zev pulled away from the curb. Next to me, Lena's eyes were closed, and her head was resting against the seat. She wiped absently at her mouth, winced, and dropped her hand. I caught the smear of red across her skin. A tremor ran through me. At first, I thought it was my phone vibrating with an incoming text, but when I checked the blank screen, I realized it was just me. Reaction was setting in. The anxiety that had been my constant companion since Lena went missing was swept under my relief that she was sitting next to me, battered but alive. "God, Lena. You scared the shit out of me." My voice was shaky and just above a whisper.

She didn't open her eyes, but her lips curved the tiniest bit. "Scared the shit out of me too," she mumbled.

The GPS announced the next turn and estimated our time of arrival. I opened my mouth to ask Zev to mute it, but he beat me to it. The electronic voice fell silent.

Under my hand, my phone vibrated. I checked the screen and saw Evan's response. "Evan's going to meet us at the hospital."

She made a soft humming sound of agreement, and Zev shot me a look through the mirror. "Keep her talking," he mouthed.

I nodded then reached out to cover one of her scratched hands and squeezed. "Hey, Lena, don't fall asleep on me."

"Not sleeping. Just resting my eyes." The soft slurring of her words contradicted her claim.

"Uh huh, sure." It came out droll. "Tell me about Keith and Theo."

A sigh escaped her lips as she rolled her head in my direction and opened her eyes. "Only if you tell me how you ended up partnering with Dark and Broody here."

"Deal." Heat rushed over my face, and I didn't dare look at Zev. Not that it mattered. Lena knew me too well. "But you first."

She studied me for a moment before wry amusement settled in. "Fine. I'm assuming you accessed my case files?"

"Not me, exactly."

Her eyebrows rose. "Evan?"

"Yep," I confirmed. "We saw the referral from the doctor about Keith's limp dick."

That dry comment earned a flash of humor before she licked her lips and continued. "While that's accurate, it's actually called an Acrapous hex. It's a preferred revenge for disgruntled ex- or soon-to-be ex-lovers. Despite Madeline and Keith's diversified past relationships, I was able to narrow it down to Keith's ex, Madeline, or her newest boy toy, Theo. I had some questions I wanted to ask Keith."

"Questions you wanted to ask before your wrap-up appointment scheduled for Monday," I guessed.

"Exactly," she confirmed. "Except when I got there, I didn't know that it wasn't Keith who answered the door."

Confused, I frowned. "What do you mean?"

She grimaced. "How deep did you and Evan dig on Theo?"

"Not so much on Theo since we were focused on you and Keith." That reminded me of what we found on Lena. I shot a glance at Zev to make sure his eyes were on the road and not the mirror. With the coast clear, I turned to Lena and mouthed, "Clarke Family?"

I didn't think her face could get much paler, but it did. Her hand shot out and gripped my arm, her broken nails scratching my skin. Her panicked gaze flicked to Zev and back to me in silent question.

I dipped my head in a tiny nod and covered her hand with mine before giving it a comforting squeeze. Knowing a prolonged silence would clue Zev in, I cleared my throat and picked up the conversation. "By now, Evan might have more on Theo, but..." I trailed off, hoping it was enough of a lead-in to swing the conversation out of dangerous waters.

Lena's grip tightened then eased. She pulled her hand away and fisted it in her lap. Her shoulders straightened, and her jaw took on a familiar obstinate line. "What about you, Zev? What do you know about Mr. Theodore Mahon's abilities?" Her voice was sharp, carrying a hint of belligerence.

Knowing Lena was uncomfortable with Zev knowing about her ancestry, I still wanted to warn her that antagonizing the man was not smart.

Zev used the rearview mirror to meet Lena's gaze, then he turned back to his driving. "He holds a minor ability in illusions."

"Minor or not, it's enough," Lena countered with a hint of embarrassed anger. "He opened that damn door, wearing Keith's face, and I didn't catch on until it was too late."

Remembering the scene at Keith's house, I finally put some of the pieces into place. "He'd already killed Keith?"

She nodded then winced. "He invited me in and suggested I head to the living room. I hit the archway, saw Keith's body sprawled in the wreckage. It was so unexpected, I just stood there like an idiot. It gave him enough time for the bastard to knock me out." She turned her wan face to the window and stared out morosely. "I woke up in that damn shed, locked inside that damn circle, saw Keith's body dumped off to the side, and knew I was in deep shit."

And knowing my friend, that would not sit well with her. "And Theo?"

"He was just waiting for me to wake up." She turned, her face hard. "When he finally decided to make an appearance, I asked what he thought he was doing; he was all too eager to share. It seems that while Keith worked for LanTech, he ran across some proprietary information worth serious money. Unfortunately, that information was locked under a complex Arcane cipher. The kind that would require a skilled Key to open."

"So he what? Gets himself cursed to lure you in?" *Talk about going to extremes.*

"Not me, specifically, but yeah, that's exactly what he did," Lena said.

"Delusional dick," I muttered. "Why?"

"I don't think it was his idea," she said. "From what I could gather from Theo's I'm-so-clever diatribe, he made the mistake of heavily investing in one of Keith's businesses. When it went under, it left Theo in rocky waters and pissed as hell at Keith. He was going after him, hard. Threatening to expose his dirty laundry. Keith offered the information in lieu of cash if Theo would keep his mouth shut. When Theo got a peek at the cipher, he knew they would need someone with serious skills who wouldn't squeal to someone with a bigger checkbook."

"So they went to the Guild." Because while the Guild was mercenary in nature, its reputation on maintaining confidentiality was impeccable.

"Yep." She picked at a nail. "Theo convinced Keith to agree to the Acrapous hex, telling him it was a sort of test, to make sure whatever Key they got was legit."

I didn't know enough about hexes to assess that, so I asked, "Is that kind of thing that complex?"

It wasn't Lena but Zev who answered. "It's on the lower end of the top level of complexity, but I don't think the complexity was the point, was it?" He directed that last to Lena.

She grimaced. "No, they needed someone with a delicate touch."

I shifted in my seat, feeling left out and stupid. "Explain that for those not in the know here."

Lena explained, "When reversing curses, whether they're a cipher or a hex, you have to be able to gauge magical pressure." Reading my confusion, she switched gears. "Think of it like a magical bomb tech. Some bombs are simple—cut the red wire and save the world. Some have multiple redundancies. If you don't take it apart in the right order, you go boom. Some rely on pressure plates, too much or too little—"

"You go boom," I repeated. "I get it."

She managed a wan grin. "Right, in this case, both the cipher and the hex required a delicate Arcane touch because of the way they were crafted."

"And they needed your magic fingers."

"Exactly."

A low-grade headache was setting up shop, and I pressed the heels of my hands to my eyes for a minute. "Okay, so that explains why they needed you." I dropped my hands and blinked away the tiny spots as my vision steadied. "Why'd Theo kill Keith?"

Her forehead furrowed, and the lines around her mouth deepened as she frowned. "That's a good question that I don't have an answer for. What I do know is whatever Keith did pissed Theo off, they argued, and Keith ended up dead. Which wouldn't have been my problem if I hadn't chosen that particular moment to knock on Keith's door."

I winced. "Bad timing."

She huffed out a sound of amusement. "That's one way to think about it."

"What about the Drainer's Circle?" Zev broke in.

"What about it?" she asked.

"That spell is highly advanced." At the GPS's warning, he slowed and made a turn. "Much more advanced than I'd expect someone like Theo to be able to pull off."

"It was already set and primed when I woke up," she explained. "I think he had someone else cast it." Her eyes narrowed in consideration as she tapped her fingers against her knee. "Actually, now that I think about it, he definitely had to have had someone else do it."

That earned a sharp glance from Zev. "Why?"

Her fingers stilled. "Because that first day he had me, Theo screwed up."

"How?" This time, I managed to get my question in before Zev.

"He smudged one of the circle's sigils while he was casting a translocation spell on Keith's body." The hand resting on her knee curled into a fist, and her voice turned hard. "It was a minor mistake. One he eventually caught, but before he did, I was able to adjust the spell's intended location enough to drop the body somewhere obvious."

That explained the body drop that had reeled me into this mess. "You did a damn good job." When she gave me a quizzical look, I grinned. "It landed in the lobby of the condo."

She blinked, bemusement washing the lines of stress away for a brief moment. "No shit?"

"No shit."

"Uh. Nice." Her pleased expression faded under obvious exhaustion. "He left me in that spell for hours, letting that dirty magic suck bits and pieces of me away in a slow drip. He needed me weak enough to be compliant, but not so weak I couldn't do what he wanted." She reached out to me. I grabbed her hand and held on, both of us taking comfort from our tight grips. She looked at our hands and blinked rapidly. "I knew you, or the Guild, would be looking for me, so I needed a way to buy myself time." I squeezed, and she lifted her head and gave me a weak smile. "When he finally showed back up, I reluctantly agreed to work on the file. It took some acting and a few tears, but he finally believed me and produced a flash drive that contained the locked files. I worked as slow as I could, but Theo's impatient, not stupid."

"That couldn't have been easy." Zev turned on to the winding road that led to the hospital. "Trying to work while being drained."

She shuddered, and her grip tightened. "It wasn't, and the Drainer's Circle made it twice as difficult." She let go of my hand and dropped her head back against the seat. "I got through most of the hex on the files, but I knew if I undid the last of the cipher, Theo would just kill me, so I created a magical tripwire tied to me, one that would destroy the drive and all the information if triggered."

Her simple explanation hit me hard, and I bit back my sharp protest.

Zev had a completely different reaction. "That's brilliant."

I glared at him, but when I turned back to Lena, it was to see a hint of color seeping into her cheeks.

"Necessary," she corrected self-consciously. "As far as I was concerned, if I didn't survive, neither would that information. Then I told Theo what I did."

Unable to check myself, I snapped, "You blackmailed a psychopath."

"I wanted to keep breathing," she shot back. "And it worked."

Zev broke in before the two of us could get into it. "Do you know where the drive is now?"

Lena shrugged. "Probably with Theo, why?"

Zev followed the hospital signs to the emergency room entrance. "Because the information on that drive belongs to the Cordova Family."

Lena turned to me with raised brows, silently questioning his claim.

I confirmed with a slight nod then aimed my next question at Zev. "How likely is it that Theo knows we broke Lena out?"

"Pretty damn likely." He turned in to the lot near the emergency entrance and parked.

"Yeah, that's what I thought." I sighed. "He could stash the drive anywhere and ghost."

"If he was smart, he'd keep the drive close," Zev said. "It's his only bargaining chip."

"Well, if he has the drive on him," Lena chimed in, "you can track his ass down and find out."

Zev undid his seatbelt and twisted around so he could see her. "What do you mean?"

Instead of answering him, she turned to me. "You said Evan's going to meet us here?"

"Yeah, he should be right behind us," I confirmed.

She turned to Zev and studied him for a long moment. "Promise me, when you get ahold of Theo, you'll make him hurt for me?"

Zev held her gaze and solemnly said, "I swear."

Lena considered him for a moment then nodded decisively. "Good. When Evan gets here, have him track my Guild signature. I used it when I set the tripwire."

I blinked at my friend, then I threw back my head and laughed.

CHAPTER NINETEEN

LENA'S normal resilience was no match for the results of spending three grueling days at the mercy of a Drainer's Circle. She tried to get out of the SUV and all but fell into Zev's arms. He ended up carrying her through the emergency room doors, while I rushed in behind him. Like a well-rehearsed dance, the emergency staff whisked Lena into the bowels of the hospital, where a Guild-approved doctor would ensure her health. Since I wasn't technically considered family, I was told I could see her once she was brought back to her room. The admitting nurse took in my rough appearance with a critical eye and asked if I required treatment. I declined, and she sent Zev and me to the waiting room.

On the way to the lounge, everything caught up to me in a swamping wave, and I stumbled. Only Zev's quick reaction kept me from adding more bruises to my collection.

"Whoa, Rory. You okay?"

"Sorry." Embarrassed by my clumsiness, I ducked my head as he tucked me against his side. Despite our differences in height, we fit. "Just tired."

His arm around my waist tightened, and for a brief, unsettling moment, I felt strangely safe. "Let's find a seat."

He stopped us in the lounge's entryway, taking in the other occupants. There weren't many. Two kids, probably under ten, played quietly in a corner next to an exhausted-looking man, most likely their father. On the other side of the room, an older woman held tight to the hand of a younger one, while she worked a set of rosary beads. The TV in the corner was on a home improvement show, but the volume was low, making it difficult to hear.

Zev led me to a loveseat in the middle of the room that was angled to see the TV. "Let's sit here."

"Works for me." So long as I could sit, I wasn't picky. I sank down and discovered the couch was fairly comfortable. I sat in the corner at an angle, one knee propped on the couch, one foot on the floor. I braced an elbow on the armrest, dropped my head into my hand, and closed my eyes.

The cushions shifted as Zev settled in on the other side. For a few minutes, I simply drifted but it didn't take long for the quiet to gain weight. I could all but feel him watching me. When I forced my eyes open, I found I was right. His position mimicked mine, except one of his arms was draped along the back of the loveseat. There was a slight frown on his face, and something intense lingered in his dark eyes. Whatever it was, it left me off balance. I frowned. "What?"

My snippy question erased the complicated look and replaced it with amusement. "What what?"

"You're staring at me," I groused, feeling my cheeks heat. "Stop it."

His amusement broke into an appealing grin. "I'm not staring. I'm just thinking."

What are we? Thirteen? "About?"

That grin turned wicked. "You."

Reverting to adolescence, I rolled my eyes and muttered,

"Whatever." The dull headache from earlier had stepped it up a notch, and I could feel my scraped knees stiffening up. I avoided his too-perceptive gaze and picked at the torn material of my slacks. "What happens now?"

He didn't dodge the question. "Once Lena's man gets here, I'll have him track Theo and the drive."

Without correcting his assumption about Evan, I shot him a look. "And if that doesn't work?"

He cocked his head. "Then I'll go back to my original plan and hunt Theo down."

His intention to hunt solo came through loud and clear, and I found myself both irritated and strangely hurt. The irritation was easy. I had my own grievances to address with Theo, but I was realistic enough to understand that mine meant little to nothing in light of the ones Zev and the Cordovas held. Lena was safe and sound, which meant my part in this mess was technically done. Unfortunately, I wasn't quite ready to let it go or, to be more honest, let Zev go. It was beyond stupid. He lived in a world that would eat me alive, but as I studied him from under my lashes, I couldn't ignore that I was tempted to risk it. And since I couldn't quite let him go, I asked, "When you find Theo, what will happen to him?"

He arched a brow. "If he survives?"

I nodded.

"He'll be brought before the Arcane Family Court on charges of murder, intent to murder, larceny, kidnapping, and use of illicit magic." There was little inflection in Zev's voice, almost as if he were running down a checklist of offenses.

Since I wanted Theo to pay in very painful ways, I pushed, "Which means he'll what? Get locked in a cell somewhere and rot?"

Zev's smile was scary. "In this situation, that's too easy.

Just take my word for it—he won't ever bother you or Lena again."

I dropped my gaze and nervously picked at a torn piping on the armrest. "What about the local authorities? Do I need to worry about them showing up on our doorstep?"

"It'll be taken care of."

I was sure it would, but Detective Brenner was going to be pissed that Family politics and arrogance outranked his authority. But that wasn't my problem. Frustrated, sad, and so mixed up I just wanted to leave, I muttered, "You have an answer for everything."

"Not everything."

At that ominous response, I looked up and got caught in his gaze. "What do you mean?" My question came out on a breathless squeak.

He leaned in, bracing his hands on either side of my bent leg. My world narrowed down to his face, the stark lines that disappeared into the neatly trimmed beard, the dark eyes that burned with an unsettling intensity. My heart pounded, and my mouth went dry, but when he traced a fingertip down the side of my face with infinite gentleness, my heart raced for an entirely different reason. "I don't know what it is you're hiding."

"I'm not hiding anything." I managed the lie without flinching.

The sinful curve of his lips left me torn between whimpering in fear or whimpering in want. "I don't believe you."

I jerked back, losing that delicate touch, not that I had room to go anywhere as I was all but trapped on the damn loveseat. "I don't care what you—"

"Where's Lena? Is she okay?" The rest of my denial was cut off as Evan rushed into the lounge and aimed straight for Zev and me.

Grateful for his interruption, I turned away from Zev and

his too-knowing gaze. I scrambled off the loveseat. "She's going to be fine. They're checking her out now."

Evan's panic receded, and his shoulders hunched as he dropped into a nearby chair. He ran his hands through his hair, leaving it on end. "Thank God." His lifted his head, nudged his glasses back in place, and pinned Zev with a hard stare. "You'll get the asshole that took her, right?"

"I will," Zev said as he stood to join us. "But to do that, I need your help."

Evan sat up, his knee bouncing. "Whatever you need."

I took the chair next to Evan and was grateful when Zev continued to stand. "Lena said she tagged the flash drive and that you would be able to track it by her Guild signature. Do you know what she's talking about?"

His face scrunched up in thought, and he rubbed his chin. "Yeah, I'm pretty sure I do." He looked around. "I need a computer."

"I'm sure the hospital has a business center around here." I patted his knee and left the lounge to ask the nurse at the desk. When I returned, Evan stood with Zev, and whatever they were discussing was done in low voices. They both fell silent at my approach. "Second floor, to the left of the elevators, near the chapel."

Evan looked at the doors then back to me. "You'll stay and keep me posted?"

I nodded. "As soon as they get her assigned to a room, I'll let you know."

"Okay, good." He turned to Zev. "Let's get this done." He didn't wait but headed toward the elevators.

Zev didn't follow immediately. Instead, he stepped into my space. Refusing to give ground, I lifted my chin and glared. "What?"

Those whisky-dark eyes roamed over my face like a physical touch, which was bad enough, but then he smiled with wolfish intent. "I'll be in touch."

He didn't wait for response, which was a good thing, since I was having a hell of a time finding my voice. That didn't stop me from watching him and his undeniable gorgeous ass waltz away. He stepped inside the elevator and turned toward me. Holding his gaze as the elevator doors slid shut, I muttered a mature "Whatever."

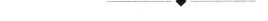

The Guild-approved doctor wanted to keep Lena overnight for observation. He said with time and rest, her magic would revert back to its normal levels. His biggest concern was dehydration, so they hooked her up to an IV and pumped her full of liquids and antibiotics to stave off infections from her various cuts. Evan came back without Zev and waited with me until they finally got Lena in a room. He didn't say much, other than to confirm he was able to lock on to whatever signal Lena had established. I'm sure Zev was out doing what he did best—hunting. As miffed as I was to not be at his side, sticking with Lena was more important.

When we finally got to her room, Lena was out of it, but neither of us felt comfortable letting her wake alone. When it was obvious we weren't going anywhere, one of the nurses offered me a pair of scrubs. Since my skin was starting to crawl under the dust, dirt, and blood, I took them and made use of the shower in the attached bathroom, leaving Evan on watch. I spent just long enough under the spray to rinse off the layer of grit and grime from the day's adventure. Later, when I got home, I could indulge in a long soak to appease my aching muscles.

When I walked out in my stylish baggy scrubs, I found the Guild director sitting in my chair and Lena awake and propped up in bed. Sylvia listened to each of us as we recounted what had happened, who was involved, and our half-confirmed guesses on motives. There was another round of Q-and-A as Sylvia homed in on specifics that would allow her to hold her own when she dealt with the fallout from Madeline Thatcher, the Phoenix PD, and the Cordovas. When we were done, she got to her feet. "Lena, be prepared for the Cordovas to request your assistance with the flash drive."

Lena didn't quite mask the flash of worry, but being the loyal Guild employee she was, she said, "I'll be happy to help, but I want hazard pay."

Sylvia's smile was razor sharp. "Not to worry. The Guild will ensure the Cordovas pay for your expertise and any hardship incurred." Her gaze swept over Evan and me. "I want your official reports on my desk no later than ten tomorrow, understood?"

We both nodded.

"Good." She turned to me. "Rory, walk with me?"

Since it wasn't really a question, I shared a worried look with Lena then turned to follow the director out. As we waited for the elevator, Sylvia said, "I received a phone call this morning."

It took a second to switch gears. *Why would a call to Sylvia involve me?* Then, remembering my evening with Sabella, I couldn't stop the burst of nerves. "Oh?"

"It seems you provided outstanding professional services under unforeseen difficulties and left quite the impression. It's my understanding you should expect a contract to be delivered within the next few days." Sylvia gave me an amused look. "Congratulations."

I couldn't quite contain my pleased grin, but I managed a relatively calm "Thank you for providing me the opportunity."

The elevator doors slid open. Sylvia stepped inside then turned to face me. "Thank you for proving my confidence was not misplaced." She hit a button. "Good luck, Rory." As the doors closed, she added, "You're going to need it."

I all but floated back to Lena's room, my head spinning with the implications of Sabella's contract. The niggling worries generated by the journal lingered but weren't enough to completely douse my elation. I pushed through the half-opened door and came to a stop. "Oops, want me to come back?"

Evan straightened from where he was leaning over a red-faced Lena and with remarkable composure said, "It's good." He looked at Lena, brought their laced hands up to his mouth, and pressed them to his lips. "I'm going to head into the office and get a few things tied up. Do you want me to come back tonight?"

"No, I'm good." She tugged at her hand, and Evan slowly let her go. Despite the hectic color on her cheeks, she gave me a stern look. "You can go home too, Rory. I'm good here. I'm just going to sleep so they'll let me go home tomorrow."

I was already shaking my head. "Sorry, babe, I'm sticking."

Evan aimed a narrow-eyed glare at Lena, who missed it because she was watching me with clear exasperation.

I decided it was best to nip the looming argument before it could take a breath. "Just indulge me, okay? I promise I'll stop hovering once you're home."

She flopped the hand without the IV in it. "Fine, but if you're going to stick around, see if you can get me something more substantial than Jell-O. I'm craving some serious carbs."

"I'll see what I can do," I promised.

Evan patted the bedrail absently. "All right, I'm out." He waited until Lena turned to him and added, "I'll call you in the morning."

"Sounds good." Lena watched Evan until he was gone.

I retook my uncomfortable chair and propped my feet against her bedrails. "So, Lena, got something you want to tell me about our friendly neighborhood electrogeek?" I teased.

Proving she was well on her way to normal, she nailed me in the face with a pillow. "Nothing to tell."

Clutching the pillow to my stomach, I waggled my eyebrows. "I don't know about that. Rumors are flying around the Guild that you have a mystery man on the hook."

She snorted, but her blush deepened. "Look, it's just... complicated."

Hearing her discomfort, I let her off the hook. "He's a good guy, Lena." I waited until she met my eyes and said, "He cares about you, and he'll go out of his way to keep you safe."

She frowned. "Where's that coming from?"

I looked at my toes, flexing them against the rail as I debated how far I wanted to take this. Lena and I both had secrets we were trying to keep, but the thing with secrets was they never stayed that way. Thanks to Evan's research, both he and I knew Lena's history, which was bad enough. The fact Zev had dug just as deep, if not deeper, and Lena would be working with the Cordova Family in the near future, worried me. Taking a deep breath, I dove in. "When Evan and I were looking for you, he stumbled across your sealed records." At her sharply indrawn breath, I looked up. Her face was back to pale, and the sheet was caught in her white-knuckled hands. My words tumbled over each other as I rushed to reassure her, "It doesn't change a damn thing, Lena. For Evan or for me."

"Why?" Her question came out shaky, but there was a ribbon of heat under it.

"Because Evan was worried, I was worried, and we needed all the information we could get to find you. No way in hell were we leaving you swinging in the damn wind. The thing you need to understand is we weren't the only ones poking around." I sat up and leaned in, gripping the bedrail. "Evan thinks one of his searches tripped something for someone else, but he couldn't go any further without raising more flags. He was worried, but he didn't want to go deeper and possibly put you in more danger."

"Dammit, Rory."

I held her furious gaze. "We know Zev knows. He brought it up to me during one of our discussions."

She studied me. "Anyone else?"

"I don't think so."

A slew of low, vicious curses fell from Lena's mouth. When she wound down, she closed her eyes in defeat. "I want nothing to do with the Clarkes. Nothing. They were shits to my mom and me. I was relieved when they renounced me, because the Guild was my family. I don't want anything to do with the Families."

"I get that," I said.

She opened her eyes and turned her head to look at me. "Do you?"

"Yeah." I swallowed hard and shared. "You're not the only one with secrets, Lena." My gaze skittered to the door, a nervous check to ensure we were alone, then I lowered my voice. "Have you ever heard of a Prism?"

Her eyes widened, and she turned to her side, bringing us closer. "Seriously? I always thought those were just made up. You know, wishful thinking."

"Nope, it's real. I'm real," I admitted, even as a panicked voice in my head screamed at me. "There's not much information out there about it, and I barely understand how it works."

"Not a surprise. Most stories surrounding that ability are considered myths." She eyed me shrewdly. "The one thing all the stories agree on is that if a Family gets their hands on a Prism, it doesn't end well for the Prism."

"I know."

"Do you?" Apprehension replaced wonder, and she covered my hand on the bedrail, the warmth of her touch seeping into my chilled skin. "If that's true, you can't tell Zev, Rory."

I dropped my forehead against our hands. "I know, but I think he's on his way to figuring it out."

"Then you need to avoid him at all costs," she warned.

I lifted my head and gave her a sickly smile. "I'd love to, but unfortunately, I owe him a favor."

She studied me, then proving she really was my best friend, she said, "You like him."

There was no use denying it, so I didn't try. Instead, I tugged my hand free and slumped back in my chair. "It's such a mess."

"Yeah, it is," Lena agreed. "But if anyone can figure a way out of it, my money's on you."

I blew out a breath and wished I had as much faith in me as she did.

CHAPTER TWENTY

A FEW DAYS LATER, Sabella's contract arrived by secure courier, along with a sealed letter on thick stationery. I was home alone as Lena was out to dinner with Evan. It was their first "real" date and their first foray into making their relationship public. I was happy for both of them, but I knew the future wasn't guaranteed, especially since they worked for the Guild.

I'd spent the days immediately after rescuing Lena typing up reports, answering questions, and fruitlessly waiting for Zev to call. He never did. I tried to lose myself in the mysterious journal, but my thoughts were too fragmented to concentrate.

I reviewed the contract, which appeared fairly standard. When Sabella was in town, I would be her on-call driver. Her requests would take precedence, and the compensation made my heart and my bank account deliriously happy. Before I signed, I needed to review it with a Guild lawyer. I took Sabella's letter, dropped onto my sofa, and tucked my feet under me. As I broke the seal, a buzz of magic woke mine. It quietly hummed under my skin, and although I braced and waited for something to happen, nothing did. I pulled out a thick piece of linen paper. Sabella's handwriting flowed over the page in bold strokes.

Dear Rory,

I apologize, I intended to invite you to lunch to do this properly. However, an unexpected situation required my presence at home. I do hope you're enjoying my gift. I ran across it in a small monastery library, where it appeared to have been forgotten. Perhaps for the best, all things considered. I'm sure you have many questions, and I'll be happy to do my best to answer them when I return. Until then, a word of advice from an old woman: be careful who you trust, dear. Some things are coveted to a dangerous extent. There are whispers that such items command unrelenting demands, and those who can afford to meet those demands will do so at any cost. I would so hate to see such a gem shattered under the unrelenting pressure.

Until later,
Sabella

Stunned, I read the letter—twice. "Holy shit." My attention shifted to the leather-bound journal on my coffee table, and my earlier excitement dimmed under a rising tide of anxiety. A shattering realization hit. The journal had been delivered before I'd even met Sabella. *So how did she know?*

My mind whirled with questions as I tried to adjust to my new reality. First Zev, now Sabella. It looked as if my secrets weren't as secret as I thought. After my initial panic receded, I re-read the letter. It didn't take a genius to read between the lines. I took small comfort from the fact that she appeared to be on my side—at least for now. I wasn't naive enough to believe it was out of the goodness of her heart. The part about unrelenting demands, if I were to hazard a guess, would confirm that Prisms were still hunted. By Families or other interested parties, it didn't matter. History proved no price was too high to obtain one. That did not bode well for me at all.

I looked at the contract lying next to the journal. I would definitely have the lawyer look it over. I needed to take my time analyzing the pros and cons of working for Sabella. No way did I want to sign anything without ensuring I wasn't setting myself up for unending servitude. Sabella wanted something from me, but the thing was, I wanted something from her, as well. For the first time, I had access to actual information about what I could do. Not to mention, as Zev explained, allies were everything in his world. Since it looked as if I would be part of that world in more than just a professional sense, I needed to make sure I had the right weapons— and the right connections—to survive.

As for Zev... well, I owed him a favor, and I would pay up. I had a reputation to uphold, after all. Unlike Zev and his empty promise. I hadn't heard a thing from him, which left me vacillating between anger and disappointment. My fascination with him was stupid, but logic held little sway over emotions. Still, I was working on snuffing out that pesky crush, one bite of chocolate at a time. Give me a few more days, maybe a week, and he would be an interesting memory.

And if you believe that, I have a bridge I could sell you.

Before I could indulge in a schizophrenic discussion on my unhealthy infatuation with Zev, there was a knock on my door. I tucked Sabella's letter into the journal then stuffed both under the couch cushion before heading toward the door. I checked the peephole and dropped my head against the door with a soft thump as I stared unseeingly at my bare toes, unsure what I was feeling. "It figures."

Another knock had the door vibrating under my fore-head. Blowing out a long breath, I straightened, undid the locks, and pulled open the door. "What are you doing here?"

Dressed in a faded concert T-shirt and equally faded jeans, Zev leaned against the doorjamb. "I told you I'd be in touch."

"Ever heard of a phone?" I grumped, trying to ignore the way my hormones sat up and panted at the wildly sexy picture he presented.

He straightened, put a hand on my door, and pushed it wider. "Let me in, Rory." He dipped his head down when I stayed stubbornly in place, and put his mouth close to my ear. "Otherwise, I'll give your neighbors something to talk about."

I fought back the shiver that erupted at his nearness and prayed my T-shirt was up to the job of hiding my body's reaction. With a frustrated growl, I spun on my heel and stalked back to my couch, leaving him to follow. As the door shut, I dropped into the cushion and folded my arms over my chest. I watched moodily as he strolled in and made himself comfortable at the other end of the couch.

"So, how's things?" he asked, propping his ankle on a knee.

"Shouldn't that be my question?" I shot back, doing my best to ignore how his position tightened his jeans over a rather impressive package. *Down, Rory. No drooling.*

"Did you miss me?" He grinned, and I realized the lines of strain I'd become used to seeing on his face were gone.

Fighting a telling blush, I rolled my eyes, exasperated with him and myself, but there was something about this version of Zev that made it hard to hold on to my mad. "Were you gone? I didn't notice."

He laughed. "Liar."

Since he was right, I shrugged.

His grin faded, but he continued to study me. "I would've

stopped by earlier, but things have been hectic. I wanted to let you know I got Theo."

"I figured you would," I said. "Is he going to get his day in court, or is he making time in hell?"

Something heated in his gaze. "You're a bloodthirsty thing, aren't you?"

"I'm not very forgiving of those who hurt my family," I admitted without shame.

"I get that," he said.

I bet he did, and the fact he did made him even more fascinating. Doing my best to stay on track, I asked, "Did you get the drive as well?"

"Yeah." He looked around the condo. "Is Lena here?"

"She's out." I tried to ignore the burst of disappointment at what I suspected was the real reason behind his visit. "But I can give her a message."

"No, that's okay. Emilio wanted to make the request through the Guild." He paused, and if I hadn't known better, I might have thought he was uncomfortable, but this was Zev, a man who was never out of step and always in control. His attention came back to me, and he arched a brow. "This how you spend your nights?"

"When I can." I refused to be embarrassed by my less-than-exciting lifestyle. "It helps offset the few unexpected turns my life has taken lately."

"And what kind of turns would those be?" Something changed in his eyes, and a subtle tension sprang up.

Is he flirting with me? I licked my lips, and his gaze followed, like a cat spotting a tasty treat. Before I could rethink, I said, "The dangerous kind."

Heat rose under his cheeks as he shifted, angling toward me. "Do you like it?"

I blinked, trying to drag my attention away from the temptation he presented. "Like what?"

His voice deepened, taking on a note that tempted. "Danger."

I swallowed back my clamoring hormones, trying to focus on anything other than the rising sexual tension clogging up the room. "I don't know." It came out husky, and it was an outright lie. I wanted the thrill of pitting myself against the odds. Even here, in this very dangerous arena, despite knowing how much it would complicate—everything. It felt a lot like racing, when I rode that breathtaking edge between control and disaster.

"Want to find out?"

It took a moment for his question to sink in, but when it did, it swept aside logic and beckoned like a sexy, sweet, low-slung sportscar, leaving behind the pulse-pounding thrill that left me higher than a damn kite. It was too much and not enough. But staring into his wicked eyes, I knew I was going to go for it. Curiosity might kill the damn cat, but a cat had nine lives, right? Why not find out? Before my courage could bail, I fisted a handful of Zev's T-shirt and dragged him close as I leaned in.

I curled my other hand around his neck and took the taste I wanted. I brushed those full lips with mine, lightly tracing them with my tongue even as the rasp of his beard set every nerve ending alight. I licked over those lips that had haunted way too damn many of my over-enthusiastic thoughts. There was the faintest hint of something intoxicating, like the spicy burn of a good whiskey, and it started a slow burn deep inside where dirty Rory lived. She perked up.

Even though the hard muscles under my hand didn't relax, he didn't push me away. In fact, I took my time tasting him and teasing myself. Yet when he continued to hold still and stiff, doubts began circle in for the kill. Unwilling to force myself where I wasn't wanted, I traced those stubborn lips one last time, loosened my grip on his neck and shirt, and started to edge back.

A low growl rumbled against my lips, and his hand gripped the back of my head, holding me where he wanted. Suddenly, instead of trying to hold him close, I was holding on for dear life as my world tumbled into a fiery heat that threatened to burn everything to ash. His mouth opened, and he took over with a ferociousness that left me breathless. He shifted my kiss from teasing to devouring and demanding. Happy to let him indulge, I let everything else disappear under the onslaught.

As suddenly as it changed, it stopped. He tugged my head back, forcing our mouths apart. Not far, because he dropped his forehead against mine, and I could feel his breath against my wet lips. His dark eyes stared into mine. Emotions I wasn't sure I was ready to tackle swam in the heated depths. We stared at each other as the inferno he ignited slowly banked.

"You're trouble." His hand tightened in my hair.

It didn't hurt. In reaction, my body pressed closer to his. His eyes flared, and for a moment, I caught it—what he tried to hide. Zev loved the chase too, and he'd just caught my scent. Naughty Rory cackled in wicked glee. Unwilling to let him off the hook, I smiled. "So are you." *So fucking much trouble I will probably regret it.* Eventually. But it would be so much fun until then.

I got a hard, quick kiss, then he was gone, my door shutting behind him.

◆

- YOU HAVE ARRIVED AT YOUR DESTINATION -

◆

Thank you for strapping in for GRAVE CARGO. Craving the open roads? Hitch a ride with Rory in **RISKY GOODS** and race through the twists and turns of an unexpected assignment, a jealous ex, & a game-changing serum with Rory.

Buckle in and enjoy the ride, now available in Kindle Unlimited.

◆

Want to know how Rory and Zev met? Then don't miss out on exclusives & new release information by subscribing to Jami's newsletter at: https://www.subscribepage.com/Jami-Subscription-Books

Do you want to share your exciting discovery of a new read? Then leave a review!

Or you're welcome to swing by and visit Jami's website at: http://jamigray.com

◆

ARCANE TRANSPORTER BOOKS

Urban Fantasy Series

Binge this urban fantasy thrill-ride today!

Need to ensure you delivery, magical or otherwise, makes it to its destination? For guaranteed delivery, hire the best in the west, Rory Costas, Arcane Transporter. (Independent contractor - not responsible for damage incurred in transit.)

Check out this series at
https://www.amazon.com/dp/B088FCSVKB

◆

GRAVE CARGO

When a questionable, but lucrative delivery job takes an unexpected turn, will Rory survive the collision or crash and burn?

RISKY GOODS

A dead mage, a missing friend, and an unpredictable alliance merge into a volatile package sending Rory careening through the Arcane elite's deadly secrets.

LETHAL CONTENTS

Rory and Zev's final adventure crashes into shelves August 2021

ABOUT THE AUTHOR

"Taking a refreshing approach to fantasy magic, this fast-paced, economical thriller is told from a highly likable perspective." —Red Adept Editing

 Jami Gray is the coffee addicted, music junkie, Queen Nerd of her personal Geek Squad, Alpha Mom of the Fur Minxes, who writes to soothe the voices crammed in her head. You don't want to miss out on her multiple series that combines magical intrigue and fearless romance into one wild ride -- Arcane Transporter, Kyn Kronicles, PSY-IV Teams, or Fate's Vultures.

amazon.com/author/jamigray

facebook.com/jamigray.author

bookbub.com/authors/jami-gray

goodreads.com/JamiGray

twitter.com/JamiGrayAuthor

instagram.com/jamigrayauthor

Printed in Great Britain
by Amazon

80484226R10159